THE BOOK OF BROKEN HEARTS

Also by Sarah Ockler

Bittersweet

#scandal

THE BOOK OF BROKEN HEARTS

SARAH OCKLER

Simon Pulse
New York London Toronto Sydney New Delhi

This book is a work of fiction. Any references to historical events, real people, or real places are used fictitiously. Other names, characters, places, and events are products of the author's imagination, and any resemblance to actual events or places or persons, living or dead, is entirely coincidental.

SIMON PULSE
An imprint of Simon & Schuster Children's Publishing Division
1230 Avenue of the Americas, New York, NY 10020
First Simon Pulse paperback edition May 2014

Also available in a Simon Pulse hardcover edition.
For information about special discounts for bulk purchases, please contact Simon & Schuster Special Sales at 1-866-506-1949 or business@simonandschuster.com.
The Simon & Schuster Speakers Bureau can bring authors to your live event. For more information or to book an event contact the Simon & Schuster Speakers Bureau at 1-866-248-3049 or visit our website at www.simonspeakers.com.
Interior designed by Mike Rosamilia
Cover designed by Regina Flath
The text of this book was set in Adobe Caslon Pro.
Manufactured in the United States of America
2 4 6 8 10 9 7 5 3 1
The Library of Congress has cataloged the hardcover edition as follows:
Ockler, Sarah.
The Book of Broken Hearts / by Sarah Ockler.—First Simon Pulse hardcover edition.
p. cm.
Summary: Jude has learned a lot from her older sisters, but the most important thing is this: The Vargas brothers are notorious heartbreakers. But as Jude begins to fall for Emilio Vargas, she begins to wonder if her sisters were wrong.
[1. Love—Fiction. 2. Family life—Fiction. 3. Argentine Americans—Fiction.] I. Title.
PZ7.O168Bo 2013
[Fic]—dc23
2012033041
ISBN 978-1-4424-3038-9 (hc)
ISBN 978-1-4424-3039-6 (pbk)
ISBN 978-1-4424-3040-2 (eBook)

For Zoe Strickland,
my favorite bookworm ever

CHAPTER 1

The law of probability dictates that with three older sisters, a girl shall inherit at least one pair of cute shorts that actually fit. Agreed?

Bzzz! Thank you for playing! Please try again.

If these things could talk, they'd be all, *Hi! We're Araceli's old cutoffs!* And I'd go, *Congrats on fulfilling your destiny, because you totally cut off circulation to the vital female organs! High fives!*

Actually, they were so tight up in there that if they could talk, it would sound more like, *Umph mphh mphh hrmm.*

What?

Exactly.

"Ready to do this?" I killed the engine and smiled at Papi across the front seat. He didn't say one way or the other, just squinted as I leaned over to do my lip gloss in the rearview.

"You look old, *mi querida.*"

"Says the guy who microwaves his socks?"

"They were cold." He shrugged. Seriously. Like *I* was the crazy one in this operation.

"Lucky you didn't start a fire." I hopped out of the truck and hooked the leash on Pancake, our golden retriever, who was suddenly doing this shake-rattle-and-roll dance with his dog booty—pretty adorable.

I de-wedged my sister's ex-denim and turned back to Papi. "Ever hear of dressing the part? If they take us seriously, maybe we won't get screwed."

He appraised Araceli's shorts and the strategically ripped Van Halen tee I'd pilfered from Lourdes's castaways. "Jude Catherine Hernandez. I'd like to see *anyone* ride a motorcycle in that outfit."

I stifled an eye roll. *Viejito* hadn't ridden a bike in thirty years. I, on the other hand, was totally up on this stuff. I'd bookmarked practically every Sturgis video diary ever posted, and thanks to a few Red Bull–and-Oreo-fueled YouTube all-nighters, I was approaching expert status in the vast and shadowy realm of motorcycle culture.

Leather, chains, and flagrant bralessness? Bring it.

Papi squinted at me again. "You look like—"

"Your favorite daughter? Tell me about it." I slipped an arm around his waist. Aside from my unequivocally pro-undergarment stance, I felt at least 87 percent biker-babe legit as I navigated Fifth Street, shoulders tucked neatly under the arm of a man old enough to be my father.

Okay, in all fairness, he *was* my father, but still. Manufactured authenticity? Phrase of the day, people!

"Duchess Custom Cycles." Papi read the sign just as I caught our mismatched reflection in the glass. He'd insisted on wearing an insulated flannel shirt and his complimentary THANKS FOR SUBSCRIBING TO THE WESTERN CHANNEL, PARDNER cowboy hat, despite the fact that it was five hundred degrees outside, and I would've gotten more coverage from a skein of yarn and some duct tape.

Sweet Jeremiah Johnson, what a pair!

Papi opened the door, and I hobbled in with Pancake, still trying to coax out those unforgiving shorts. People probably thought I had some kind of medical issue, which was ironic considering the whole reason I'd gotten myself into this rollicking high-plains adventure in the first place.

Despite its royal moniker, Duchess met my research-supported expectations. Dusty. Grimy. Wallpapered with scantily clad women draped over motorcycles. I *so* blended in, but once the door shut behind us, my nose was assaulted by the tang of motor oil and sweat, and my mind flashed through all the things I *should've* been doing the summer after graduation: dorm-supply shopping. Summer theater at Upstart Crow. Sipping frozen Java Potions at Witch's Brew and flirting with the East Coast kayakers who flooded Blackfeather, Colorado, every June.

Papi's warm hand on my shoulder tugged me back to reality. We'd reached the service counter. A glass door behind it offered a view of the garage, a wide concrete space scattered with bike parts and rags and grease-smudged mechanics.

The guy who emerged through the door had a small mouth hidden behind a dried blond shrub of a goatee that made me think of the tumbleweeds that cruised Old Town all summer. He wiped his hands on a dingy cloth as he greeted us, eyes lingering judgmentally on my shirt.

Jeez. I guess Pancake was just being nice when he gave my outfit the patented three-bark approval this morning.

"We need some info on restoring a vintage panhead," I said. "And a mechanic who can work at our place. Blackfeather Harley thought you could give my dad a better deal."

The guy's smile warmed when I said "dad," and I relaxed. But only a little, since my shorts were still trying to ride off into the sunset via Butt Cheek Pass and it was a challenge to stand still.

"We can sure try, darlin'." He spoke around a gnawed-up toothpick that had probably been in his mouth since the seventies. "Name's Duke. Whatcha got?"

"Sixty-one Duo-Glide. Bought her in Buenos Aires from the original owner in seventy-eight." Papi rattled off the specs, right down to the odometer reading and the customizations he'd done before he biked through the homeland when he was seventeen.

The story was a sock rocker for sure—I hadn't even heard it all yet—and Duke's face lit up at the telling.

Adventurous.

Daring.

Totally badass.

This was the Bear Hernandez everyone knew and loved. Not the guy cooking his socks or forgetting the way home from work. Papi's eyes shone as he spoke, and my heart thumped hard behind Eddie Van Halen's face.

The old man was still in there somewhere—I knew it.

The bike would bring him back. We just had to get her running again. A few replacement parts, paint job, good as new.

I handed over my cell to show Duke the picture.

"Wow," Duke said. "You had her in storage all this time?"

"*Sí.* She's been idle since . . ." Papi squinted at Pancake as if the answer were written in those big brown dog eyes. "Pretty sure Reagan was in office last time I rode. She won't turn over. Brake lines were going too, if I remember right."

"The tires are all soggy," I said helpfully, "and some of the pipe things on the side are loose." I tugged my shirt down over the strip of belly that showed whenever I took a deep breath. *Pipe things. Soggy tires.* Apparently my extensive research didn't cover the technical terms.

Duke inspected the photo. The paint was fading, she was caked in rust and dirt, but it wasn't hard to imagine her glory days. Baby blue and cream, chrome that must've gleamed like white light. She was probably strong once, really tore up those Argentine mountain roads.

And then my parents got married. Moved to the States. Had Lourdes. Araceli. Mariposa. And eight years after that, me.

Surprise!

Out in the garage, an engine growled and the mechanics cheered. Pancake whimpered and curled up at my feet.

Harleys. It was hard to picture Papi riding one of those things, but I guess he was pretty hard core back in the day. He had a posse and everything: Las Arañas Blancas. The White Spiders.

"*Queridita.*" Papi grinned when the rumbling stopped. "That's the sound of happiness, yeah?"

Actually my idea of happiness involved less machinery and testosterone than your average Harley offered up, but I returned his smile. Despite my wardrobe malfunction and the general dangers of hanging out with Papi in public these days, we'd already enjoyed a fine breakfast at Ruby's Mountainside Café and managed to walk all the way from the truck to Duchess without Papi trying to steal a car or kiss another man's wife.

Real bang-up day so far.

"Good news and bad news." Duke returned my phone. "Good? She's a real beauty, and we can definitely fix 'er up."

Papi was suddenly looking out the front door like he needed to know the exits, needed a quick way out, and I held my breath, hoping that whatever came out of Duke's mouth next didn't spark one of Papi's meltdowns and send him running into the street.

Mom would kill me if I lost him again. She'd seriously crush up my bones and throw me down the side of a mountain, and the Holy Trinity of my all-knowing sisters would stand there shaking my ashes from their hair and rolling their eyes about how even postmortem I couldn't follow directions.

Keep him close to home, Jude. Keep him calm and focused.

But they weren't there when I found the bike in the storage barn last week, when I cast off boxes of Christmas decorations and old report cards and peeled back the dusty blue tarps and asked Papi to tell me all about it.

They didn't see the light in his eyes, flickering on after months of darkness.

And other than a little dignity and the ability to walk normally for a few hours on account of these shorts, I wasn't planning to lose anything today.

"The bad news?" I asked.

"Time and money, honey." Duke swished the toothpick from one side of his mouth to the other. "Repairs, paint, accessories . . . that's a helluva restore. I'm not sure we can beat the big boys much on price. Hate to say this, but you'd probably get a better deal tradin' up, gettin' the old man something newer."

Heat flooded my face. "He's not old."

"It's she. And a sixty-one's goin' on more than fifty years, darlin'. Not a lot of miles left, if you catch my drift."

I catch your drift, all right.

I looped my arm through Papi's and leaned on his shoulder. Pancake let out a soft whine.

"We aren't trading up." I'd already been through all that with Blackfeather Harley. "Look, I'll be honest with you here, Mr. Duchess—"

"Duke."

"Duke. We don't have a ton of cash. What if we use rebuilt parts?" I met his gaze and held it, hoping this wouldn't require any waterworks. Calling up a few tears was an option, but the biker-babe mascara made the prospect less appealing.

He stroked his goatee, hopefully considering our predicament. At least, how our predicament looked from the outside: Sticker shock. A girl trying to help her daddy with just enough babysitting money to cover the basics.

"Problem isn't just parts." He was still going to town on that toothpick, which seemed like some kind of motorcycle guy code; I'd seen it in the videos. "It's labor. Only got one guy experienced on vintage bikes, and he ain't that cheap. Ain't that available, either—he's booked till fall. When you lookin' to get 'er done?"

"I'm going on a road trip in August," I said. Fingers crossed Zoe and Christina hadn't finalized plans without me. "So, before then?"

Duke sucked in a breath. "Gonna be tight. For an off-site gig, at my lowest rates, I could only spare my junior mechanic. He's not completely certified yet."

I peered into the garage. Guys were stationed at different motorcycles and dirt bikes, most of them dressed in jeans and raggedy T-shirts, bare arms coated in grime. The conversation was muffled by the glass, but their easy banter was unmistakable.

Duke thumbed through the glass at a dark-blue bike, most of which had been stripped to its steel bones. A guy knelt before it—a little younger than the rest, maybe, but equally sure of himself. One arm was deep inside the bike, the floor around him littered with tools and rags.

"That's him in the bandanna," Duke said. "Good kid, knows his stuff. But like I said, barely got his training wheels off."

"Doesn't look like a kid to me." I subtly shifted my hips. Damn. These cutoffs were on a *mission*; my ability to concentrate was becoming seriously compromised. "Besides, we don't care how old he is. Just that he can do the work for cheap."

Papi nodded, but his eyes were still far away.

Duke tapped on the glass and waved the young mechanic forward.

The guy got to his feet, wiped his hands on a rag that hung from his back pocket. His head dipped low as he opened the door and I couldn't see his eyes. Just stubble. Dimples. Scar across the bottom of his chin. His arms were etched with jagged white scars too.

Dangerous stuff, this biker gig.

"How long you been working on these bikes?" Duke asked him.

"Eh . . . forever?"

"*Here*, smart-ass. For me."

"Like, two or three months, I guess. Why?" All his attention was on the boss, but my skin tingled like I was being watched. Not in a creepy way—a familiar one. Like maybe I'd seen this guy before, but with the bandanna and the grime, I couldn't place him. Definitely not from school or summer theater. Someone's cousin, maybe?

"Not ready, junior." Duke was totally baiting the poor guy. "Not for a sixty-one hog."

"You *kidding* me? A sixty-one?" He finally turned to face me, a grin stretching across his face. His dimples were kind of disarming full-on, but I stood my ground as he looked me over.

My skin heated under the scrutiny. I really wished Zoe had helped me prepare this morning. I didn't even like Van Halen, and she would've smartly pointed that out.

Dressing the part? Really, Jude. Someday your theatrics will be your undoing.

"Sixty-one panhead," I finally said.

His eyebrows jumped in either surprise or appreciation. Maybe both. "You *ride*?"

"No. It's—"

"She's mine," Papi said, his mind returning from its little side trip. "And as far as I'm concerned, if you want the job, it's yours."

The mechanic started yammering at his boss in Spanish, deep and low. Puerto Rican, the accent was, faster and less meandering than the Argie stuff I'd grown up with.

He was trying to convince Duke that he could do the job. Needed the *dinero* for some big bike trip this summer.

"Gentlemen," I said. The mechanic looked up at me again, but I kept my eyes on Duke. "We're not asking for a museum piece. We just need to get this thing rebuilt. So if he can help—"

"I can help." He turned back to Duke, his scarred forearms flexing as he gripped the counter. "I rebuilt my own hog last year."

"That's an eighty-seven, kid. Sportster besides."

He shrugged. "Aside from the kickstart, mechanics ain't changed much."

"Duke, please," I said. "We *have* to get this thing running."

Without permission, those on-call waterworks pricked my eyes. Maybe it was ridiculous to put so much hope in restoring the bike, in believing it could really fix Papi. But it was our last shot—the one thing the doctors had overlooked, the faint glimmer of *maybe* that the medical research and case studies had somehow missed.

I cleared my throat and tried again. "What I mean is . . . it's imperative that we complete the restore as planned."

Papi shook his head, his smile finally returning. "My daughter . . . she has a way with words."

Duke eyed me skeptically, but he was clearly under the spell of our father-daughter charms. Even the toothpick stopped shuffling. "Okay, what the customer wants, the customer gets. Even if it's the kid."

"It's the kid," Papi confirmed. He was beaming again, totally back in the moment. "You're hired."

"You won't be sorry." The boy shook Papi's hand and then reached for mine. I pressed my palm to his automatically, but as my skin warmed at his touch, something clicked inside, something familiar and dangerous, and I jerked my hand away and stared at it as if I'd been stung.

Freak show!

My cheeks flamed, but before anyone could question my bizarro reaction, Duke grabbed the boy's shoulder. "You'd better be ready for this, Emilio."

Emilio?

My head snapped up, jolted by a flash of recognition. "What's your name again?"

"Emilio." His lips formed the word, each syllable sliding into my ears with a rush of memory and white-hot guilt. Those caramel-brown eyes. Black hair curled up around the edge of that smudged bandanna. He wasn't smiling now, but the dimples were still there, lurking below the surface like a dare.

I'd been warned that those dimples would be my undoing. Trained to avoid them most of my teen life, a feat made easier when he'd bailed inexplicably out of Blackfeather High two years ago, a month before he was supposed to graduate.

Yet there he was. More grown up, scruffy along the jawline, filling out his T-shirt in all the ways he hadn't before. Practically almost *ogling* me.

That real bang-up day I was having?

Crash. And. Burn.

The only guy in all of Blackfeather who could help—the guy we had just so desperately hired—was the only guy in all of Blackfeather I was bound by blood, honor, and threat of dismemberment from every female in the Hernandez family to unilaterally ignore.

I'm not kidding about the blood part. There was an oath and everything, carefully scrawled into an infamous black book that once held all my sisters' secrets.

I almost laughed.

Of *course* it was him.

Emilio fucking Vargas.

CHAPTER 2

I, Jude Hernandez, vow to never, ever, under any circumstances within or outside of my control, even if the fate of humanity is at stake, even if my own life is threatened, get involved with a Vargas. . . .

Back in the blissfully boy-free zone of our kitchen, I stabbed a tomato until its guts leaked out. It'd been five years and I was the only Hernandez sister left in the house, but the ancient oath echoed clear as a hawk in the canyon.

"Rotten," I whispered.

"Oh, they're just a little soft." Mom shook a saucepan of peppers and mushrooms into a sizzle behind me. *¡CALIENTE! ¡CUIDADO!* OVEN AND STOVE FOR COOKING ONLY. DO NOT USE ALONE. The index card on the range hood curled in the steam. "How was Papi today? Did you guys fish?"

Ugh. Fishing and board games—Mom's idea of summer fun. It was only June, and Papi, Pancake, and I had already fished every living thing out of the Animas. And *Viejito* totally cheats at Scrabble. You should see the words he makes up for triple-letter scores. *Hola* and hello, *amigos*. Some of that stuff isn't in the English *or* the Spanish dictionary.

"We went into town for breakfast," I said. "Walked around Fifth, checked out some of the stores."

Mom's pepper mix sizzled a bit louder. "See anything cute?"

And the award for the understatement of the year goes to . . .

"No one. Nothing." I turned on the faucet, RIGHT FOR COLD/*FRÍO*. LEFT FOR HOT/*CALIENTE*. "We ended up at that motorcycle garage. Papi hired a guy, this kid who works there."

Once Papi and Duke had agreed on an hourly rate for Emilio and signed the paperwork, I rushed us out of Duchess, and Papi hadn't said another word. When we got home, I changed into my normal clothes and he parked himself on the couch for a cowboy movie marathon. Now I needed to get Mom's stamp of approval on the motorcycle plans without actually naming names. I was pretty sure Vargas was still a four-letter word in our house.

For those of us who remembered what it meant, anyway.

"Mi amor." Mom's accent got stronger when she was worried or upset, and I turned to watch her lips, just in case. "Maybe you shouldn't plant seeds in his head about fixing that old junker. It's expensive, and Papi . . . It isn't good to have strangers at the house all the time."

Recently she'd started discouraging visitors—mostly well-meaning neighbors and Papi's former office buddies—telling them Papi was tired, busy, unavailable. Now she mentioned "strangers at the house" again like I'd been nonstop ragin' it every day since graduation. Sure, those Scrabble matches got intense sometimes. And one day, Pancake knocked his food right out of the bowl, spilling it all over the floor. *Cray*-cray!

"Don't worry," I said at the sink, PRESS DOWN TO TURN OFF WHEN DONE. The whole thing tied my stomach in knots too, just not for the same reasons. Still, this wasn't about strangers and it wasn't about some oath and an evil boy. It was about taking care of Papi. "I'll keep an eye on things. And Papi's really excited to work on it—something to do this summer besides fishing."

Mom sighed and lifted the pan, flipping the veggies perfectly. With everything still steaming, she spooned the mix into circles of dough and folded each expertly, sealing the edges with the tines of a fork. I hated that she worked so many hours only to come home and cook, but that was her thing, she'd insisted. Her anchor to normal. Papi used to say that he fell in love with her cooking first, her soul second, and maybe that's why she still did it. I'd pinned my hopes on the motorcycle, but maybe Mom thought the empanadas would help him remember, that the half-moon sight of them would bring him back.

"Hmm. We should ask your sisters about the mechanic, *queridita*. No?"

"No! I mean . . . They're, like, *super* busy, and we don't need to stress them out over my summer plans with Papi. I can totally handle this, Mom."

Mom finally nodded and I returned to my mushy tomatoes. They reminded me of hearts, and I blinked at the hazy memory of Lourdes's prom corsage crushed in the garbage. And then, seven years later, Araceli's face, streaked with tears.

That whole family is cursed, Mari had said on Araceli's night. *Dark hearts, every one.*

Thou shalt never, ever, get involved with a Vargas? It was one of those things we were supposed to accept without question from that night forward, like the way Mom pressed a fork into her empanadas because that's how Abuelita taught her. It didn't matter if there was a better way, something new to try. It was just how it'd been handed down, as much a part of the family history as our olive skin and long brown tresses.

Well, Mari chopped her tresses and went bombshell blond, but not every tradition could be overturned with scissors and a box of Nice 'n Easy number 104.

The oven door creaked open, heat washing over my bare legs as Mom slid in the empanadas.

"Twenty minutes," she said. "How's the watercress coming?"

I layered red onion rings over the tomatoes. "Done."

"Looks perfect." She winked over my *ensalada de berros* as if she'd known it would be perfect all along.

If our house was ever attacked by zombie bunnies, Pancake would totally sound the alarm, but for now the coast was clear, and he lounged on the floor with his nose against the screen door and eavesdropped on our dinner conversation.

Papi was saying something for the third time about the blueberry pancakes we'd eaten at Ruby's, and the poor dog kept snapping his head back and forth between Papi and the door, Papi and the door. Pancake-*bunnies*-pancake-*bunnies*-pancake-*bunnies*.

When Papi got to the part about Duchess, I gave him the hush-hush symbol before he could name Emilio, and he stuck out his tongue and tugged his ear like we were umping a baseball game.

"Are you okay?" Mom asked him.

"*¿Que?*"

"Okay?" she said louder. "Something wrong with your ear?"

He waved her off and dug into the watercress with his silverware.

"*Dios mío*, use the tongs." She abandoned her chair and dished out his salad, poured the oil and vinegar too.

Sometimes I wondered what it would be like to fly away, as far as I could, like Lourdes and Celi had done, first chance they got. Not just Denver, where I was supposed to go this fall for college.

Away away.

"*Ay*, Rita. Not so much dressing." Papi dumped the excess onto her plate. He smacked her butt and she shooed him off, but she was totally smiling.

"You never make empanadas anymore." Papi manhandled a few more onto his plate.

"Por favor," Mom said. "We had them last week."

He wagged his finger. "You're trying to trick me, woman."

Spain. That's where I'll go. Or maybe South America, look up Papi's old biker buddies, follow the trail he blazed all those years ago.

"We did," Mom said. "Juju, tell him."

"I don't remember," I said.

"That's because we didn't have them." Papi reached for another empanada. Now that calories had been demoted on the list of Things Likely to Kill You When You Least Expect It, he could eat a few more. "When I die, bury me with a plate of these."

Mom laughed. "I would not let perfectly good food go to waste in the ground. Speaking of wasting money, what were you saying about this Duchess boy?"

"Seems like a good kid," Papi said through a mouthful of food. "His name was . . . what was it, Juju?"

"Finish chewing," Mom said.

"Something . . . simple." I scooted my chair closer to Papi. "Oh, Eddie. That was it. Eddie." Mom might not remember the name of every last Vargas, but no sense taking chances.

"How much does this simple Eddie charge?" Mom asked.

"He's cheap," Papi said.

"What if you do it yourselves?" Mom scooped another empanada onto my plate. "Maybe you could order the parts from this Eddie, and read the manuals—"

"Don't be silly. Juju and me, rebuild a bike from scratch? Oh, *mi amor*, you're too much."

Papi was right. If either one of us tried to fix the Harley alone, we'd end up with the world's most expensive toaster.

"I'm telling you, it's a great deal. And it'll feel good to work on her again." Papi knocked on his head. "I remember everything about that bike. We'll show El Demonio who's boss, eh, Juju?"

That's what he called it—the Demon. The evil thing eating its way through his mind, devouring his memories. I pictured it that way too, some hell-bound red dragon, shadow and fire, carving a path of utter ruin.

The doctors had another name for it: early onset Alzheimer's.

I watched him closely, and I wondered if he saw anything, if the words and images turned to smoke as he looked on, helpless. Or if it was more like trying to open a deleted file on the computer, something you thought was there last time but couldn't be certain, and all you got was that annoying message, over and over.

File not found.

I waited for him to finally ask why we'd left Duchess in such a hurry, or to say something about Eddie-slash-Emilio, how he'd seen the family resemblance and changed his mind.

But Papi kept on chewing and smiling. He had no idea who Emilio was.

. . . never, ever, under any circumstances . . .

Dios mío, the oath was a silly thing. The candles. The knife.

The burnt hair. The black book. Mari was such a drama queen. Plus, my sisters would've said anything to make Celi laugh that night. Plus, I was twelve years old—pretty sure no court would uphold a contract signed by a kid under duress. Plus, if anyone wanted to get technical, hiring a Vargas to rebuild Papi's bike was certainly not the same as "getting involved" with one, which I would never do in a million years, oath or not. I stood by my pro-undergarment stance 100 percent—definitely not compatible with the Vargas lifestyle.

"So you like this boy, Juju?" Mom asked.

"What? No! Why would you think that?"

She squinted at me over the rim of her wineglass. "I don't understand. Why hire him if you don't like him?"

"I *like* him. I just don't *like* him, like him. Like a boyfriend."

"Boyfriend?" Mom set down her glass. "Juju, what on earth are you talking about?"

I grabbed my water glass and chugged. For, like, ten minutes. Then I set it on the table and waved off her confusion. "Bad boyfriend. Good mechanic. Since we need a mechanic, and not a boyfriend, we're in luck."

"Juju . . ." Her brow was furrowed, eyes darting from Papi to me. "Do you trust this boy to work on the bike? *No estoy seguro. . . .* Is he a good idea?"

No. Under no circumstances, in Spanish or in English, is Emilio Vargas a good idea.

But across the table, Papi's face was untroubled, his eyes

full of excitement and possibility, and I knew we'd done the right thing today. Papi's soul was tied up in the Harley, his very essence. Emilio Vargas's name set my teeth on edge, but we needed him. He was our *last* good idea. Our only hope.

My only hope was that the youngest in the family of notorious heartbreakers had no recollection that one time, in a galaxy far, far away, we were *this* close to becoming family.

"Sí," I said, and Papi was totally glowing. "It's a great idea."

CHAPTER 3

The storage barn was one teetering pile away from an episode of *Hoarders*, but there was an old workbench and tables that Papi had set up back when he was still allowed to use power tools. He and I had spent the morning clearing out space, and now the Harley rested on its kickstand beneath a dingy blue tarp right in the middle of everything.

"This is your girl, huh?" Emilio beamed at us over the bike, and I felt completely exposed, like I was wearing an even skimpier outfit than yesterday.

Does he know who I am?

Not possible. He hadn't seen me in two years, and even when we went to the same school, we never hung out. I was glued to Zoe, and he'd spent his BHS days surrounded by an impenetrable wall of girls who buzzed around him like spazzy little electrons.

And before that? We never had the chance to meet on

official family business. His brother Johnny had seen to that.

I squared my shoulders and shook off the cloud of nerves and guilt. We weren't here to reminisce about how I never got to wear my junior bridesmaid dress, which was the color of lilacs and was still hanging somewhere in the storage barn, clean and pressed.

"Do the honors," I said.

Emilio peeled back the tarp until the bike stood naked before us. She was dull and banged up, but beauty still shone beneath all those miles, all that time. Emilio ran his hand along the length of her, his feather-light touch lingering at the curves. His forehead creased with intensity as if he were communicating with her very soul.

"Do motorcycles have souls?" I asked.

"Better believe it." Papi was at the workbench rifling through old tools, his hands covered in dust, eyes alert. The barn seemed to have a clarifying effect on him. Maybe it was the faint smell of oil and gas, the remembered clang of tools on metal. Or maybe he just liked being away from the note cards Mom had tacked onto every potentially dangerous object in the house. The barn was a label-free zone.

"They have their own magic," Papi continued. "Especially Valentina—she's something else."

"Valentina?" I asked.

"That's her name. She's been with me a long time, lots of places. Did I ever tell you about Paraguay? We outran a jaguar together. That beast chased us down the road for I don't know how long." Papi wiped his eyes. "If you don't believe in God? That's the day you find religion."

I rolled my eyes. A jaguar? Honestly.

Emilio didn't say anything, just squinted at Valentina, tapping and rubbing, watching and listening. I'd seen people treat horses that way, but not motorcycles. Papi didn't seem bothered by it though. Maybe it was normal biker-guy stuff, like the toothpick thing.

I pulled the cell from my pocket and snapped a picture. Emilio looked up.

"It's for my father," I said.

"Lots of girls want my picture."

Papi laughed.

"Actually, I wanted a picture of the bike, but your giant head got in front of it." I turned back to Papi. "You be quiet. I was taking it for you."

"Talk to me, Valentina." Emilio knelt on the ground and pressed his ear to the gas tank.

What a show-off!

"She saying anything?" I asked, hopping up on the workbench.

Emilio glanced up at me, then back to the bike. "I can't hear her."

"That's weird," I said. "You must be easily distracted. It's pretty quiet here most of the time. Except when Pancake spots a rabbit and goes nuts. Or when it rains. Then it's like someone dropped a bunch of quarters on the roof, and you can't hear yourself think, because—"

"Juju?" Behind me, Papi dusted his hands together. "Let the man work."

My cheeks went hot and I clamped my mouth shut.

Fine. I could observe in silence. *No problema.* None whatsoever. *This is me, being quiet. Letting the man work.*

On the dirt-dusty floor, Pancake yawned and stretched out on his belly. Together we waited, stealth mode, until Emilio finally waved Papi over for a conference. The two of them huddled near the engine, speaking a foreign language. Like, a not-Spanish one.

I hopped off the workbench. Apparently I wasn't very helpful in the motorcycle restoration department, but it felt weird just sitting around looking pretty, as they say. Plus, my butt was asleep.

Emilio stopped speaking and looked up as if I might try to sneak in a few words, but I didn't. He and Papi needed quiet Jude, so quiet Jude they got.

"Sodas," I mouthed, pantomiming the act of drinking one with my right hand while I pointed toward the house with my left.

Yes, my friends, this is what six years of advanced drama looks like!

When I got back to the barn, Emilio was on the floor examining some parts he must've taken off the bike. Papi watched intently, but he'd gone still, his face drawn and pale.

"Come outside and take a break," I said to them. Out loud this time, no more interpretive dancing.

We headed over to the picnic table, where I'd set out Cokes, a cold spread of leftover empanadas, and a bowl of Doritos.

Papi slumped in his chair and reached for a chip. He turned it in his fingers and crushed it, but when the crumbs hit the table, he stared openmouthed as if he'd expected some other outcome.

"Hope they're not stale," I said. "Have some Coke, Papi."

Across from us, Emilio crunched loudly, and I prayed he was too engrossed in Blazin' Buffalo and Ranch–ness to notice Papi fading out.

"Are these bad?" Papi mashed his thumb into the mess on the table.

"They're not exactly healthy." Emilio grabbed another handful. "But they're awesome."

Papi crammed a few chips in his mouth. "I'm not really a morning person," he said, lips dotted with crumbs. "I like camping."

My neck went hot and prickly. One minute Papi was talking about jaguars and chrome piston covers, which he hadn't thought about in decades, and the next he was in outer space. He was like a GPS in the mountains, alternately navigating impossible roads with ease and then losing the satellites.

"We should all go sometime. Lourdes, do you still have that old tent?"

Searching for signal . . . searching for signal . . . searching for signal . . .

"It's Jude, Papi. I don't know where the tent is. Probably in the barn."

I tensed and waited for Emilio to bolt, to come up with some urgent need that would take him anywhere but here. Maybe Mom was onto something, trying to keep Papi tucked away from the world. Not because we should be embarrassed of him. But because everyone else would be embarrassed *for* us, and watching them squirm was worse than enduring the uncomfortable squirming ourselves.

"Love camping." Emilio reached for an empanada. "Only in the summer though. Anything below fifty degrees and I wimp out."

"Remember when we camped at Rocky Mountain, Lourdes?" Papi asked.

I stared at my hands, twisted together so tightly my fingertips turned white. "It's *Jude*, Papi."

"Jude wasn't born yet. Mom was pregnant with her. Don't you remember? Mom couldn't go on the big hikes, and you and Mari wanted to stay in the tent with her while Celi and I climbed Twin Sisters. What a beautiful view—we saw bighorn sheep. Celi almost gave me a heart attack, she got so close with her camera!"

I smiled. It seemed like a good memory; I would've loved to have been there.

But I wasn't.

Lourdes lived in Mendoza now—she'd been out of the country for twelve years already. I barely remembered the times she'd lived here, sharing a room with Mari, who moved to Denver six years ago. Celi was the last to go, and she'd been in Manhattan four years already. They'd all gone off to live productive lives—winemaker, literary agent, executive assistant—and I'd been alone with my parents ever since.

I looked around at our once-crowded picnic table, and suddenly I felt the absence of my sisters like a pressure on my heart. I closed my eyes and tried to remember them exactly as I'd seen them at this table last—two years ago, huddled around Papi as he made wishes over fifty candles. Lourdes couldn't come in person, but she'd attended via Mari's laptop on Skype, and she cheered louder than anyone when Papi blew out the candles, all but one extinguished.

"Jude?" Emilio's voice brought me back. When I opened my eyes, my sisters vanished. All that remained in my memory was that single flame, burning bright beneath the smoke of the others.

"Jude?" Papi repeated. He smiled with his mouth full, and my heart sank.

Please bring Papi lots of happy birthday luck and good health. The end.

"I'm beat." I faked a yawn. "Should we head inside?"

Papi stared at me so long I could almost see the wheels turning behind his eyes, the pieces slipping in and out of the puzzle that never quite clicked into place anymore. "Okay, *querida*."

Emilio was in the barn when I got back, checking out Valentina's speedometer and scribbling notes onto a yellow pad.

"You're still here?" The question was out before I could stop it, words thick with surprise and unexpected relief.

"You think I'm gonna eat and run? We got a job to do here, you and me." He smiled and set the notepad on the workbench, wiped his hands on his jeans. Everything he did was so confident, determined, and when he met my eyes again, my heart gave an involuntary shudder. "Everything okay with your pops?"

"He's . . . It's fine."

Emilio nodded. "I knew it. You needed an excuse to get me alone. Next time just say so, *princesa*. I'll take you somewhere nice and quiet."

The skin around his eyes crinkled when he laughed, and my stomach tried to react with a little zing, but I shut *that* nonsense down with a quickness. Just by talking to this boy and sharing the same air, I was breaking some serious sister code.

Um, Universe? If I'm betraying my sisters, please cause a power outage or freak rainstorm or some other natural disaster. Preferably a super obvious one that leaves no room for interpretation. Anything? Anything at all?

"You and your pops were smart to hire me. I'm really good." Emilio raised his eyebrows in a hopeful arc, making him look about five years younger but doing nothing to diminish his charm. He knew it too—wore that flirty little grin like a badge. "Can't wait to get my hands inside this baby."

"I'm *sure*." I matched his smile, and then deadpanned, flipping open my phone calendar. There was a text invite from Zoe—coffee tomorrow at Witch's Brew with Christina—but I ignored it. I couldn't think about friends right now. Papi's mini-meltdown was an alarm bell, a reminder of how little time we had to get the bike restored, to reconnect Papi with his old memories before he lost any more. "If you're done congratulating yourself, I need to know how much time we're talking. We don't have all summer."

He pulled back almost imperceptibly, but I noticed the change. *Good*. Now that he knew he wasn't dealing with some softhearted little damsel, we could get down to business.

"Time?" I said again, finger poised over the touchscreen.

Emilio rested his hands gently on the bike. "I won't know how much work she needs until I get a good look inside, then we'll need to order parts. I know this great place for rebuilt stuff online, and—"

"Look, Emilio. That's your name, right?" By now I was in full-on actress mode, channeling every heartbreaking babe I'd ever played onstage. "Can you get this thing running by August or not?"

"Absolutely."

"Good. Then we'll see you here tomorrow at—what time did you say?"

"I didn't." Emilio was laughing again, shaking his head.

"I'm at Duchess tomorrow. Think you can wait a whole 'nother day to see me?"

"No. I mean yes. I mean—for your information, I have plans tomorrow." I hastily accepted Zoe's invite and continued scrolling through my calendar as if there were more invitations to consider. *Busy, busy!* "I'm just trying to get your schedule straight for my father. I'm a partner in this restore, and I intend to manage your work *very* closely. Got it?"

Emilio took a step toward me, his smirk widening. "Whatever you say, *princesa*. But if you're gonna work *very* closely with me, you better stop dressing like that." His eyes trailed down my pink lace cami and white capri pants, his stupid dimples like a warning beacon. "Things are gonna get dirty up in here this summer."

CHAPTER 4

Christina's big summer plans involved cramming in shifts at Witch's Brew and checking out the rock climbers who cruised through before their trek up the East Animas cliffs. She'd claimed all that careful observation would enhance her sociology studies at UC Berkeley.

Zoe and I were supposed to be her research assistants. In quotes.

So far, it looked like Zoe had been holding up her end of the deal—after I got to the café this morning, it took five minutes to snag her attention from the pack of boys at the counter.

I'd been trying to put in enough time with the girls to hold my place, to let them know I still wanted in, still thought of them. But things were getting tougher with Papi, and ever since he stopped working, Mom had been taking more shifts at the NICU up in Willow Brush, which meant long hours for all of us. I hadn't seen my besties in weeks.

I'd accepted the invite yesterday to prove something to Emilio—what, I didn't know—but I was glad I had.

"I missed you guys," I said. And that was the truth of it.

"I missed you too!" Zoe said, and Christina nodded, all sun-kissed and adorable in her purple Witch's Brew apron. There was a little emblem on the front beside her name tag, a black witch riding a broom against an all-white moon.

"I wanted to call you, but I didn't know . . ." Christina's eyes darted over to Papi, parked at his own table in his leather Arañas jacket, recently unearthed. Her smile had faltered when he walked in behind me earlier, but she pulled it together fast, bringing him a free blueberry Scrying Scone and a cup of Dark Moon roast. When he'd asked about her summer plans, she pretended she didn't hear and scooted back behind the counter to help a caffeine-jonesing rock climber.

I set my frosty Java Potion and a bag of salted caramels on the table. "What's up with the Dunes? Did we settle on dates yet?"

Zoe smiled so big and bright, all ten million of her freckles lit up, and her red curls seemed to bounce in place. "Yay! I *told* you she wouldn't bail!"

She'd meant it for Christina, but our coffee witch was busy watching Papi, holding her breath like he might wig out again.

Not that I blamed her. Last time she'd seen Papi, he was accusing her of trying to poison him at the BHS family picnic.

A turkey sandwich. That's how it all started.

One of the volunteers had mislabeled it as roast beef, and Christina gladly passed it to Papi as such.

That little error changed everything.

The Turkey Sandwich Incident (TSI), Mom and I later called it. Everyone was there to see it. All the graduating seniors. Parents. Siblings. Teachers. The principal.

And here go my friends: Shock. Confusion. Fear. And then the worst one: pity. I hadn't even told them about the diagnosis yet—Mom wanted to keep it in the family as long as possible—and in the span of five minutes, all the things that made me *me* got erased. I'd gone from Jude Hernandez, best friend, play person, bookworm, bad drawer, salty-snack connoisseur, to Jude Hernandez, Daughter of Crazy Pants.

He wasn't crazy. He had Alzheimer's. And he didn't like turkey. *Really* didn't like it.

Neither did I, anymore.

"Wouldn't miss it," I said with a hefty dose of enthusiasm. "When do we leave?"

"August twentieth," Zoe said, "give or take."

That gave us more than two months to get the bike running.

"Perfect," I said.

Zoe beamed. "Should we hit up Target tomorrow? Stock up on road-trip reinforcements?"

"I work a double tomorrow," Christina said. "Friday?"

"You guys have to stock up without me." I gave them

the highlights version of the bike project, skipping over the name of our mechanic. Emilio and his brothers had been a topic of more Jude-and-Zoe middle-school gabfests than the Cullens, the Lightwoods, or any of the other mysterious yet fictional bad boys we dreamed about back then, and she'd freak if she knew he'd resurfaced. At my house. For the entire summer.

"I need to stick close to home," I said. "Keep an eye on things for my dad."

"For the whole summer?" Christina said.

I popped a few caramels and shrugged. "The guy promised it would be done before our trip."

"But it's our last summer." Zoe's freckles dimmed. "What about the play?"

Upstart Crow was doing *Alice in Wonderland* this summer, starring Zoe as the Queen of Hearts. Six months ago, she and I had grand plans: She'd be the Queen, I'd be Alice, and we'd spend weeks rehearsing to get it absolutely perfect. A real curtain call on our last summer.

When I backed out of auditions, I promised I'd still help backstage, rehearsals, costumes, whatever I could do at the theater. Now even that would be impossible.

"I can't," I said.

"Okay. I get that you have to help out at home," Zoe said, "but you just graduated. And after this we'll be at college, and then we'll have real jobs and a mortgage and all that sucky stuff. This is our last chance for a normal teenage summer."

I chewed on my straw. *Normal teenage summer? What does that even mean?*

"At least she's coming to the Dunes," Christina said.

"She better." Zoe bumped my knee with hers, and I swallowed the lump in my throat, waited for it to lodge back in my chest where it had settled after Papi's diagnosis in January. I'd told Zoe and Christina soon after the TSI, but they didn't really get how someone as young as Papi could have a disease associated with grandparents, with frail old bodies bent and bleached by time. Even I didn't get it. Papi still had the wavy black hair and tanned skin of his youth; he was broad shouldered and strong, and every time I looked at him, some part of me still believed that one day he'd decide enough was enough and shake it off.

Apparently, today was not that day.

Out of the corner of my eye, I caught Papi beelining for the door. He hadn't finished his scone, though when I got up close, I noticed he was wearing a good bit of it on his shirt.

"Papi, you okay?"

"Eh?"

"Can we hang out a few more minutes?"

He watched me a moment, then finally returned to his table by the window.

"Sorry," I said when I got back to the girls. They exchanged a nervous glance, and I fumbled for something to rekindle the conversation. "Any more ideas about the trip?"

Zoe leaned back in her chair. "We're thinking of renting a

car so we don't have to worry about breaking down."

"Good idea. What else?" I slurped up my Java Potion, waiting for her to continue.

"There's some cool stuff to see on the way there, like—"

"Jude?" Christina's face was tight and pale. "Your dad's . . . digging in the trash."

I followed her eyes across the coffee shop. Sure enough, Papi had both hands in the trash can, elbows deep.

"I need something." He glared at me as if it should be obvious. "It's not here. I think . . . I have to go now."

The sun was deceptively cheerful, and as soon as we got outside, he stopped and basked in the light. Behind us, one of the other coffee witches swept a family of tumbleweeds off the sidewalk. Papi watched them catch the air current and mosey on down the road.

"This way." He crossed the street to Grant's Pharmacy and ushered me inside. He grabbed a shopping cart and the warning bell in my head gave a faint tinkle, but before I could ask any more questions, Mari called.

Mari was not the kind of sister you casually forwarded into voice mail.

"Ready for Mari's Internet Dating Fiascoes, take seventeen?"

She launched into the story without waiting for a response, talking fast while I trailed Papi through the store—he cruised past the coolers, through the foot-care aisle, past the vitamins and fish-oil capsules, right to baby central.

"So not only was he missing a tooth," Mari was saying when we reached the diapers, "but he was totally married."

"*Eww.*" It was the only word I'd managed so far, and Mari giggled.

"I know, right? Like he couldn't get a crown or something?"

"I meant the married part. Hang on." I covered the mouthpiece and turned to Papi. "Almost done?"

"Ah!" He smiled and pointed to his head. "Wrong aisle. This way."

". . . the last guy at least had all his teeth." Mari chattered on, oblivious. "But he lived in his mother's basement in Capitol Hill, so obviously *that* was going nowhere."

"Papi, what are you looking for?"

"Papi's there?" Mari said. "Let me say hi."

"We're . . . shopping." I left out the part about us standing in the feminine-products aisle, scanning pink boxes as if they revealed a secret code while some poor kid stocking pregnancy tests tried not to stare.

"What else are you guys doing today?" she asked.

"Coffee with the girls. Maybe . . . fishing? I don't know. What about the basement guy?"

Papi grabbed a box of tampons off the shelf. "Four girls," he told the stock boy. He waved the pink-and-white box like a flag.

"Who's he talking to?" Mari asked.

I switched the phone to my other ear and reached into the cart to retrieve the tampons. "Just the stock guy."

"We need those, Juju." Papi took the box from my hand and dropped it back into the cart, then added a few more. The store kid smiled awkwardly. Thankfully, I didn't recognize him from school.

"Anyway," Mari said as if we weren't approaching code-red in the tampon aisle, "I'm deleting my Match profile."

I tried to steer the cart away, but Papi wouldn't budge.

"Do yourself a favor, son." His voice rose as he swiped boxes of feminine-hygiene products into the cart faster than I could put them back.

"Juju?" Mari asked. "What's going on?"

My throat tightened as I held off a sob. I couldn't do this without her, without Celi or Lourdes. Mom was working so much and Papi was getting worse and everything was falling apart. . . .

"Papi's upset," I said. "He's freaking out and—"

"Where are you?" Her tone went high alert. "Can you call Mom?"

"She's at work. What do I do?"

"What about Zoe, Juju? Jude!" Mari was frantic. "Do I need to call the police?"

Police? The word sent a jolt through my heart, shook me out of my panic. Cops would make things more embarrassing for Papi—for all of us. I had to handle it. We could buy the tampons if we had to—stock up for the next decade if it would get us out of here quickly.

I took a deep breath. "No. I got it covered. Sorry . . . false alarm. But you're breaking up. Call you later!" I clicked the phone off and slipped it into my pocket, reaching for Papi with my other hand.

"If you ever have girls," he told the stock boy, "buy shares in this company. By the time you're my age, you'll own Tampax, Kotex, and any whatever-ex out there."

"Okay, Papi," I said. "Good advice. Let's get home for lunch."

"Lourdes, your sisters will kill me if I go home without this stuff." His voice was getting louder with every word.

"We'll come back later," I said. "I don't know what kind they like." The phone buzzed against my hip bone. Mari.

"It's this kind. I'm sure." He dropped a different box into the cart—a pregnancy test.

"They definitely don't need that." I tried to put it back on the shelf, but he grabbed my arm.

"What are you doing?" he asked.

"It's a pregnancy test, Papi. I thought we were getting tampons?"

And that wraps up the top-ten things a girl should never have to say to her father. . . .

Papi snatched the test from my hands, chucked it back into the cart. "Young lady, I think I know what kind of shoes my own daughters wear."

The lump was back in my throat, threatening to choke off the air. My phone buzzed and buzzed and the overhead lights hummed and I gave Papi's hand a gentle squeeze and leaned in close to whisper in his ear. "Please, Papi. I'm starving. Can we go?"

"I'm not hungry." He slipped out of my grasp and spiked a package of yellow-wrapped pads into the cart.

"Jude?"

I turned toward the voice at the end of the aisle: Zoe, hands on hips, red-gold curls lit by the fluorescent overheads. "What's—"

"Oh, good! Mariposa is here. Is this the kind you like, *querida*?" Papi reached for her as she approached, holding up another package of pads so she could see.

"Papi," I said gently, "this is Zoe. Mariposa isn't here."

"Zoe?" He looked at her as if she were a stranger, as if she hadn't spent most of her childhood camping out in our backyard and sneaking ice cream sandwiches from our freezer. I nodded slowly, praying that Zoe wouldn't say anything to further scramble the circuitry between his ears.

His face filled with recognition. "Do you . . . do you girls need a ride to school? Or . . . no. First I have to get some things for Araceli, then . . . are we at Burger Barn?" He drifted off, his eyes suddenly red and watery.

I wanted Zoe to leave. To turn around without saying another word, to forget she'd come here. Because if anything was worse than seeing a grown man lose it in the tampon aisle, it was seeing a grown man cry because he didn't remember how he'd gotten to the tampon aisle in the first place.

Zoe didn't move, and Papi turned his head from side to

side as if that would help him get his bearings. The stock boy returned to his arranging, but he was straightening the same boxes over and over, his neck and ears bright red.

Papi continued to look around, baffled and humiliated, and I closed my eyes, silently repeating the mantra the social worker doled out after we got the news: *It's not my father, it's the disease. It's not my father, it's the disease. . . .*

"We're at the pharmacy," I told him. "We had Burger Barn the other day, so let's try the Cantina. I've been craving their chips and guacamole."

I touched Papi's elbow, and his eyes cleared. He looked from me to Zoe with renewed focus, sharp and determined.

"My daughters asked me to pick this stuff up for them, can you believe that? But I do it. Because we do what we can, right?"

Zoe forced a smile. "Jude, um, let's get coffee another day. I'll tell Christina . . . um . . . call me when you get home, okay?"

Her eyes were glassy and frantic, and she zoomed toward the door as if the place were on fire, and a woman behind us whispered to her companion, "I think that's her father, poor thing."

"Let's go eat." I tugged on Papi's shirtsleeve, but he shook me off immediately.

"Jude Hernandez, you will settle down and behave yourself in public."

I was five years old again, wilting in the Colorado heat, whining to go home after a long day of errands. People were watching us; the burn of their collective stare scorched my skin. My phone kept buzzing in my pocket, and my tongue was fat and stupid and useless. "Papi—"

"*¡Cállate!*" His command was short and firm, and I did as he ordered: Shut up. He dropped another box into the cart and I stared at a crack in the floor, wishing it would expand and swallow me down into the deep red earth with the dinosaur bones. But it didn't, and people kept passing by and jostling me, and Papi was loading up the cart and—

"It's my favorite Hernandezes." Emilio clomped down the aisle, arms loaded with enough candy and chips to feed the whole garage. When he noticed the disheveled pyramid of boxes in our cart, his eyes went wide.

I didn't have time to worry about my own mortification. Papi was three minutes from a full-scale nuclear meltdown. We needed to vacate. *Rápido.*

"We're leaving," I said. "Just had to get some things . . . for my mother. And my aunts. And all my cousins." *Even though they live in Argentina, where they grow their own tampons.* "Ready, Papi?"

Papi turned to Emilio, his fingers closing on another pregnancy test. "Do you have kids, *júnior*?"

Emilio looked at me with raised eyebrows, but I didn't have answers. Was there a right one? A wrong one? Anything could snap him back to reality or send him into the abyss.

"No, sir," Emilio said. "No wife yet either."

Papi clucked his tongue. "Good-looking guy like you? I don't believe it."

"I know, right?" Emilio loosened up, his smile genuine. "Glad I ran into you guys. I found this vintage Harley blog and—"

"Harley? I used to ride. Sixty-one Duo-Glide," Papi said.

Emilio's eyebrows drew together, but I shook my head, like, *Don't ask, just play along,* and he pressed on. "Yeah, I heard."

"Life throws different things at you though. Can't hold on to the past." He held up the pregnancy test and tossed it into the cart. "Do you kids know if they have the . . . What are they called?" Papi made a balling-up gesture with his hands.

"What are you looking for?" I asked.

"You know. The . . . thingies. For the . . ." He closed his eyes, face contorted with concentration and frustration. "Damnit! God damnit!"

Emilio met my eyes across the cart. My skin crawled with panic, but his gaze didn't waver. "Sing, Jude."

Papi made a fist and slammed it against the cart handle, pounding and pounding, cursing with every blow. The stock boy finally got up from the floor.

"Miss?" he said. "Do you need me to call someone?"

Emilio held up a finger, put the stock boy on pause. "Jude, does he have a favorite song?"

"I don't—I have no idea."

Does he?

Papi kept on hammering the cart, and I scanned my memories as far back as they would go, searching for a note, a lyric, a verse. My mind served up happy birthdays, television theme songs, Mom's tango CDs, but nothing I could remember him singing, nothing he cranked up the car radio for.

Everyone has a favorite song. . . . Why don't I know his?

"I should get the manager," the stock boy said.

"We're fine," Emilio told him. "Jude, sing something. We need to distract him, get him calmed down."

I cleared my throat and started singing "Many a New Day" from *Oklahoma!*, which I hoped Papi would appreciate, since he'd been on that western kick. My voice was shaky at first, but Papi stopped pounding, smiled even, and I kept on.

Never have I wept into my tea over the deal someone doled me. . . .

At the end of my Grant's Pharmacy concert debut, Papi abandoned the cart that only moments earlier had been his entire world. "You're an angel, Juju. How come you don't sing anymore?"

I shrugged, but inside, shame clawed my stomach. I'd manipulated him. Tricked him like you would a little kid throwing a tantrum, offering up a shiny new toy to get him to stop.

"Well, you should." Papi put his arm over my shoulder. "You hungry, *queridita*? Can we get some lunch?"

Just like that, the rage and confusion lifted, and everyone in the store returned to their prescriptions and greeting cards and sunburn-relief gel as if nothing had happened.

Calm followed chaos, a temporary relief, false and tricky.

That's how El Demonio rolled.

CHAPTER 5

"How'd you learn so much about motorcycles?" I sat on the workbench and flipped open a Coke. Now that Emilio had finished the whole bike-whisperer gig, I really hoped my job as silent spectator was over, especially since Papi was down for an afternoon nap and Emilio still hadn't mentioned yesterday's Great Tampon Incident, and one more falling feather of silence would crush me.

Emilio shrugged. "My pops was into bikes. And my uncles. None of my brothers liked 'em, though." He held my eyes for a second, and something crossed his face like a shadow. Regret, maybe? Guilt? I swallowed back my own, hoping he wouldn't bring up my sisters.

"What's up with your dad?" I said. "Still riding?"

Emilio wiped his forehead with the back of his hand. "He's in Puerto Rico with my grandma. I only see him for Christmas."

"Where's your mom?"

"She's here with me."

"They're divorced?" I didn't remember Celi saying anything about that. Maybe it was recent.

"No, still together. They're just . . . weird." He looked like he wanted to say more but then the shadow passed and he motioned for me to come closer. "Check this out."

I knelt beside him and peered into the guts of the bike. He pointed to an accordioned piece below the gas tank that looked like a giant *V* capped with twin metal plates.

"You know why people call Harleys different nicknames, like panhead or shovelhead?" he asked.

"This one's a panhead." I'd looked that up first thing, no way I'd forget.

"Yeah, but why?"

I took another sip of Coke, scanning the archives for a clue. *File not found.* "I forget."

"It's the shape of these rocker arm covers." He popped off one of the metal plates and handed it to me. "See how they look like pans?"

I nodded, and he pulled a manual from a stack he'd brought and flipped to a page in the middle that showed all the different models.

"That's a shovelhead," he said, pointing. "That one's a knucklehead. Valentina's a Duo-Glide panhead, which means she has the pan-shaped covers and the kickstart. You have to jump on it to get her going."

"Like yours," I said. I'd noticed it when he left here the other day.

"Exactly. But mine's an aftermarket addition. It could start with the key, but I like the jump. In sixty-five, Harley rolled out the Electra Glide, which was the first one with an electric starter." He dropped the manual and pointed again to the bike, his whole face lighting up. "Now the Duo-Glide is an FLH model, the H meaning high compression—more power than the FL bikes. 'Duo' is 'cause it's the first Big Twin with suspension in both the front and the rear . . ." He trailed off and looked away, running a hand through his mop of hair, bandannaless today. His face was still glowing. "Sorry. Your pops probably told you all this, right?"

"Only a little." Papi hadn't gotten into the mechanics or the Harley history, but he'd told me everything else about Valentina. How he'd saved up, searched for months for the right one. "She spoke to me, Juju," he'd said. "Called my name." To hear him tell the story, it was no less than magic, an ancient jewel fated to him by the prophecy.

"Not for nothing?" Emilio said. "It's cool as hell you guys are doing this. Not a lot of girls would be into it."

"Girls can't be into Harleys?"

"That's not what I—"

"What can we be into? Being barefoot in the kitchen and pining over you?" I'd meant it playfully, but it came out sharp, and Emilio raised his eyebrows.

"Hey, don't let me stand in the way of your dreams or anything."

I opened my mouth to put that jackass in his place, but

instead of my witty retort, a giant belch escaped.

"Nice!" Emilio laughed. "You went primal for that one, *princesa*."

"It's the soda! And why do you keep calling me princess?"

Emilio flashed me another dimpled smile, but then he just shrugged and turned back to the bike. He poked and prodded, leaned in close to check out the engine.

And then he started humming. One note, two, the first line, the second . . .

Beauty and the Beast, tale as old as time. It was last year's school musical. I'd starred as Belle.

"How do you—"

"Saw the show," he explained. "My cousin Ben played the candlestick guy."

So he does *recognize me from school. . . .*

My stomach twisted when I thought of Emilio watching me twirl around stage in Belle's big yellow dress, cavorting with talking candles and clocks. The whole thing seemed so ridiculous now. And Ben was his cousin? God, there were a lot of Vargas boys. Even though Ben's a Ribanowski, not a Vargas. Still. I wondered if my sisters knew how broadly this dynasty of heartbreakers spanned? We could be talking nationwide pandemic here.

Emilio looked at me over his shoulder, still smiling like he was plotting some big practical joke. "Anyway, I just think it's badass. I don't know any other girls who'd spend their summer restoring a vintage panhead with their pops. That's all I meant."

His dimples diffused the tension, and my shoulders sank under the weight of Papi's secret. Emilio had to know something was wrong with him—there was no logical way to explain the pharmacy meltdown, the random trips to the moon in the middle of a sentence.

"My father . . . This isn't some summer bonding project."

Emilio's face was open and curious, not judgmental. I wanted to tell him the truth, the family secret Mom tried hard to protect, the one I wanted so badly to destroy with the roar of Valentina's rebuilt engine. But the words burned my throat, as if naming the disease out loud would unleash another cloud, darker than the one that had already settled over our family, and I let them turn to dust on my tongue.

"Sorry about yesterday," I finally said. "He gets tired sometimes. Kind of throws him off."

Emilio held my gaze another moment but didn't press. When he asked me to help put away the tools and manuals like it was no big deal, I was so relieved I could've hugged him.

But obviously *that* wasn't happening.

"The good news?" He wiped his hands on a rag. "This is a big project. I'll need to strip her down to the bones, clean her, and build her back up, one piece at a time."

We left the barn and walked toward his motorcycle, parked next to Papi's old truck, and Emilio grinned. "You'll be seein' a lot of this pretty face around here."

"How is *that* good news?"

He took a step closer and stared me down, unblinking, and my stomach flip-flopped.

"Jude, I never thought I'd feel this way, but . . ." He held his hand over his heart. "I think I'm in love . . ." His eyes drilled right through me, and my breath hitched as he licked his lips and leaned in close. . . .

"With empanadas," he whispered.

I jerked away fast. "That was a one-time deal."

Emilio shifted toward me, closing the space between us again. "Hey, for real. This is a cool project. Best thing I ever got to do." He twirled his keys around his finger, the star on a Puerto Rican flag key chain glinting in the sun, silver where it should've been white. "Leave the oil pan set up. The old stuff needs to drain out."

"No problem. Do you need a—"

The words evaporated the second I saw Mom's dark-gray Jetta motor up our driveway.

"She never comes home this early! Um . . . leave." I met his eyes. The amusement there didn't reflect the panic that must've been blazing through mine. "No, seriously. Can you go?"

Mom killed the engine and got out of the car in one swift motion.

"I think she already saw me." Emilio stiffened. "Should I be worried?"

It was too late. She was already walking toward us,

eyeing us up with every step. *Please don't notice the family resemblance. . . .*

"Let me do the talking," I said.

"*Hola, mi amor.*" Mom kissed my cheek and gave Emilio the side eye. "Where's your father?"

"Taking a nap. This is—"

"Emilio," he said, and I winced, hoping he wouldn't say the *V* word.

Mom looked at him a moment, assessing. "Are you . . . one of Jude's boyfriends?"

"*Mom!* God." Mari was the one with the string of random dudes all through high school. The only boy I'd ever brought home was Dylan Porter in tenth grade, my first-last-and-only boyfriend, ancient history. "Don't be weird. He's the mechanic. The one we hired to fix the bike."

"Oh! Sorry, *querida*," Mom said. "I was confused. It seems like you two are old friends already."

"Tryin' my best, but she keeps shootin' me down." Emilio flashed another dimpled smile and leaned in close, our arms brushing. Beneath the faint smell of gasoline and metal, a warm wave of leather and fabric softener wafted up. His muscles tensed as if he were trying not to laugh.

I was trying not to *die*, not that anyone cared.

"Are you staying for dinner, Emilio?" Mom asked. "I'm making *milanesa napolitana*."

"He can't," I said before she launched into a description of her mouthwatering creation. I should've seen it coming.

Feeding people—friends, family, notorious bad boys—was pretty much her holy mission in life, a mission that even trumped the no-strangers-in-the-house rule. "He has a thing."

Emilio was laughing now. "I do?"

"Yeah, you know. Your thing!" I stared at him with wide, desperate eyes. *Basketball practice, chess club meeting, monster truck rally . . . Make something up!*

"Right. My . . . thing. Guess I forgot."

"Some other time, then." Mom watched us for, like, five hours. "Oh! Look at me, talking off your ears. I'll leave you alone to say good-bye. Nice to meet you, Emilio. I don't know why Juju said your name was Eddie. You don't look like an Eddie. Emilio suits you so much better—"

"Mom! Go inside before you hurt someone."

She was practically blushing. What was *with* the women in this family? Vargas was like Hernandez Lady Kryptonite!

Thank God I had my father's genes.

"Good thing I'm such a charmer with the parents," Emilio said once Mom was gone. "Otherwise, this boyfriend thing wouldn't stand a chance." Emilio winked, straddled the bike, and jumped on the kickstart, which I now knew, thanks to his helpful lesson, was just for show.

Who's this hottie you've got working at the house?

What's Mari talking about? Hottie?

OMG, what's Lourdes talking about? Do you have a new boyfriend?

FINALLY! I hope you're being careful!

It had been less than two hours since Mom met Emilio, and already my public Facebook wall—yes, public, thank you!—glittered with my sisters' peanut gallery commentary. Was nothing in this family sacred? Five women, and after decades of shared news and gossip, it was still like the nonstop telephone game. At least Mom had left out his name. So far.

Delete, delete, delete, delete.

I thunked my head on the desk and closed my eyes, my sisters' questions flashing behind my eyelids. No, I didn't have a boyfriend, so no, there was no need to be careful. And if my sisters found out just who this hottie not-boyfriend was, they'd kill me anyway. Lourdes would be on the next plane to New York, Celi would meet her at JFK, they'd rent a Prius and speed all the way to Denver without stopping once to pee, they'd snag Mari, and the Holy Trinity would be on the scene by morning, looming over me at the breakfast table, hands on hips, demanding an explanation.

"It's fine," I said to the family of stuffed owls on my bed. Emilio was temporary. A means to an end. As soon as the bike was running, he'd be out of my life, and "Vargas" would never again pass my lips.

Over.

Done.

Terminado.

I nodded vigorously as if that would help the words settle in, and it worked for about ten seconds. But in all that rattling, I'd shaken loose an image my mind had captured and stored without permission—Emilio, winking at me and jumping on the kickstart, the bike roaring beneath him. My treacherous little beast of a heart fluttered.

I took it for what it was: a warning. The heart—in all its infinite wisdom (with some backdoor bribery from the hormones)—was totally edging in on this Vargas boy situation, and the heart didn't know the meaning of *terminado.*

CHAPTER 6

Emilio Vargas was officially a no-show.

Papi, Pancake, and I had waited for two hours the following morning before I finally grabbed the keys and zoomed us all down to Duchess.

Forget summer theater. I was starring in a lovely little production from the comfort of my own head.

All the world's a stage!

"Here to complain about the kid already?" Duke looked up from his magazine and smiled when we approached the service counter. "Ain't even been a week."

"Just wanted to look at some accessories," Papi said. He'd agreed to let me handle this since Emilio and I seemed to "hit things off." Yeah, I was about to hit things off, all right. Starting with his head.

Duke directed us to a row of shelves stocked with chrome bike parts and dusty manuals that looked like they'd been there since the Industrial Revolution. Or at least the eighties.

"Is Emilio working today?" I asked.

"Yep. Go on back." Duke nodded at the glass door. "Just stay close to the wall—too many loose parts and sharp edges back there."

I didn't know whether he meant the bikes or the boys, but I heeded his advice and pushed through the doorway. All eyes were on me as I scanned the crew. No sign of Mr. No-Show.

"E!" one of the guys yelled. "*Tu novia está aquí.*"

Your girlfriend is here? I can't believe he told them about that.

"Ro-milio, Ro-milio!" one of the other guys said. The rest giggled. They were worse than Zoe and me on a Pixy Stix bender.

Emilio entered through a propped open door at the back of the garage. He punched the first guy in the arm as he walked past, and I let out a big ol' sigh, totally rocking my poker face.

There was only one problem.

Freaking Ro-milio wasn't wearing a shirt.

He nodded when he saw me and turned to grab his T-shirt from the back of the blue Honda I'd seen him working on that first day. He had a tattoo on his left shoulder, black words and numbers, too far away to make sense. There was a nasty scar on his lower abdomen and another on his right shoulder. An accident, probably, and I wondered what happened, but I looked away when I realized the Romilio-calling guy was totally watching me.

What a creeper!

I mean, the guy. Not me. Obviously.

Emilio yanked the shirt on in one fluid motion. "Duke know you're back here?"

I forced myself to focus on the shiny tools spread out near the Honda. "He said it was okay."

"Cool. So . . ." He rubbed a hand over his bandanna and all that "I'm about to hit off his head" stuff evaporated.

"Where were you today?" I asked. "My father waited for two hours."

Emilio shook his head. "I ain't on with you till day after tomorrow."

"You aren't?" I pulled out my phone calendar. "I must've gotten the dates mixed up. I could've sworn . . . No, you're right. We ain't—aren't—on again until the day after tomorrow. Which is when we are."

"You sure about that, *princesa*?" Emilio's eyes held a playful spark. "Maybe you should write it down on paper this time."

Behind him, three of the guys whispered to one another in Spanish and laughed, which only magnified the mortification. It was obvious they didn't know I could understand them, and the one guy kept saying how hot I was and if Emilio screwed it up, he'd be happy to mend my broken heart. And then *something something something* naked.

"Oh, Ro-milio!" one of the guys squealed. The high-pitched whir of the big drill muted their chuckling, but Emilio was unfazed, still staring at me with that mischievous glint.

"I don't like you," I said. "Just so we're clear."

"Did I do something wrong?" he asked. "Did I offend you?"

"No, I—"

"I'm not good-looking enough for you?"

"No. I mean yes. I mean . . . I don't like you *that* way."

"What way?" He smiled.

"The way your friends think I like you. Because I don't."

"Funny." He rubbed his stubbled chin and stared at the ceiling as if he were pondering the world's problems. "Someone must've hacked your Facebook account."

"Huh?" It was all I could croak out before my throat closed up. Seriously, it was like anaphylactic shock up in there.

"You can't take Internet security for granted, Jude. If someone hacked your account, you should report it. People could misunderstand your intentions. Get the wrong idea about you and me."

I coughed and glared back at him like all the mountain lion warning signs on the hiking trails instructed. Make noise. Stare confidently. Make yourself appear larger than you are. "There's *no* idea about you and me. I don't like you. Not as a boyfriend. Not as a friend. Not as anything. Okay?"

"Okay. So . . ." He loosened his bandanna and retied it, pulled it snug. "Why are you here again?"

I stamped my foot on the concrete floor, totally five-year-old. What was my problem? I'd been around boys forever—kissed a lot of them too, and not just Dylan Porter. Granted, the others were for school plays, but still. Composure, people. I had it in spades.

The drill let out a few short chirps and I jumped. Being in the garage was clearly affecting my brain—the chemicals and lack of sunlight and probably noise pollution had something to do with it too.

"I came to clarify a misunderstanding about your schedule," I said, "but obviously the concept of adult conversation is foreign to you, so I'll leave you to your motorcycles and expect you the day after tomorrow. And I don't know what kind of health codes you're used to violating here, but at my house, you *will* wear a shirt."

The *tu novia* guy—Samuel, I thought someone had said—laughed. *"Chica loca,"* he told Emilio.

I flashed him a wicked grin, straight out of the Mari Hernandez Complete Guide to Melodrama. "I'm a crazy girl? Is that right?"

All the mechanics turned toward me with dopey boy-grins like they'd bought front row tickets to the show. But they had another thing coming. I was *not* there to be anyone's matinee.

"Si quieren ver una película, traten Netflix," I said. Then I poked Emilio in the chest. *"Pasado mañana. No llegues tarde."*

Day after tomorrow. Don't be late.

If I remembered the Spanish phrase for *jerkoff*, I would've added that too.

"*¡Adiós!*" I pushed past him and marched back into the shop.

Duke looked up from his reading. "Forgot you were back there, hon. You all right? Boys didn't give you a hard time, did they?"

I shook my head and returned his smile, but something was off. . . .

Papi. Pancake.

"Where's my father?"

Duke looked around the shop. "Huh. Must've stepped out."

I paced the entire floor, even though it was obvious Papi and the dog weren't there. Duke checked the restroom, but that was a dead end too. I stuck my head back through the doorway into the garage. "Has anyone seen my father?"

The guys shrugged and looked around, but Papi wasn't there. He wasn't anywhere. He must've wandered out while I was arguing with stupid Emilio, who now looked at me with a mixture of curiosity and mild alarm.

I bolted out the front door.

"He can't be far." Emilio was right behind me, scanning the sidewalk in both directions. "Bookstore and Grant's that way and the ice cream place down there—those are the most likely spots."

"How do you know? He could be anywhere."

Emilio raised a hand to shield his eyes from the blazing sun. "Those are the best choices."

"It's your fault he took off in the first place. If you weren't so busy trying to show off—"

"Jude." Emilio grabbed my arms. "Let's find your pops, okay?"

I wanted to tell him I was certainly capable of finding my own father, but clearly I wasn't, and Emilio had already taken off toward Uncle Fuzzy's Creamery.

"Papi!" I almost collapsed as the worry dissolved into relief. "Where were you?"

Papi strolled up the sidewalk with Pancake and Emilio, spooning mint chocolate chip ice cream into his mouth. "Felt like a sundae. I didn't know how long you'd be with the boys."

"You scared me!" I smeared the tears leaking out of my eyes. Emilio must've thought I was ridiculous, crying on the sidewalk on a beautiful sunny day because my father—a grown man who'd once ridden a motorcycle all over South America without a GPS or anything remotely like a plan—had walked two blocks down the street with the dog.

Papi put his arm around me and hugged me close, his hand cold from the ice cream cup. "I'm sorry, Jujube. I didn't mean to worry you."

"You can't do that, okay? You have to tell me. You can't—"

"I'm *okay*. I'm all right, *querida*." He patted my shoulder once more and trotted over to a bus stop bench with Pancake to finish up his sundae.

"You okay?" Emilio asked. "I gotta get back."

"Yeah, I . . . sorry I snapped." I kept my voice low, eyes on Papi. "I'm supposed to watch him. He's . . . I should've been more careful."

"What else?" Emilio asked.

I shook my head. "Just that I'm sorry."

"Nah, you wanna say more. I can tell. Your lips press together when you're thinking."

"They do not." I clamped my mouth shut, then immediately opened it. Closed it. Opened it. Then I didn't know what to do because Emilio was probably right and *that* thought drove me nuts, so I just stood there with my lips slightly parted.

"Jude?" Emilio stepped closer, his body blocking out the sun, eyes serious, and my heart sank. I couldn't handle it again. The looks. The whispers. The overbearing silences that crept in whenever people figured out that something wasn't right with Papi. I didn't even know Emilio, and I could already see it happening.

He put his hands on my shoulders, and I braced for the letdown. *Sorry, Jude, maybe next time. . . .*

"We cool?" he said. "For the—"

"Sorry," I said again. "The Facebook thing . . . my sisters . . . They don't . . . um . . . live in town," I finished up.

Random!

"That's . . . nice. I'm talking about the bike. Still on for Wednesday? Shirt required?" Emilio smiled, and it was like, stubble, dimples, scar.

Damn.

"Wednesday," I said with a firmness that I hoped masked the awkward. "Shirt required."

CHAPTER 7

I was still rubbing the morning from my eyes on Wednesday when I caught Papi's silhouette in front of the patio doors. GLASS DOORS. ➔ ➔ ➔ SLIDE OPEN BEFORE WALKING OUTSIDE.

He turned toward me, squinting like I might be a shadow, and I took in his outfit: Gray pants with a crease above each knee from the hanger. Pale-green button-down, cuffs undone. Shiny black shoes, untied. His cologne took a moment to register.

Cologne. That's what had woken me up, I realized. The scent had become unfamiliar, a near stranger in our house revisiting after months away.

"Papi?" I stepped into the light. *"¿Hacerte un café?"* It was his favorite old joke, the power of suggestion he'd wielded for years when my sisters were still around. *Get yourself a coffee!* In other words, *Make me some coffee!*

But he didn't smile this time, didn't wink and wag his finger like I'd finally beat him at his own game.

"No." He looked at his hands, forehead creased with concentration. "I'm . . . I think I'm late for something. An appointment?"

"Your appointment is tomorrow. See?" I directed him to the dry erase calendar we kept on the fridge now. "You got the date wrong, that's all."

He checked his watch and looked back out the doors. Pancake nudged his leg and gave a short yelp.

"No big deal. I did the same thing the other day with Emilio, remember? I thought he was late and—"

"There's a staff meeting." Papi's face was pained with the effort of searching, seeking something that would never be found, and when I finally figured out what it meant, a dark ache bloomed in my chest.

He wasn't confused about his doctor's appointment tomorrow. He'd gotten ready for work, same as he had every weekday for thirty years until a few months ago when they kindly suggested he take an early retirement—a diplomatic way of putting him on disability.

"You don't have that job anymore," I said gently. "Now your job is to hang out with me all day."

He probably just needed a break. A day to mellow out, avoid the crowds of Old Town, take his mind off Valentina's problems.

"How about a Scrabble rematch?" I said. "You up for getting your butt kicked, *mi viejito*?"

Papi stared at me so long I thought he was trying to place

me, to remember where he'd last seen my face. I'd been careful about giving him his medications, taking him for walks in the sun when he was up for it, just like the doctors instructed. But this was the second major misfire this week.

He was getting worse.

"I think I'll watch some TV, maybe have some coffee. Okay?" He smiled, but his eyes were glassy. A blush seeped into his cheeks, and I turned to the pantry, DRIED AND CANNED FOODS ONLY, and rummaged for the coffee filters as if I hadn't noticed.

Clint Eastwood was a familiar guest in our living room, and his signature rasp and gunslinging badassery blazed a trail through my skull all morning. After *A Fistful of Dollars*, I slipped out onto the front porch for a slightly less blazin' coffee break, leaving Papi to watch his favorite—*The Good, the Bad and the Ugly*—for the hundredth time.

I'd been out there a couple hours, drifting in and out of half sleep in the golden butter sun, when a once-familiar sight pedaled up the driveway. I thought I was dreaming, ten years old again, waiting for Zoe to get here after dinner so we could run down to the Animas and wash our dusty feet and Kool-Aid mustaches.

Zoe parked her bike alongside the house and clomped up the porch stairs with her backpack. I blinked at her in the sun, still halfway between awake and asleep, the hazy dreamworld where anything was possible. *Is she really here?* I scanned her face and silently counted her freckles, an old habit.

"Morning, sunshine!" Zoe beamed as she fished a stack of papers from her bag. "It's the script! Help me read? I have to make notes and—"

"You see, in this world there's two kinds of people, my friend," Papi and Clint Eastwood simultaneously warned through the open windows behind me, the TV volume shooting up exponentially. "Those with loaded guns, and those who dig. You dig."

Papi howled with laughter. It was his favorite part, right near the end.

"Hope you don't mind a little competition on those lines." I stood from my wicker chair and stretched. "This is a really good part. Wanna watch? It's the end, but it's funny."

"No, but . . ." Zoe's eyes darted around me to the window, and when Papi cackled again, she took a step backward. "Isn't your dad, like, working on the bike? Where's the motorcycle guy?"

"In the barn." When Emilio arrived after breakfast, I'd sent him out back alone to give Papi his TV break. It seemed like a good idea at the time, but now that Zoe was standing on the porch with all those questions, I wanted to be out there with him, passing him tools and listening to the sound of dust collecting on the old boxes.

"Zoe, it's *Papi*," I finally said. *The guy who built our tree fort and called in sick to work to camp out for our Angry Hermits tickets.* I let the thought float silently between us and watched Zoe crunch the numbers, predict the possible outcomes.

They'd played out across her face in the span of eight seconds, and by the time we hit nine, I was reaching for the door without her.

"I'm coming." She slipped in behind me, and then she was through the entryway, marching toward the kitchen, straight past Papi.

"Hey, Mr. H.," she called once she got herself situated at the kitchen table. It was a safe distance away. He didn't hear her.

"I know she's supposed to be this total psycho," Zoe was saying, "but I'm holding back until the end. Do the super-polite thing all along, and then, BAM! Bring out the crazy. Totally unnerving, right?"

"Totally." I dumped a box of pasta into a pot of boiling water as Zoe scribbled notes in the margins of her script.

"What about the off with her head bit? Like, should I go, 'Off with her *head*,' or, '*Off* with her head'? Or maybe, 'Off with *her* head'?"

"Maybe the second one?"

"*Off.* Yeah, that's what I thought too. What about—"

"Hey, girls," Papi called from the living room. "Did you know they call these movies spaghetti westerns?"

"Yes," we said in unison. It was the third time he'd made the proclamation and the whole reason we were having spaghetti for lunch—Papi's request.

He muted the commercials and shuffled into the kitchen. He'd shed the dress shoes after breakfast and was rockin' a pair of Mom's slippers, which were too small on him and covered in peach and yellow roses. "In the sixties the Italians made all these cowboy movies. They filmed them in Italy and Spain, and if you look closely, you can see some of the actors speaking Italian. They recorded the English after. Isn't that something?"

"That's awesome, Papi," I said.

Zoe buried her face in her notes, scribbling and scrawling, deep in thought, and Papi shuffled back into the living room. Gunfire broke the silence once again.

I slid open the GARBAGE ONLY—NO DISHES OR CLOTHING trash compactor. A glossy, magazine-size pamphlet glared at me from beneath this morning's coffee grounds—I must've been too worried about Papi to notice it before. There was a white-haired couple on the front, hands clasped over the woman's knee. Behind them, a woman not much older than Lourdes smiled awkwardly, her hand on the man's shoulder.

I pulled out the brochure and shook off the coffee mess. Bright purple letters marched along the bottom of the page as if they had nothing to hide, nothing to be ashamed of.

Transitions: Talking to Your Family About Long-Term Care Options.

"Why do you think the Queen is so bitchy, anyway?" Zoe asked. "Crappy childhood?"

"Probably," I said, but I was barely listening.

Transitions, as it turned out, was a care facility in Willow Brush, the town where Mom had been working those extra shifts, about an hour and a half north of us. It had a medical staff, a rec room, a ballroom, swimming lessons, yoga, a salon, and most important—since it was spelled out in all caps—A SPECIAL WING FOR ALZHEIMER'S PATIENTS! And if the shiny photos could be believed, these special patients were happy, well fed, and extremely compliant.

And as old and weathered as fossils.

Zoe rambled on about the Queen's tortured backstory, and I flipped through every wrinkled page, reading about the challenges of caring for this "special population," patients who wandered aimlessly at night, forgetting where they were. These Transitions people were super equipped to "manage" them. They locked the doors and windows, padded sharp corners, corralled them into "safe zones."

My teeth clenched. I imagined cattle and horses locked behind an electric fence, eating out of a shared trough, counting down the hours till the slaughter.

At the end, I found the note. Beige card stock, folded in half, tucked inside the back cover.

Handwritten. As if she knew us.

Dear Rita,

I'm so glad we had the chance to talk. I've enclosed the brochure and application packet you requested. Please don't hesitate to contact me if you have any questions or would like any additional information on the Transitions facility or staff.

You, Ted, and your daughters are in my thoughts during this difficult time. Know that I'm here when you need me.

Sincerely,

Janice McMullen

Ted? No one called him Ted. He was Papi or Bear or at the very least Teddy. And who was this Janice person? What right did she have to put us in her thoughts? She didn't know *anything* about us. Because if she did, her letter would've apologized for bothering us with this useless brochure. Papi wasn't some crusty curmudgeon who needed his food pureed, and the only ballroom dancing he'd ever done was tango with Mom, moves they showed off only at weddings after a few too many glasses of Malbec.

Guilt seeped into my stomach.

The last thing I'd wanted to do was tell Mom about Papi's pharmacy meltdown the other day, but we'd made a deal after the diagnosis. Freak-outs, prolonged disorientation, severe mood swings—all documentable evidence. The doctors said that keeping an accurate report could help them track the progression of his illness and modify his treatment plan accordingly, but I thought it was busywork, something to keep us distracted from the fact that there *was* no treatment. It was like drawing a treasure map upside down, dashes and arrows and *X*s that led straight into the sea no matter which way you turned it.

I'd kept my promise, told Mom and Mari about the Grant's episode that very night, and now I realized they'd be looking for this stuff—the random outbursts. Getting dressed for a job he no longer held. Too tired to help Emilio with the Harley. It wasn't about treatment anymore. It was ammo; every wrong turn or confused expression another excuse to stash him away.

I tore up the note and dropped the pieces into the trash. Then I went after the brochure, shredding it page by page until the old people turned to ash and the poisonous words became individual letters, neutral and harmless.

"Are you okay?"

"Huh?" I'd almost forgotten Zoe was there. "Sorry. The Queen . . . yeah. She probably had a bad childhood."

Zoe crinkled her nose. "We were talking about costumes and makeup."

I looked at the torn bits of paper in my hands. Then back to Zoe. Back to the paper. Everything went blurry.

If Janice thought for one second we'd let Papi turn to dust at that place . . .

"Jude? What are you doing? What is that?"

I mirrored Zoe's concerned gaze. She'd stopped staring at her script long enough to notice things weren't right on my side of the world.

"Mom must've brought it home from one of their appointments," I said softly. I told her about the letter. What it meant.

She didn't say anything at first, and I dumped the rest of the brochure into the compactor and flipped the switch, DO NOT TOUCH, until everything turned to gray pulp.

Transition that, *Janice.*

"I'm sure it's nothing." Zoe shuffled her papers and wrapped her fingers around the edges, fanned the corners against her thumb. "They probably give it to everyone who's . . . the patients and spouses and stuff."

I blinked against the images. *Crisp white sheets. Metal beds. No sharp edges . . .*

"Don't think about it," Zoe said. "If your mom actually needed it, she wouldn't have thrown it away. Right?"

The pasta was bubbling over in the pan, water hissing on the burner. Some of the noodles had stuck to the bottom, and I stirred and scraped, suddenly desperate to loosen them.

"She's taking him to an appointment tomorrow," I said once I'd freed the noodles. "Maybe it has something to do with—"

"Stop. Know what you need? A day off," Zoe said brightly. "You're driving yourself nuts. Come to rehearsal tomorrow. We're doing a full run-through with the scripts. You can watch—you'll love it." Zoe smiled as if I were already convinced, as if her plans for the so-called normal teenage summer would fix everything.

We're painting the roses red. . . . We're painting the roses red. . . .

I promised her I'd be there, and before I could confirm the time, the huge grandfather CLOCK NOT PHONE BOOTH in the hallway chimed one, a single gong that flash-froze the words on my tongue, and in its echo a line from Janice's note resurfaced, hammering my brain with sudden, glaring obviousness.

I've enclosed the brochure and application packet you requested. . . .

It wasn't just the glossy brochure—there was more. An application packet.

And Mom had *requested* it.

"Ready for the report?"

I jumped and turned to find Emilio peering through the kitchen screen door.

"I got the front end disassembled," he said. "Inside's in good shape. Nothing we can't clean up."

I heard the words, knew Emilio was talking about the bike. But my brain was stuck in first gear, unable to shift from the images in the brochure, the letter from the woman who thought she knew our family.

"Jude?" Emilio's tone changed, his voice tighter. "Are you—"

"So, I'm Zoe." My best friend batted her eyes at Emilio until recognition dawned on her face. "Wait, you're—"

"Emilio." He opened the door then, crossed the kitchen to where I stood at the sink. Again, I saw it all happen—Emilio's sneakers on the tile floor, Zoe fidgeting at the table, noodles tumbling in hot water that splashed and sizzled on the stove—but it was like watching from outside the window, and suddenly Emilio was next to me, his soft gray T-shirt brushing my arm as he leaned to turn off the burner.

"Everything okay?" he asked.

I stared dumbly at his hand on the counter, focusing on a streak of oil across his index finger.

"Maybe you should sit down, Jude." He put his hand on my arm, and I finally snapped out of it and turned back to the pot on the stove. The water had gone calm and milky.

"Lunch," I said. "I was making . . . What were you saying about the bike?"

I felt his eyes on my back, but when I lifted the pot and shifted to drain the water, he stepped out of the way and continued.

"I was saying the guts are in pretty good shape, but we're missing some flange nuts."

"Flange nuts."

"They hold in the bolts," Emilio said. "*El jefe* might have some extras in the barn somewhere."

"I'm about to call him for lunch. You hungry? I made a lot." I tossed the pasta with a jar of sauce in a giant ceramic bowl, and Emilio smiled, big and goofy. I directed him to the bathroom to wash up, ANTIBACTERIAL SOAP: TWO PUMPS ONLY!

"Emilio Vargas?" Zoe whispered once he was out of earshot. Her eyes were wide with shock. "The motorcycle guy is Emilio Vargas?"

"Shh!" I set the steaming bowl of pasta on the table.

"Dark hearts, every one," she teased. Not that I needed the reminder. That was exactly how Mari had first described the Vargas boys. Back then, standing outside Celi's door in the middle of the night, I'd felt the words like an electric shiver up my twelve-year-old spine, and it was the same when I'd recounted the whole story to Zoe the following night. They were the right words, she'd agreed. Two devilishly handsome brothers, years apart, each destined to break a Hernandez heart. It *did* seem like something out of a book, straight from the black-and-silver cover. *In a world of smoke and flame, caught in a centuries-old battle between good and evil . . .* Maybe the Vargas boys were vampires or fallen angels, Zoe and I had wondered. That particular fantasy had lingered on the edge of our dreams for months, whispering to us in the dark hours of our backyard campouts.

But Zoe wasn't reminiscing now.

"You hired Emilio Vargas? And you never told me?"

I set out plates and silverware, hoping she wouldn't see the guilt in my eyes. "Guess I forgot."

"How could you forget Emilio Vargas?"

"That's what *I'm* sayin'." Emilio crossed his arms and leaned against the doorway between the hall and the kitchen.

"We were talking about something else," I said.

He flashed that killer smile. "Something else named Emilio Vargas?"

Zoe scooped her stuff off the table and shot me a wounded look. "I told Mom I'd help her in the garden today, so I'm out. Thanks for your help with the script."

She didn't say good-bye to Papi but stopped at the door and leaned down to scratch Pancake behind the ears. Zoe looked up at me once more, maybe giving me a chance to explain, to ask her to stay, but I didn't move, and she walked out the door and hopped on her bike without another word.

Logically, I knew Papi's illness was progressive. The doctors told us he'd deteriorate, mentally and physically, until we could no longer care for him at home. They didn't know when, just that it was coming. I felt it too. Every day, a little piece of him vanished. He could still use the bathroom and feed himself and all the other stupid stuff you never think about until you can't do it anymore, but he might not remember that he'd watched *The Magnificent Seven* two days in a row, or that he didn't need lined flannels in the summer. Perhaps he put on Mom's slippers this morning because he got frustrated trying to tie his own shoes.

Or maybe he thought they were *his* slippers.

Progressive. Degenerative. Destructive. The "ives" had been batted around like a tennis ball all year.

But to look at him now, doing his Spanish accent cowboy impersonations for Emilio and talking about those missing flange nuts and which part goes where . . . How could someone so whole and alive be shriveling up inside? My brain hurt to contemplate it, and I forced myself to stop, lest the demon sense my thoughts and try to prove its mettle.

I didn't need more proof.

"In this world there's two kinds of people, right, Juju?" Papi brandished his fork like a pistol. "Those with loaded forks, and those who pass the spaghetti. You pass the spaghetti."

I rolled my eyes as I handed over the bowl, but tears gathered behind my lids.

Who will sit next to Papi at Transitions and watch the cowboy movies? Do the nurses know all the quotes? Do they know about the Italians and the spaghetti?

I slipped over to the sink and pretended to blot spaghetti sauce from my shirt as Emilio and Papi puzzled over Valentina. Papi knew he'd replaced the bolts when he first got the bike because it was the same day he'd joined Las Arañas Blancas. He recalled how the leather smelled when he first pulled on that jacket, how quickly it warmed in the Argentine sun.

I closed my eyes. Valentina was so important, held so many memories. Maybe I didn't understand the demon illness, but I knew without a doubt that reconnecting Papi to his past was the only way to bring him back to the present, and with Mom already screening places to stash him . . .

In the words of John Wayne in *The Cowboys*, "We're burning daylight."

"I'll clean up," I said when Emilio brought me his dishes. "You get back to the bike."

Emilio frowned. "No coffee? I thought you Argies were all about the coffee."

"*Hacerte un café*, Juju," Papi said.

"Make it yourself," I told Emilio.

"Yours tastes better," Papi and Emilio said simultaneously. They both laughed. *So clever, these biker boys!*

"It's just Dark Moon roast from Witch's Brew." I filled the pot with water and dug out a clean filter. "Ten bucks a pound, there for the taking."

"Wow," Emilio said. "You really know how to take the magic out of it."

"Fine. It's not *just* Dark Moon. It's half dark, blended with thirty percent espresso and twenty percent Solstice Spice. That's my special blend. Magic enough for you?"

"Abracadabra."

"Someone is on a mission," Papi said playfully, and I returned his smile. The bike would be finished this summer and Papi would be fine, and Janice and all the other concerned medical professionals could take their long-term care facility and shove it, while the rest of us ate empanadas and laughed about that one summer Papi almost lost his mind.

CHAPTER 8

"We'll be a few hours," Mom said. "The doctor wants us to meet with another specialist."

"What about Janice?"

Mom stiffened.

"Papi said something about a Janice," I said quickly.

"She's a new social worker. She's helping with some of the . . ." Mom waved her hand around, searching for the right word, which I hoped wasn't *transitions*, because that would make me lose my waffles, and then I'd seriously fa-*reak*, because they took an hour to cook perfectly and they were so delicious that I didn't even mind when Papi smothered his with mayo instead of butter.

" . . . adjustments," Mom finally said.

Papi emerged from the upstairs bedroom, fumbling with his cuffs as he clomped down the stairs. The button-down shirts and khakis Mom dressed him in for appointments were a far cry from the mismatched flannels I let him get away with.

"These stupid things." He was grumbling and mumbling, turning his wrists like there might be some yet-to-be-discovered secret to buttoning the sleeves.

"*Ay*, we're late." Mom reached for his cuffs, but he shook her off.

"Bear, there's no time—"

"Then don't dress me in these shirts." If he remembered the shirt from yesterday's nonexistent staff meeting, he didn't say, and now his brow furrowed as his fingers tried unsuccessfully to push a tiny button through a tiny hole.

"Do it in the car," Mom said. "We have to go."

"I'm not going anywhere half dressed." He squinted at the buttons; his fingers seemed to be getting fatter by the second.

Mom was a powerhouse. On an almost daily basis, she held colicky newborns, sang and rocked them for hours. She patiently inserted breathing tubes and changed diapers the size of cocktail napkins. She conducted important, lifesaving tasks amid entire nurseries of crying babies.

She'd birthed and raised four crying babies of her own.

But here in our living room, two little plastic buttons were about to wreck her; her eyes were wild and desperate, cheeks the waxy red of store-bought apples.

"What would Clint Eastwood say?" I stepped between them and steadied Papi's hands. "Wear a fancy shirt like this, and people might think you've gone respectable."

"Wouldn't want that."

"Your secret is safe with me, *viejito*." I winked, and he

forgot his frustration with the buttons as I did them up. "Call me when you have news. I'm going down to Upstart Crow."

"Oh? I thought you weren't doing the play this year," Mom said.

I scooped up my backpack, heavy with a bound manuscript Mari had sent last week—perks of being her authors' target audience—and a bag of white cheddar popcorn. No telling how long I'd be sitting in the audience today, watching the same scenes on repeat. "Just helping Zoe."

"*Bueno, mi amor.*" Mom went about her daily search for sunglasses (on her head), purse (kitchen table where she'd set it five minutes ago), keys (in hand). She was more scattered than usual, her mind clearly on Papi and whatever the hospital had in store: *Draw a face, draw a clock, what's your address, repeat this tongue twister, need more drugs?* Papi, on the other hand, was unfazed. Now that his shirt was all done up, he kneeled on the floor and called for Pancake.

But before Papi'd gotten his dose of pooch slobber, Emilio was rolling up the driveway. He met us at the door. Mom was on company behavior with a welcoming hello, and Papi followed with a fist bump, which Emilio gladly returned.

Oh, it's like that *now?*

"Hey, Jude." He tried to hit me with those dimples, but I was all, *Shields up*!

"Didn't you get my text?" I asked. "I'm going out for a while, so . . ."

"*No problema.* Got everything I need in the barn."

"It's too beautiful to be cooped up today," Mom said. "You guys should go on a hike or a picnic."

"Good idea." Papi winked at me. "Take a load off."

Zoe used to tell me I was lucky to have such "liberal, cosmopolitan" parents. Now I just wished they'd send me to my room, forbid me to be home alone with any boys like normal parents did.

"Aren't you late?" I said.

"Oh!" Mom's eyes bugged out. "Yes! Bear, let's go! *¡Vamos! ¡Vamos!*" She kissed me and made me promise to take the *ensalada rusa* from last night's dinner on our picnic. "Have fun today, *querida*. Enough for all of us."

Back in the house, the only sounds were Pancake's nails on the linoleum and the endless ticking of the grandfather clock.

I dumped my cheddar popcorn into a turquoise bowl on the island counter between us and dug in. "Sorry if Mom got your hopes up, but I'm going into town. You're on your own today."

Emilio leaned across the counter, elbows resting on the white tile. "What about our picnic?"

"Have some popcorn." I opened the fridge to scope out the beverage situation. Top shelf, COLD DRINKS AND YOGURT. "Want a Coke?"

"Nope."

I felt him right behind me suddenly, and I turned to face him, holding two sodas like a double-fisted barrier at my chest.

He took the cans and put them back in the fridge. Shut the door. Leaned against it. His gaze swept my face and finally settled on my eyes. "Wanna get out of here for a while?"

He didn't blink or look away, and the footprint of his words lingered in my ears, pressed pictures into my mind. *I'll climb on the back of that black motorcycle and slide my arms around you, and you can take me away, over the mountain passes, through eons of rock and tree and all the ancient places, and the wheels will kick up red dust, and the wind will blow it from my hair, and we'll outrun our yesterdays and tomorrows and I'll never ever look back. . . .*

"I don't . . . Where?" I backed into the counter. He followed, keeping just enough space between us to confuse me. Was he hitting on me? Were we friends? Did friends flirt like this? Was he just looking for a way to pass the time, to get out of work today? "What about—"

"You'd be doing me a huge favor," he said. "I need a bike lift from Duchess. Samuel was gonna bring it up in his truck later, but if you took me down there now, we'd save a bunch of time."

A favor. Of course.

"Besides," he continued, "what kind of boyfriend would I be if I didn't take you out?" Emilio's eyes locked on mine, like, *Target acquired! Prepare to launch!* "We ain't even had our first date, our first kiss. . . . I'm strikin' out."

"Surprising, considering how romantic you are, bringing a girl to the motorcycle garage. *And* making her drive. Nice first date."

"You want me to drive, *princesa*? Take you for a spin on the bike?" He twirled the Puerto Rico key chain around his pinkie and smirked. Everything he did seemed like a dare, an invitation to some secret place where time didn't exist and boredom didn't stand a chance.

"I'll pass," I said.

"Thought we had something special, you and me."

"Yeah. My father's paying you to be here. *Super* special."

He made a face like a wounded puppy, and I abandoned the popcorn bowl and most of my good judgment.

"I'll take you," I said. "But I only have an hour. And this isn't a date; it's a favor. Which means you owe me."

"Any other conditions?" He raised an eyebrow. Only he still hadn't quite mastered the trick, so it came out less charming and more menacing.

"You practice that eyebrow thing in your bedroom mirror, don't you?"

That rascally eyebrow dropped, and I swear his face turned pink, but with the stubble it was hard to tell.

"That mean you're stalking me? You been at my house? Maybe you snuck in my room?" He took a step closer, invading my space with his fabric softener scent, and for a second I imagined his room, how it must've looked when he woke up this morning . . . gray T-shirt tossed over the edge of the bed. Wild hair rumpled and crazy. His morning face, that deep sleep-scratchy voice, my fingers tracing the scars on his shoulder, his abdomen . . .

"Hey," he whispered. "You don't have to sneak around. I'd let you in."

I almost choked. Was that a popcorn kernel? Those things could be pretty dangerous.

"Does that stuff actually work on other girls?" I asked. "I bet you practice *all* your favorite lines in the mirror, huh?"

Emilio shook his head. "Don't need a mirror. I know how I look."

"Yeah, like an idiot." I called for Pancake and walked outside, Emilio trailing behind. Fresh air, that's what the situation called for. Nothing a little sunshine couldn't cure.

"Sure you don't want a ride?" Emilio jerked his thumb toward the motorcycle.

"Positive."

"Your pops was this trailblazer, right? And you won't ride anything that ain't got four wheels. You really his kid?"

I laughed, but the mention of Papi and his old life clawed my insides. I wish he'd wear his Arañas jacket to the doctor appointments instead of stuffy corporate shirts. He looked pretty hard core in the jacket, even all these years later. Maybe then the old A-heimer's would get the memo and run the other way, like, *Oh, we'd better not mess with* this *muchacho!*

"I roll with Pancake," I said, "and he doesn't do motorcycles. Right, boy?" Pancake totally agreed, evidenced by all the tongue lolling and tail wagging as I got him situated in the truck's backseat.

Emilio and I climbed in front. As soon as he clicked his

seat belt, he noticed the shifter on the floor between us. "You drive stick?"

I pressed down the clutch, started her up, and revved the engine. Like, three times.

"*Ay, Dios mío*, this girl." Emilio rolled his eyes and I shrugged, like, *Hells yeah! Motorcycle restoration, driving standard . . . nothing this girl can't rock!*

I caught my reflection in the rearview as I backed out of the driveway.

Pretty ridiculous.

The lift was a massive orange ramp with an adjustable platform, presumably for the motorcycle, and through the window I watched Emilio and Samuel haul it to the truck. Emilio caught me scoping him out, but instead of making a big show of it, he smiled, soft and sweet. I was the first to look away.

Moments later the big softy reappeared at the service counter where I'd been updating Duke on the restore progress. "All set," Emilio said, and after we'd said good-bye to Duke, he led me and Pancake out the front door, his hand warm on my lower back.

The truck bumped down Fifth Street and past Old Town limits, but Emilio hadn't spoken. He was fidgety, tapping his fingers on his thigh, bouncing his knee. He rolled the window down and back up again. Twice.

"You okay?" I asked.

"Good." *Tap-tap-tap.*

"You sure?"

"Yep." *Tap-tap.*

"You know you're acting weird, right?"

Emilio looked out the window, fingers tracing the row of ponderosa pine that lined the road. "I'm not weird. I just . . . I dunnohajurivesterd."

"What?"

He groaned and turned toward me, jaw clenched. "I don't. Know how. To drive. A standard."

"Give it more gas. Now slowly release the clutch and . . . nope. Back to clutch. Clutch. Clutch!"

We bucked into a stall—the fiftieth? The hundredth? I'd lost count after twenty. Even Pancake looked a little green under his golden-blond coat. I tried not to think about the damage the lift was probably causing the pickup bed, everything clanging around like the apocalypse. At least there wasn't any traffic.

Emilio started her up again, bucked a few more times, stalled. He pressed his forehead against the steering wheel and groaned.

"Get out," I said. "I have an idea."

We switched places, and I directed him to grab the shifter and close his eyes.

"I'll shift for you," I said. "Pay attention to how it feels and what the engine sounds like when I do it."

His face was tight and serious. When I set my hand on top of his on the shifter, he flinched, but his eyes stayed closed.

"Relax," I said. "Whenever I shift, I'm pressing the clutch down. I'll tell you which gear we're hitting. We'll start in first." I started the engine, stepped on the clutch, and shifted to the top left, hoping my hand wasn't sweaty as we cruised down the desolate road.

"Second." I pulled the shifter straight back, our speed steadily climbing. "Third."

I caught his excited smile and pushed us all the way to fifth. We were only going fifty, and the truck growled at the high gear, but the windows were down, and Pancake had his head out, tongue lapping up the breeze, and the sun toasted my arms and Emilio was laughing and the wind rustled my hair and I thought, for just this one time, just this one minute, *Fuck yeah. This is what it's all about.*

And then I remembered it wasn't, and I downshifted and piloted us to the shoulder.

"Standard one-oh-one." I slid my hand off his.

Emilio opened his eyes. "Lesson's over already? I was just getting it down."

A pair of magpies swooped in front of the windshield and disappeared into the ponderosas.

"We should probably get back to Valentina before you're too tired to work," I said.

"I don't get tired," Emilio said. "Two words for you: Hard. Core."

"Yeah? All that 'hard core' talk means a lot coming from a muchacho who can't drive stick."

Emilio faked a tough guy look, lips curling into a mock sneer for an instant before he cracked up. The sun glinted in his eyes and his grin stretched wide, dimples lingering.

It was like a sunset, the brilliant red ones over the canyon, and in the temporary silence he reached over and grabbed my hand, held it on the seat between us.

I waited for an explanation, a punch line, a dare, but he wasn't revealing anything. His lips looked so soft and utterly kissable and his gaze drifted lazily to my mouth and for one nanoparticle of a nanosecond I felt myself leaning toward him. . . .

No. My parents were at the doctor's and Papi was probably getting poked with needles and I was teetering on the edge of a fantasy with a notorious heartbreaker of a boy I wasn't even supposed to acknowledge, one breath away. . . .

I slipped my hand from his and steered us back onto the road.

"Damn," he said. "Shortest date ever."

"I told you this wasn't a date." I tried to arrange my face into a sarcastic smirk. Chances are it looked more like I was second-guessing this morning's waffles, but it had the desired effect, because a flash of disappointment shot through Emilio's eyes and he looked away.

We rode home in silence, my mind replaying the driving lesson, the feel of his fingers beneath mine on the shifter, his touch as he squeezed my hand, and about twenty-seven other highly inappropriate thoughts involving—

"—nuts?" Emilio was saying as we coasted into the driveway.

"I'm . . . um . . . what?"

"Did *el jefe* find those missing flange nuts?"

I coughed. "Flange nuts. Not sure. I'll ask when they get back from the doctor."

Emilio picked at a dried patch of yellow paint on his shorts, but he didn't move to get out of the truck. I opened the driver's side door and Pancake rocketed out from behind me into the backyard after a little gray rabbit, like, *Thank God we're finally home! Because . . . bunnies!*

The engine ticked and sighed, and Emilio stopped messing with his shorts and looked at me.

"Jude, is your pops . . . Why does he . . ." He ran his fingers through his hair, not finishing his question but waiting for an answer nevertheless.

Pancake zigzagged through the grass like a total spaz, and I stared out at the old barn, the bristlecones that seemed to be consuming the north side of it, the broken-tooth Needle range in the distance, the jewel-blue sky sparkling overhead. Papi'd been patching up that barn forever, adding a new board here, nailing down a loose one there, but the trees kept sneaking up on us anyway. The mountains loomed heavy and huge, and I felt it now more than I ever had before—that cosmic insignificance, the terrible, comforting knowledge that if you stood too long in the same place, the dirt would gather at your feet, and the earth would swallow you one cell at a time, and in a hundred years you'd still be standing there admiring the scenery when the final speck of dust covered your eye.

"He gets worn out sometimes," I said, all the old excuses gathering on my lips like a summer storm. "He works really hard. We're always telling him to slow down."

"I thought he retired," Emilio said.

"I mean here, the stuff he does around the house." I emptied myself out onto the driveway and unlatched the pickup gate so Emilio could get his lift.

"Hey, Jude?"

A tiny silver-green hummingbird zipped overhead, and I tracked it and hoped he wouldn't ask any more questions about Papi, why he drifted off, why he wandered, why the doctors kept insisting he'd one day forget any of this had ever happened.

"Thanks for the driving lesson," Emilio said. "I think I'm pretty good, right? Not bad for my first time, anyway." He mimed the act of steering and shifting, brow deeply furrowed, and I couldn't fight my smile.

"Much smoother on the ground than on the road." I rubbed my neck and rolled my shoulders. "Feels like I lost a rodeo."

He laughed, and then the silence drifted between us again.

"So I kind of need some help with this," he finally said, gesturing toward the lift.

"Too heavy for you?"

"No. Just awkward."

"Like you." I smirked as I grabbed one end of it, and the two of us penguin-walked it into the barn.

“Don’t let this go to your head,” he said when we’d finally dropped the thing, “but today was pretty fun for a nondate. Next time I’m getting a nonkiss.” He winked and walked backward toward Valentina, those maddening dimples daring me all the way there to disagree.

CHAPTER 9

Sorry abt rehearsal. Call me?

Zoe had ignored my texts all afternoon, sent my calls straight into voice mail. Not that I blamed her. Like so many things now, all I had were a bunch of lame apologies. *Sorry I lost track of time and missed your rehearsal. Sorry my father freaked out at the class picnic and scared everyone away. Sorry I'm spending my summer thinking about motorcycles and medications and that stupid Transitions brochure. Sorry I didn't tell you about Emilio. . . .*

All our years together in drama club, in summer theater, crushing on the boys from the private schools in the valley, taking bets on who'd get the lead roles, the kissing scenes . . . it felt like a lifetime ago, and now I was floating in another world a million years from normal. If things were normal, I would've called Zoe the moment I'd recognized Emilio at Duchess, spilled out all the gory details. And if things were normal, she'd make a list of pros and cons with a line right down the middle, with the oath on the con side. Dimples, hair, eyes, body, smile, scars, motorcycles, sense of humor, and other general adorableness? All pros.

"Nine against one," she'd say. "Choice is obvious."

Only it wasn't obvious. It wasn't even a choice. It was strictly business, an agreement with a defined end point. It was ridiculous to give that half-second kissing fantasy another thought. . . .

The phone buzzed in my hand, and I jerked so hard I almost flung Zoe across the room.

Only it wasn't Zoe. It was Mari.

"I just talked to Mom," she said. "Papi did all the tests, but now they're waiting to meet with another dementia specialist to see if he's gotten worse." Mari took a breath and let it out slowly. "How you holding up?"

"Fine. Hanging in."

"Mom said that cute boy was at the house again today. What's the deal? You holding out on me, sister?"

"As usual, you're all getting lost in the translation," I said. "There's no deal. He's helping us fix up Papi's motorcycle."

"Mom thinks you like him."

"Mom watches too many soaps."

"What? She never watches TV."

"At the nurses' station she does. They all do." I said this with all kinds of authority even though my extensive knowledge of nurses' station activities came almost entirely from the soap operas Zoe and I used to watch in middle school. The irony was not lost on me.

A few seconds passed, Mari clicking away on her keyboard. She was probably looking up the nurse's station thing. Mari liked to be in the know.

"So here's the big news," she finally said. "I'm coming home for a few weeks."

"Seriously?" I bolted up in bed, instantly light. I hadn't seen Mari since graduation more than a month ago, and the visit was sad and strained because after the picnic stuff, Mom wouldn't risk taking Papi to the ceremony.

Mari's announcement floated into my heart. I was already picturing lunches together, walks to the river, book talks . . . but then I remembered that whole *never, ever, under any circumstances* business and my heart plummeted. She'd figure out who Emilio was and it would be, as they said on the mean streets, which I'd never been on but had seen on TV, *on and poppin'*.

The oath had been Mari's idea. She was especially proud of the blood part.

I swallowed the lump in my throat. I couldn't believe what I was about to say to my favorite sister. My flesh and blood, the girl who'd taught me how to do French braids and make Mom's empanadas and memorize the answers to Mrs. Fisk's freshman history tests because, year after year, they'd never changed.

Yes, Hell? This is Jude Hernandez. Just phoning in my reservation. Table for one, near the fireplace if you've got it . . .

"Cool if you want to visit," I said. "But you don't have to stay that long. We're fine."

"It's too much for you, Juju. Look what happened at the drugstore. What if that happens again?"

I twisted my legs into the fleece blanket on my bed. "Papi has episodes sometimes. Like, one or two times. The doctors said that would happen."

Mari sighed a whole tornado into the phone. "You can't do this by yourself. Mom shouldn't expect—"

"She doesn't. I want to. It's summer—I have time. Just come for the weekend."

Devil-Jude sat on my shoulder throwing rocks at Angel-Jude on the other side. Things were getting seriously cartoon-esque.

"The girls and I talked about it," Mari said. "I'm the closest one—it's easy for me to get there. Celi can come in the fall before you go to school. That way you don't have to spend all your time with Papi."

"But I *like* being with Papi." Talking to my sisters always aged me backward. Suddenly I was five years old, crying in the driveway as they drove off to Uncle Fuzzy's without me. *Not this time, Jujube. We'll bring you back some chocolate peanut butter cup!* "What about your Internet dates? Your soul mate could be right around the corner."

Mari groaned. "Around the corner in his mother's basement. I'm going cold turkey on boys for a while, how's that? Unless you're hiding any more cute ones in Blackfeather."

"No! I'm not. I mean, there are no cute boys here. Zero. Not one."

Pancake flashed me a wounded look. *What am I, chopped liver?*

"Except for Pancake," I added hastily.

"Jude, you're being weird."

"I'm . . . What about your clients?" I asked.

"I'm all set up to work from there. Ooh, did you read that book yet?"

I thought of my backpack stashed under the kitchen table, the manuscript inside untouched since I'd packed it this morning. "I will. I'm reading it tonight."

You're awesome! Devil-Jude was totally giving me the thumbs-up, her smile glinting mischievously. She had a gold tooth, that's why. Angel-Jude hung her halo in shame, and it drooped over her hair, dull and dented, because hers was fake gold. Clearly, Devil-Jude's work paid better.

"You *have* to read it tonight. It's so good! Super-hot boys, no vampires." Mari clicked away on her keyboard. She was at her office, but I pictured her how I always did, wrapped up in her cloud pajamas, manuscripts everywhere, legs stretched out on the love seat in her Denver loft. We'd spent two weeks together on my winter break, huddled on that love seat watching Netflix and ordering Thai food, which was impossible to find in Blackfeather. Mari had let me read some of her submissions, and she sold one of my favorites a month later.

When it hits the shelves, you can tell everyone how you picked the author out of the slush pile. . . .

"I'll be a huge help with Papi," Mari said. "I've been reading tons of stuff online, and Mom keeps me totally up to date. I'm prepared. You don't have to worry."

I considered asking her to put that in writing. "If you say so."

"I say so. I'll be there by lunch tomorrow," she said. "*Besos.*"

"Ciao." I tossed my phone on the bed. A headache was setting up camp behind my eyes—Angel-Jude and Devil-Jude were still duking it out. I wanted to see Mari, wanted to trust what she'd said about being a huge help, but . . .

Let's rid the Vargas boys of their ability to reproduce. . . .

Hello, disaster. I couldn't let her come home—not yet. When Valentina was running and Emilio was on his road trip? She could totally come then. She could take a whole month off and bring a roll-aboard suitcase full of manuscripts and Mom could make empanadas and Papi could tell everyone he has this big surprise. Then we'd all go outside and he'd start up the bike and tell everyone the story of how we fixed it up, just the two of us mostly, and Mom and Mari would cheer and we wouldn't even have to mention Emilio.

But that was the future. First, I had to convince Mom to convince Mari that we were fine, that she didn't need to uproot her life in Denver just to come babysit me and Papi.

Because putting a hold on that restore? Not an option.

Angel-Jude finally flipped me off, and Devil-Jude slapped

her and nodded supportively in my direction. *You know, Jude, the boss is always hiring down here. Happy to put in a good word. . . .*

I made myself a cup of yerba maté and dug out the leftover *torta de papas*, a potato omelet piled high with tomato sauce and cheese. The kitchen was eerily peaceful, the fragrant aftermath of Mom's culinary skills spicing the air, Pancake snoring softly in the den, the CLOCK NOT PHONE BOOTH marking off the passage of night one second at a time. I closed my eyes, held the *torta* on my tongue.

It was Papi's favorite, and the last time Mom had made it was on his birthday earlier this year. He ate only a few bites—said he didn't like it. That he never liked it in all his life. They got into this whole argument that ended with Mom digging out old photo albums of previous special occasions where she cooked the *torta*, and eventually he lost and ate two servings just to keep the frown off her face.

At dinner tonight he'd eaten almost half the pan.

Now the clock struck twelve and kicked off its melodic chime. One minute later, midnight's gentle spell was broken, and I wasn't that hungry anymore.

I slid open the trash compactor, half expecting to find another brochure, maybe the missing application packet. But there wasn't any Transitions propaganda tonight. Just the usual food scraps and torn envelopes and coffee grounds. And a baseball cap, an unopened package of frozen peas, a bar of

Irish Spring, one sock, and all three *Back to the Future* DVDs from Araceli's Michael J. Fox phase.

Papi must've been wandering earlier.

"You're up late." Mom's voice was soft as she slipped into the kitchen, her usually smooth face lined with faint pink ridges.

I set the DVDs and soap on the side of the sink. The baseball cap was pretty slopped up, not worth saving. "Pass out on the couch?"

"Guilty," she said.

I made us both fresh tea and joined her at the kitchen table. Now that Papi was in bed, we could talk openly about the doctor's appointment—a topic they'd both skirted at dinner.

"His memory recall is getting worse," she said, "but not as bad as they expected. He got approved for a clinical trial. They did another brain scan and a genetic test. They're trying to learn as much as possible."

"Do you think it will help?"

"I hope so, *mi amor*." Mom fished out her tea bag and dropped it onto the saucer. "They gave him the bracelet from the Alzheimer's Association. Just in case."

The doctors had mentioned the bracelet program when they first diagnosed him, but Mom had announced right then and there that his illness didn't need its own name tag. Now she circled her wrist with her fingers, a temporary bracelet to match Papi's.

"They have my work and cell numbers, our address, and

your cell. So if he wanders off . . ." She let the rest fade, her face tight with emotion.

"They call," I said. "I remember."

"It's just a precaution," she said. "Don't worry."

I smiled gently when she looked up from her mug. "I talked to Mari today," I said. "She's coming tomorrow?"

"I think it's a good idea," Mom said, "don't you? Then you don't have to do everything by yourself. I know you miss your friends."

My friends. At this rate, I wouldn't have any left to miss by the end of summer, but I nodded anyway.

"It's good for all of us. A little break. Share the load." She drifted off again and sipped her tea.

"What happens when I leave for school?" I asked. "Mari can't move here indefinitely. And what about Argentina? We have to start getting the house ready to list, right?"

For years my parents had talked about retiring to Argentina, moving down near Lourdes and Mom's family as soon as I got situated in Denver. Last year they started talking about it more seriously, getting real estate information from Lourdes and the rest of the relatives down there, giving away things they'd no longer need. They hadn't mentioned it lately, though, and now Mom looked at me with sad, faraway eyes.

She pressed her lips together as if considering her words, then shook her head. "Let's not burn that bridge until we cross it. Are you hungry? Want me to fix you something?" She pushed out her chair. "Why are you laughing?"

"The saying is, 'Let's cross that bridge when we get to it.'"

"Oh!" Mom laughed too, but it was tinny and short lived. "Sometimes I think I shouldn't say anything."

I held her gaze, and something passed between us. An understanding maybe. A mutual realization that *not* saying stuff was even more exhausting than dragging it all out into the light, but neither of us wanted to push or pull any harder than we already had.

I thought of the brochure again. The social worker.

There was a lot she wasn't saying.

She stared at the pile of DVDs I'd left on the sink.

There was a lot I wasn't saying too.

I squinted at the woman across the table and saw her, for the first time in my life, as someone else. Not as my mother, but as a wife, a woman who'd fallen in love. Someone young and beautiful and vibrant, someone who'd packed up and left her entire family behind for an adventure in a new country, a chance to build a life together. That was love's unspoken promise—blind and hopeful, some kind of beautiful forever.

Mom smiled, but there was a new sadness around her eyes, a worry that hadn't been there this morning. All my planned protests about Mari's extended visit shrank into the shadows. I couldn't lay that on Mom. Not now.

"I'm not hungry," I said. "I finished the *torta*."

"Okay, *querida*. Then I'm going to bed." Mom rose from her chair and kissed the top of my head, and I closed my eyes and listened to the familiar swish of her socks against the tile floors, soft as falling dust.

My sisters were wrong to name the Vargas boys in the oath. Names had nothing to do with it. *All* boys were destined to break your heart.

CHAPTER 10

Pancake, what a trooper. He'd been standing sentry at the front door all morning—he thought something exciting was blowing in, *pobrecito*. A cloud of red dust swirled up the driveway right before lunch, and his tail started helicoptering, and he was all, *Oh boy oh boy oh boy something's happening ohhhh boy!*

Then Mari's car rolled up, and he plodded into the kitchen and nosed my leg like, *Seriously? That's it? Because Jude? Jude? Jude? I was told there would be bunnies.*

"I feel you, Pancake." I set the tomato soup to simmer and pulled the empanadas from the oven. Not bad as far as last meals were concerned.

"Somebody here?" Papi said when he heard the car.

Mari had wanted her visit to be a surprise. And by "wanted," I mean "demanded."

When Papi, Pancake, and I opened the front door, Mari was there on the stoop, all sunshine and bed-head blond like she'd just sailed in from the ocean, and when she smiled and pulled us into a group hug, a few of my reservations dissolved. Like, four of them. Out of a hundred.

It was a start.

"I missed you guys so much." Her breath was soft on my cheek as she squeezed us tighter, and Papi kept saying, "Oh, oh, oh," through a big, bright grin.

"I'm glad you came." I whispered the words, and she smelled like lavender lotion and her awful cigarettes and it brought me back to when she had the bedroom across from mine and sometimes she'd let me listen to music in there while she did her homework, and I meant what I said.

I was glad she came.

Mari had just sucked down her third empanada when a rumble shook the windows. She craned her neck to look out the kitchen door and wrinkled her nose at the sight. "Who do we know with a black motorcycle?"

Heart, welcome to throat central. Make yourself at home!

I'd been planning to cancel Emilio today. I needed at least a day to persuade Mari that hiring a Vargas clearly fell outside the terms of the oath, *and* that my other sisters didn't need to know about it, *and* that it would all be finished by the time I left for the Dunes with Zoe and Christina.

¡Terminado!

But I'd totally spaced the cancellation call, and now Emilio was here, all swagger and dimples and low-slung jeans, waltzing up to the kitchen door like he was part of the family.

"Look who's here!" Papi waved him in. "Empanadas are getting cold, son. You like *jamón y queso*?"

"Love them." He shot me a devilish smile and I went all hot and bothered. Seriously, like some Southern belle, and then I had to go open up the windows over the sink and pretend all that cooking had gone to my head. Devil-Jude thought it was a real rock star of a trick.

I finally sat down again and my thigh accidentally brushed Emilio's thigh and he leaned down to pet Pancake, who in my opinion was getting a little too comfortable with this boy in the house.

"Is that the mechanic?" Mari mouthed the words across the table. "Hot!"

I tried to sink lower into my chair, but there was nowhere to go so I just grinned and hoped Pancake would start speaking French so I could be all, *Oh my God, you guys! The dog said* bonjour*!*

But Emilio started the next conversation. In English.

"Hey," he said as he took in Mari.

She extended her hand and introduced herself. "You must be Juju's friend helping with the bike."

"Yeah, must be." He smiled after they shook hands, and I quietly stomped on his foot, which was obviously the wrong response because then he threw his arm around the back of my chair. Heat radiated from his skin, and I inhaled his leather and fabric softener smell. . . .

"Emilio Vargas." *And my adorable dimples.* "Nice to meet you."

And the whole room went like this: hot, warm, lukewarm, chilly, icy, arctic deep freeze.

"Hey! Who loves empanadas?" I borrowed a page from the Book of Mom and passed the platter. Emilio scooped one onto a plate and held the platter for Mari, but she wouldn't look at him.

"Mari, don't you want an empa?" I gestured toward them all Jedi, like, *This is not the traitorous sister you're looking for. . . .*

Mari picked up a napkin, blotted her lips, refolded it, and smoothed it across her legs. "How did you two meet again?"

She feigned sincerity, but her eyes lasered us across the table. Emilio looked at me to respond at the same time Mari looked at Papi, who went on slurping his soup as if the Vargas name didn't register. Likely, it didn't.

"More salt?" *I said, This is not the traitorous sister you're looking for! Hello!* I reached for the shakers and instead hit my glass, sending a tidal wave of iced tea toward Mari. She shoved her chair backward to avoid the spill, and in one fluid motion, Emilio flung his napkin at the puddle and mopped it up. Pancake had the floor covered, licking up iced tea, crumbs, dirt, bugs, toes, anything in his path. The whole thing was over in seconds. There were no survivors.

"God. Be careful, Juju," Mari said.

"The kids are helping me with Valentina." Papi stabbed another empanada from the platter and dropped it on his plate, unaffected by my clumsiness.

"Who the hell is Valentina?" she asked.

"The Harley, *querida*."

"*Okaaaay*." Mari steamed in her chair. "I just stepped into an episode of *The Twilight Zone*."

"Yo, I love that show." Emilio pointed at her with his fork. "Ever see the one where—"

"So, lots to do today, look at the time!" I bolted out of my chair and tugged Emilio's arm.

"What about the Dark Moon magic stuff?" he asked.

"No time for coffee," I said through gritted teeth. "We have to go out back. Let my father and sister catch up or . . . whatever."

"Aw, don't go. I want to hear *all* about what you've been up to this summer." Mari flashed the kind of grin that used to send me scurrying into Mom's lap. Now it just made me a little queasy. She went on glaring, the unspoken authority of the other Hernandez sisters blazing behind her eyes, once again uniting them in their lifelong mission to be the boss of me.

"Let them go, Mariposa," Papi said. "You stay here with me. Tell me about your big-time book deals."

"It was kind of last minute," I said as we unpacked the tools. "I didn't get to tell her much about you, and it's . . . complicated." I met Emilio's eyes. *Does he really have no idea about our shared family history?*

"Pass me that headlamp?" he asked.

I found the lamp on the workbench and handed it over.

Emilio dived into the bowels of the bike, which was now propped up on the lift we'd picked up at Duchess.

"It's not just you," I said. "She's like that with everyone. Which is probably why she's still single."

"Probably." Emilio held out his hand. "Allen key? It's the black one that looks like an *L*."

"Oh, the Twizzler wrench." I pulled it out of the toolbox. "It looks like black licorice, don't you think?"

"Twizzler wrench? Don't ever let Samuel hear that. You'll be in for a four-hour lecture on tools and their proper names. I sat through that shit once. Believe me, you don't wanna know." Emilio laughed, but then everything got quiet again as he focused on Valentina, the Twizzler-slash-Allen wrench clinking softly as he removed and inspected a hundred tiny things. He didn't seem to need any more tools, so I snapped a few pictures for Papi and then busied myself in one of the teetering boxes along the side wall—a collection of fancy dessert books from Celi's brief stint as a pastry chef.

"Wrecking Ball." My voice shattered the comfortable silence, but Emilio didn't flinch. "That was Mari's nickname growing up. She's got her good points. She just goes a little overboard. A lot overboard."

Emilio grunted. I couldn't tell whether it was an acknowledgment, a laugh, or an accident; he was so focused on his work.

I abandoned the books and pulled out a stack of old homemade CDs, most of them missing their cases. The labels were scrawled in black permanent marker with Celi's loopy handwriting. *Rainy Day Blues Mix. Hot Gangsta Mess. Microsoft Word.* The last one had to be Lourdes's.

"It's funny with my sisters," I said. "They knew who they were the instant they were born, and they've never changed."

"And you?" Emilio finally said. "Always the baby girl, right?"

I chucked the CDs in the recycle pile. "More like an only child. I was born in a totally different decade."

"Me too. Thank God my bros are out of the house, tell you right now. If your sister's a wrecking ball, those guys are like . . ." Emilio puffed out his cheeks and made an exploding sound. "Nuclear bombs."

Yeah, hence all the crying at Casa de Hernandez, inspired by V-boy badasses Johnny and Miguel.

"So this is Valeria?" Mari snuffed out the last of her cigarette in an old coffee can and approached the bike. Guess Papi got tired of hearing about her book deals.

"Valentina," I said. "Where's Papi?"

"Asleep on the couch. What year *is* this clunker, anyway?"

"Sixty-one," Emilio said. "Classic. She looks a little rough now, but once we're done . . ." He trailed off, eyes alight with imagined possibilities. Mari circled Valentina, and he kept a close eye on her, shifting his body in front of the bike when Mari got too close.

"What's so funny?" he asked, and I realized I was smiling.

"Probably high from all the fumes," Mari said. "It's like sniffing gasoline in here."

"I'm surprised you still have a sense of smell," I said. "Cigarettes can kill that, you know."

"So they say."

"You should quit," I said. Emilio had gone back to work on the bike, but Mari wasn't going anywhere.

"This again?" she said. "Juju, honestly."

"I don't want you to get cancer."

Mari put her arm around me. "Enough about me. What's going on with Zoe? Mom said you guys are having problems?" She eyed up Emilio as if he had everything to do with it.

"We're . . . kind of doing our own thing this summer." Zoe had finally texted me this morning about missing her rehearsal, all *no worries, no biggie,* but it *was* big to her, just like the bike restore was big to me, and all that big stuff was slowly building up between us, and soon we wouldn't be able to cross it.

"You guys used to be inseparable." Mari glared at Emilio again.

"Key words: used to be."

Mari must've heard the tightness in my voice, because she shut her mouth and shook another smoke from her pack. She cupped her hands and lit it, the end crackling behind her Zippo.

"Chain-smoke much?"

"Not too much, since I'm still alive and everything." She exhaled through a smirk and leaned against the wall, seemingly content to watch Emilio work. I knew the feeling, but I also knew better than to joke with her about it. Mari would step in front of a charging bull for any of us, but her loyalty was blinding. Right now, that loyalty lay with Araceli, and I was the charging bull. Or maybe Emilio was the bull, which would make me . . . the pasture? No, the china shop. *Ugh.* Thank God SATs were over. I seriously sucked at analogies.

"He's just here for the summer," I whispered. "Mom doesn't even know he's a Vargas."

Mari regarded me a moment, smoke rising from the cigarette between her fingers. "Why did you let Papi hire him?"

"I didn't *let* him." I picked up one of the dessert books and fanned the pages. "Papi can hire anyone he wants."

Mari sucked in another drag. When she spoke again, her voice was hoarse. "If that were true, you wouldn't have to lie to Mom about him being a Vargas."

She was right, of course, and guilt sat heavy on my shoulders. Devil-Jude was playing in it, actually. Mom never came out to the barn—the piles of boxes stressed her out—but eventually she'd start asking about Emilio's family, especially if she thought we were becoming friends.

"You're telling on me, then?"

Mari shook her head, mouth twisting as she stamped out her cigarette. I bent down to retrieve it and toss it in the coffee can, and in that moment she stalked off toward Emilio.

"So, Emilio Vargas. Tell me about yourself. Your *familia.*" She stretched out that last word until it stung like a poison.

A slow and painful death, that's how Mari would kill. I ached for her future ex-husband.

Emilio gave her the super-short highlights version of his life, ending with the job at Duchess and how he'd snagged the Valentina gig. He kept shifting around her to get to the bike, clearly in the middle of some important diagnostic, but Mari was undeterred.

"You're what, twenty-one?" she asked.

"Nineteen," he said.

Mari ran her finger down Valentina's spine, and I swear the bike shivered at her touch. "Are you even qualified to work on this? Don't you need special training?"

"This is the training right here." He wouldn't look at her, just wiped the bike with a soft rag where Mari had touched the engine.

"Can't you get more experience at the dealership?" Mari asked. "I've seen all the tourists around here with their big fat Harleys."

Emilio looked up at me and raised his eyebrows, like, *Get this* loca *off my back already*, but when I shrugged helplessly, he gave up and came out from behind the bike. He rubbed his fingers with an old bandanna from the toolbox, but they were permanently smudged, tattoos from the thing he most loved.

"Duke's a solid guy," he said. "Throws us extra work like this and doesn't take a huge cut. I need all the cash I can get."

"College?" Mari said.

"Road trip. Grand Canyon to start, soon as I'm done."

"With your girlfriend here?" Mari asked.

"I'm not his girlfriend. And I'm going with Zoe," I said defensively. "To the Dunes."

Emilio caught my eye and smiled. "Road's no place for a girlfriend, anyway. Might not come back. Just gonna go until I run outta gas, see where I end up."

He winked at me, and before I could respond, he took a step closer and brushed the hair from my forehead, traced his finger along my eyebrow. It was such a small gesture, familiar and intimate. My cheeks flamed as if he'd pulled me into a passionate kiss.

I swatted him away.

Emilio leaned toward Mari and put his hand over his mouth, pretending to whisper. "She plays hard to get, but I know what this girl's all about."

"Seriously? Shut up!" I gave him a halfhearted shove, and he stumbled backward.

"I'm going to check on Papi," Mari said. "You two have fun with your lovers' quarrel."

"We're not quarreling," I said.

Emilio laced his fingers through my hair, right on the back of my neck, and leaned in close. His breath tickled my ear, soft and sharp, all at once comforting and dangerous. "Does that mean we're lovers?"

Emilio—probably just like his brothers—had the kind of voice that could give a girl goose bumps, and hours later his playful words still hung in the air. Even after he'd cleaned up the tools and said his good-byes, they lingered. They echoed in my head when Mom got home and opened their second-best bottle of Malbec to celebrate Mari's arrival. And finally, after I'd taken a hundred pictures and begged off dessert and crept into my room for some privacy, I'd just about stopped shivering, just about gotten him out of my system.

But then I pulled back the fleece blanket on my bed, and there it was, black and obvious on my bright orange sheets.

The Book of Broken Hearts.

CHAPTER 11

I hefted the tome into my lap and traced the edges with my fingertips. Celi was the last to have it, and I'd long thought it lost, buried somewhere in the barn's aging repository of boxes with her ballet slippers and *Veronica Mars* DVDs.

I'd given up looking for it a few years ago.

Yet here it was, pulling me back to the night of the oath, the words we'd uttered in the flickering candlelight like a spell. Nostalgia and regret emanated from the cover, straight through my fingers and into my heart. The effect was dizzying. I'd longed for this book for so many years that now, holding it against my bare legs, there was no way I wouldn't open it, nothing I'd do to stop myself from traveling back in time. . . .

I'm twelve years old, and Araceli's midnight tears are unmistakable; I hear them splashing onto her bedroom floor like raindrops through a leaky roof.

I flip over on the bed, shuffle the owls out of the way, and press my ear to the wall: nothing but Celi's muffled sobs and the murmurs of the other two. I can't imagine why she's upset. Tomorrow's her engagement party, and Johnny's bringing his whole family. Ours is here too—first time in seven years that all four Hernandez sisters are together under the same roof.

Why is she crying?

Next to my room, Celi's door is open a hand's width, enough to peek inside. The light from her night table glows orange-yellow, casting long shadows on the walls.

"That miserable bastard!" Mari paces at the foot of Celi's bed in gray cutoff sweats and a dark-blue cami, hands flitting around like wild birds. "I say we kill him. Him and every last one of his rotten brothers."

"Mari? Please. Shut. Up! No one's killing anyone." Lourdes strokes Celi's long auburn hair and gently removes a bright orange flower from behind her ear; she went out with Johnny tonight and must've worn it to look special. It *does* look special. My sister is beautiful.

"Sorry. It's . . . I hate that family." Mari crosses the room and opens the window. She leans on the sill and lights a cigarette, exhales through the screen.

"Why is this happening? I should've listened to you." Celi moans into Lourdes's shoulder, and I catch a glimpse of her face, cheeks muddy with mascara tears.

"No, honey. You and Johnny were in love." Lourdes pulls a tissue from a box on the desk and blots Celi's face. "This wasn't supposed to happen."

Mari is still hissing, her rampage resurfacing in a smoke-scratchy whisper that reminds me of the teakettle, all steam and whistle until someone turns off the stove.

"New mission," Mari says. She smashes her cigarette into the sill. "Let's rid the Vargas boys of their ability to reproduce."

"Mari!" Lourdes covers Celi's ears.

"This is more than Johnny and Miguel," Mari says. "We'd be doing the world a favor. That family is cursed. Dark hearts, every one." Mari nods when no one objects. She's made up her mind. "Celi needs—"

"Celi needs our support," Lourdes says. "Not violence."

"Celi needs a drink," the brokenhearted girl herself says. She untangles from Lourdes's embrace and makes for the door, but stops short when she spots me in the shadows. "Jujube?"

I slip inside and lean against the wall, all three sisters looking at me with a mixture of surprise and concern. My cheeks burn under their collective stare, so hot and piercing I have to look away. I focus on the flower from Celi's hair, cast to the ground, shining like a living thing against the weathered oak floor.

"It's okay," Lourdes says. "Go back to bed. Celi isn't feeling well, but she'll be okay."

"Once I get that drink." Celi tries to leave again, but Lourdes grabs her hand and she flops down on the bed, heart-ache resettling in her face. "I *hate* him!"

"Oh, honey." Mari sits next to Celi and rubs her back. "I know, I know. I hate them too." She looks up at Lourdes. "For both of you. How could they do this to us?"

My skin prickles and I rub my arms. Hazy images flicker behind my eyes from years past. Lourdes in a lemon-yellow prom dress with spaghetti straps and white roses pinned to the shoulder. A boy at the door, dark and handsome, a smile like a wolf's. "This is my boyfriend, Miguel," she said. Mom and Papi taking pictures. A limo full of girls like pastel flowers and boys in tuxedos, zooming off to the dance.

And then the yellow dress tossed on the bathroom floor, white roses smashed in the trash compactor the next morning. Late-night murmurs for weeks after. Miguel Vargas—horrible, awful, dark hearted—tried to hook up with Lourdes's best friend, right there at the dance while Lourdes was touching up her lip gloss in the bathroom. I was only five or six at the time, but even I knew what that meant.

They'd been together for months, and then it was done. Over. *Terminado.*

I approach Celi's bed slowly. "What happened with John—"

"Shh!" Mari holds up her index finger. "Don't utter that name. Filthy, vile beast!" She pretends to spit three times. Celi sits up again and copies the spitting gesture. She tries to smile but instead unleashes a storm of fresh tears that twist my heart. Celi's always crying about something—losing an earring, burning Mom and Papi's anniversary cake, watching the Lifetime movie of the week. But I've never seen her so distraught, so completely wrecked.

Lourdes and Mari slip their arms around Celi on the bed, propping her up, and I squeeze my sister's bare foot, a comparatively inadequate gesture that makes me feel like a little gray mouse.

"He broke my heart," Celi whispers. "I'll never love anyone again."

"Oh, hush," Mari says. "You need to cleanse your soul of his filthy, vile evilness. A ritual. We need to swear off that family forever."

Lourdes rolls her eyes, but when Mari is on one of her self-appointed missions, there's no stopping her.

"Go get one of Mom's candles, Juju," Mari says. "The Archangel Michael one. I need a paring knife, too."

Celi shakes her head. "This is crazy."

"It's totally not! Michael is the one for severing bad ties," Mari says. "Especially cheating bastard ties. That's why he has a sword. And we'll have a paring knife."

"A sword and a knife? Really?" Lourdes throws her hands up. "You're so dramatic, Wrecking Ball. *God.*"

Mari ignores them and ushers me into the hallway. "Hurry, Juju!"

When I return with the stuff, Mari lights the candle and directs us to sit around it on the floor. "Celi, get that filthy boy's things. Any mementos you can find. And get the book."

My hair tingles. I know what book she's talking about.

The Book of Broken Hearts.

Celi shuffles a few shoes out of the way and drags the book out from under her bed. The pages are so stuffed that they curve and bend and squiggle, and my eyes go wide as Celi traces her fingertips over the cover, black and dull, scarred with silver hearts and stars and quotes from sad poems, all of it ominous in the flickering candlelight.

My sisters guard that book like a secret, using all sorts of spells and incantations to keep me in the dark. "Only those with multisyllabic names can know the secrets of the book," Celi said more than once. "She who looks upon the book must first look upon herself in a bra," Mari teased one summer when I'd been particularly desperate for a glimpse. The whole thing started with Lourdes her sophomore year—some kind of art class project about bringing emotion to creation, mining the depths of the soul. They were supposed to keep a journal and record their personal tragedies. Heartbreak, loss, death, fears, disappointments. She got really into it, and it became more of a scrapbook than a journal, an art project all its own. When Mari got the same assignment later, they called it a tradition, and Lourdes passed the book to her, and then it went to Celi.

I know all of this because I found Mari flipping through it one night and she told me. But when I begged for my own page? "Not until you're sixteen," Mari said. "Then you'll be initiated and the book will be yours."

Here's the thing my sisters never remember: In four years, when I finally turn sixteen, no one will be left to initiate me.

Celi cracks the spine.

"When was the last time you opened this thing?" Mari asks as a few scraps flutter to the floor. "You're supposed to be documenting stuff."

Celi tucks the loose items back inside. "This is my first tragedy." Her eyes well up again.

Lourdes takes the book and flips to a span of blank pages at the back. The rest is stuffed, writing swirled across pages, photos and postcards and stickers too. I hold my breath in reverence.

Mari shuffles through the pile of Johnny's things Celi offered up. Concert ticket stubs. A bouquet of dried and blackened roses. A birthday card. A handwritten letter on loose leaf. Doodles, names, hearts. One of their wedding invitations. A few printed photos. Mari eyes up the engagement ring on Celi's finger, but Celi shakes her head, and Mari doesn't push. "That's it?"

Celi shrugs. "I have to dig up the other stuff. The rest of the pictures are digital."

"Good. Delete them. Burn the rest of his stuff later too. Anything you can find." Mari knifes deep *X*s into Johnny's eyes on the first photo.

I can't believe Celi is letting Mari destroy this stuff. Broken heart or not, these are Celi's memories. Proof that she existed, that she loved someone, even if it ended in betrayal.

Lourdes hands over the book, and on the first blank page, Mari tapes the defaced photos. She crushes some of the dried flowers, sticks on the blackened bits. At the bottom of the page, she scribbles the date with a Sharpie.

"You know what you can write in that stupid book?" Celi's eyes are suddenly fiery. "Screw Johnny. Screw Blackfeather. I'm getting out of here. New York, maybe. I'm sick of mountains and sick of Johnny and his stupid caramel eyes and his stupid face and this whole stupid wedding. I'm never getting married. Write that down. And then you can take that book and burn it, because I don't need it. No more love means no more heartbreak. Ever. Okay?"

"New York?" Mari says.

"New York." Celi means it. She's always wanted to go. The only reason she's still here is Johnny. He wants to live in Telluride, build a stone house in the sky.

"Now I definitely need another smoke." Mari tosses the book on the bed behind her and flips Celi's stereo on low. As she puffs on her cigarette, her head bops to the music, and the shadows on the wall follow her dance.

Celi scissors her fingers, motioning for the cigarette. She takes a long, crackling drag, face creased and serious, eyes smudged with black makeup. In that moment, in the smoky haze, Celi looks grown up and wounded, and I realize how young I really am in my long pink nightgown.

My sisters have a whole collection of broken hearts in a book, and I haven't even gotten my period yet.

"You know," Mari says, "we need, like, a vow or something. To make it official."

"What are you talking about?" Lourdes ties her long hair into a bun at the base of her neck. She looks like Mom.

Mari hops off the sill and grabs the book. "A contract. Something that ensures no Hernandez will ever get her heart broken by a Vargas again."

"Not to be totally obvious here," Lourdes says, "but Juju hasn't even kissed a boy. And *you* never got your heart broken by a Vargas."

"Not true." Mari thumbs through the book. "Jack Ramirez, right here. One of their cousins. I had a crush on him in eighth grade."

"Ramirez isn't Vargas," Lourdes says. "And a crush hardly qualifies as a broken heart."

"He didn't like me back."

"Mari, he was gay!"

"Technicality," Mari says. "We're doing this for Celi and Juju. Johnny's still around, and there are other brothers. Who knows how many. Juju could go back to school this fall and walk right into their trap."

Celi sniffles. "There's another brother two years ahead of Juju. And that's not counting the rest of their cousins."

"Let's do it." Mari flips to a new page in the book. She reads out loud as she frantically scribbles: "We solemnly swear that as long as we live, we shall be united in this promise against all that is scheming, lying, cheating, slimy, conniving, and worthless—"

"And stupid, hormonal, amoeba brained, and useless," Celi says. "And ugly."

Mari's forehead wrinkles. "Celi. The Vargas boys are *not*—"

"It's *my* heartbreak." Celi takes another drag from Mari's cigarette and exhales toward the open window. "Write it down," she croaks.

Mari writes it down, followed by the vow we'll each have to say out loud. When her Sharpie finally stops, she turns to our oldest sister. "Lourdes. Hair."

Lourdes rolls her eyes again, but she doesn't protest. She yanks a hair from each of our heads, finishing with her own, then winds them together and drops them into the glass candle holder. They pop and curl and fill the room with a burnt plastic smell, shriveling into nothing.

Next Mari shreds another photo and burns the tiny pieces one at a time, blowing the smoke toward the window. "Give Celi that flower."

Lourdes scoops the orange bloom from the floor and drops it into Celi's hand. The petals, once bright and beautiful, seem suddenly fragile, withering against Celi's skin as if they've only just realized they've been clipped from their roots.

"This is the last night we will ever speak of Johnny Filthy Vargas," Mari says. "Crush it, Celi."

Celi holds the flower a moment longer, then folds her fingers over it. Tears fall freely down her cheeks, and she passes the broken bloom to Mari, who tapes it into the book.

"Now we say the chant and bind ourselves with blood," Mari says.

Blood? My stomach flip-flops.

"Someone's been watching *Buffy* reruns," Lourdes says.

"Quit being babies." Mari turns the knife, blade flashing in the candlelight. "I'm not staking anyone through the heart. Just a prick."

"Mari, I'm not sure . . ." Celi keeps shaking her head.

"You guys! It's a pinprick. We did the same thing with the Birch sisters at Celi's birthday party. Remember?"

"Yeah, to become blood sisters." Celi crushes her spent cigarette into the sill next to Mari's. "And I was, like, ten."

"What ever happened to the Birches?" Lourdes asks.

"Hands," Mari says. "Juju, you first."

I hold out my hands, palms up. Mari pricks the first one right in the fleshy middle part. It stings at first, but I clamp my hand shut, waiting patiently for her to do the other hand, then Lourdes's. Celi's. Her own. When we're all sufficiently bleeding, we press our palms together and form a tight circle around the candle, Archangel Michael staring at us blankly, his red sword pointed at the sky. My sisters each recite the solemn vow, and when it comes to me, they watch expectantly.

I square my shoulders and take another deep breath. "I, Jude Hernandez, vow to never, ever, under any circumstances, within or outside of my control, even if the fate of humanity is at stake, even if my own life is threatened, get involved with a Vargas."

A breeze floats through the open window and the candle flickers, sealing our promise. My sisters smile at me; even Celi seems a little lighter.

"We have to sign this." Celi loops her name at the bottom of the page. "Official and binding under penalty of—"

"Death!" Mari raises her fist like some kind of revolutionary.

"Holy *issues*, Mari. You seriously need therapy." Lourdes signs her name and passes the book to our death-mongering sister, waving the pen in her face. "Try not to stab anyone."

My sisters giggle as Mari pretends to jab us with the pen, but at my turn, I'm deadly serious. My fingers tremble as I sign the page. I still haven't fulfilled most of their "she who looks upon the book" requirements—never had a crush, never saw a dirty movie, never danced naked under a full moon—but tonight they handed it over anyway. It's weighty and cold in my lap, and seeing my name there fills me with a new sense of belonging. I'm a part of them now, memorialized in the book, which Celi finally shuts and slides back under her bed with all the shoes.

She'll give it to me before she leaves for New York. She *has* to. And I'll keep it religiously, documenting every broken heart, tiny or significant. And even though I don't know what it feels like to fall in love, I do know this: When I finally christen the book with the story of my first broken heart, it definitely won't be from a Vargas.

No matter what happens after tonight, I will never, ever . . .

Five years later, Celi's once vibrant orange flower had faded to pale yellow, crushed and forgotten like the ancient pages themselves. Remembering it now, beyond the innocence of my twelve-year-old self, I knew that Araceli was utterly devastated that night. The knife and blood and the burning of Johnny's pictures were props, a temporary sideshow to cheer her up before the long and broken road she'd soon face: canceling the engagement party. Explaining to my parents and her friends why the wedding was off. Sorting through the rest of

Johnny's things, the once-shared dreams that would have to be untangled and rerouted for one instead of two. After that night Celi had spent weeks in bed, hardly eating, never going outside. Mari extended her stay to help care for her, and Mom took time off work to do what she could.

Her sobs woke me at night. They seeped into my dreams, turned them into nightmares. I felt like a voyeur accidentally spying on her private pain.

Even now I couldn't imagine what it had felt like for her, what it meant to be hurt by the one you loved most. Dylan and I hadn't been in love. We basically got bored with each other, broke up mutually over lunch. We'd even stayed friends—at least until the BHS picnic. After Dylan, I'd had a few random dates, a few stolen kisses at play parties, but nothing close to Celi and Johnny. Nothing like love. Never.

I ran my hand over the page again, traced the papery flower. Even if they'd passed the book on to me when I turned sixteen, like I'd always wished, it would still look exactly the same. I never would've filled up the last pages.

I'd never had a broken heart.

Images of Celi flickered behind my eyes again, all those tears, all that pain etched in her face. But what remained now from that night in her bedroom wasn't Celi's pain. It wasn't the Vargas threats or the smell of Mari's cigarettes, the blackened photos or crushed flowers or all the spent tissues. It wasn't our signatures scrawled in this relic of a book, or all the stories of heartbreak it chronicled.

It was the oath itself, the solemn promise that none of us would reopen Celi's crippling wounds by falling for the brothers of the boy who nearly destroyed her.

As if to remind me, the pinprick scars in the center of my palms ached.

Emilio Vargas. Regardless of whether he disappeared after we'd finished the bike and I never saw him again, regardless of whether Araceli ever knew he'd been here . . .

I broke the oath.

The day I walked out of Duchess knowing we'd just hired the last of the Vargas brothers, knowing that he and I would spend most of the summer together, knowing that we might even become friends . . . that's the day I'd betrayed my family.

Hot guilt surged through my chest, but when I thought of calling it all off, when I imagined tucking the Harley under the tarp and telling Papi it was back to Scrabble and fishing, I saw Papi's own broken heart bright red on his sleeve. I saw him giving up, succumbing to the demon and letting the memories of Valentina slip into the darkness, swirl into the confusing gray soup where everything else would one day, if the doctors were right, go to die.

And I knew, no matter what happened with my sisters, I'd never call it off.

Never, ever.

CHAPTER 12

"He takes it black," I said.

"Too acidic." Mari sloshed a bunch of milk into Papi's morning brew. "With all the meds, his stomach is more sensitive."

How do I not know that?

Mari set the mug on the kitchen table with Papi's new breakfast staples: lumpy oatmeal, a small bowl of applesauce, a hard-boiled egg, and a Sudoku book. His pills were there too—same ones I'd been giving him, but she had them arranged in a neat little row, smallest to largest.

"Order and repetition are important," she said when I raised my eyebrows at the spread.

My shoulders tensed, and I had to remind myself that this was Mari's way—swooping in, upending, reestablishing the rules.

Still, not everything needed to be reestablished. Maybe I messed up about the coffee. Maybe I let Papi cheat too easily at

Scrabble, watch a little too much television when he should've been puzzling out the crosswords to sharpen his brain. But Mari had to see that I was good for him, that the motorcycle project and our western marathons made him happy.

Didn't she?

I looked at her hopefully, and Mari touched my shoulder as if she could read my thoughts. "You're doing a great job, Juju. I'm just trying to help."

"I know. You *are* helping."

Mari tucked a lock of hair behind my ear. "I'm sorry if I came on a little strong last night. I guess . . . I don't know. Seeing Emilio Vargas all chummy with you and Papi? Talk about *Twilight Zone*."

"Yeah, but the motorcycle's super important to him," I said. "Ever since I found it, it's like he's . . . younger again. Back in Argentina, maybe, like he can remember—"

"I know, Juju." She smiled and squeezed my shoulder, but the light didn't reach her eyes, and I waited for her to say something about the book she'd left in my bed last night, or maybe about my sisters—how we'd better cancel things with Emilio before Celi and Lourdes found out.

"Tell Papi breakfast is ready, okay?" Mari nodded toward the living room, where Papi was dozing in front of *Good Morning America*, and I did as she asked, no objections.

"After breakfast," Mari said as we ate, "we'll walk to the river, and then—"

"Papi watches the Western Channel after breakfast," I said. Only it came out more like *pamphwafchanfast* because the oatmeal Mari'd dished up was like wet cement.

"He shouldn't flop on the couch right after he eats." Mari rested her hand on Papi's arm. "You need to get in some physical activity every day, okay?"

He shrugged without looking up from the oatmeal, a few blobs of which he'd dribbled on his place mat, probably to avoid eating it.

"After that," Mari said, "I have some manuscripts to review, so you and Juju can—"

"Work on the Harley?" I said.

Mari leaned over to refill Papi's orange juice glass. "Tell you what. Let's get settled into a routine, then we'll think about how the bike fits in. Fair enough?"

I opened my mouth to argue, but she was being so uncharacteristically reasonable that I couldn't speak. The coffee, the medications, the Sudoku book . . . Papi liked working on Valentina, but maybe she was right. Maybe we needed more time for exercise and puzzles.

Fishing and board games.

I stared at Papi's face and wished I could read his thoughts, wished I could follow the demon's path of destruction straight to its lair. I'd hunt it down, smoke it out, watch it evaporate through his ears. Then Papi would shake it off like a bad dream, stand up from his chair, and clap his hands once. *¡Bueno, queridas! Who's ready for some fun?*

"Mariposa, do you know what my odometer reads?" Papi stabbed his breakfast with a spoon like it was the least edible thing on the planet. "Nineteen thousand four hundred and six point one. All but three hundred and ninety are *my* miles. I rode through Argentina and Paraguay and Uruguay, nineteen thousand miles of roads and jungles and waterfalls and people. I started when I was about Juju's age. Did you know that?"

Mari shook her head. Lourdes probably didn't know the stories either; he'd never talked about his biking days until I'd discovered Valentina. I wondered if Mom even knew half this stuff, these formerly buried memories suddenly unearthed, yanked into the sunlight.

"It's true." He dropped his spoon into the bowl. "So I think I've earned the right to decide what to do with my afternoon, and today my decision is to work on that Harley, which has been waiting for some attention for, let's see . . . How old is Lourdes, Juju?"

"Thirty." Inside I was like, *Hells yeah, Papi!* But I totally sat on my hands because clapping might've been a little over the top, especially since it was Mari's first full day.

"Thank you, Juju. Thirty years. And another thing, my butterfly." He pushed his bowl toward Mari. "Is this what they call breakfast in the big city these days? *Dios mío*, it's prison food."

A full, genuine smile slid across Mari's face, and Papi cracked up at his own joke. Mari hopped out of the chair and rummaged for some half-moon pastries Mom had brought home from the bakery in Willow Brush.

"No use letting these get stale." She set the bakery box on the table like an olive branch, a do-over on the whole day.

As our oatmeal crusted over, we dug into the *medialunas*. I was about to grab a second one when Pancake started spazzing with his nose up against the screen door.

Seconds later a low rumble announced Emilio's approach.

Mari's eyebrows shot up under her white-blond bangs. "He's *back*?"

"We hired him. It's his job." I said it all cool and collected, but my nerves stood on end. My guilt over the oath hadn't disappeared entirely—Mari's trick with the book last night made sure of that—but a thin fog was creeping in, shadowing the details.

Attention, wayward travelers: You are now entering the twin cities, Moral Ambiguity and Gray Area. Enjoy your stay!

"That's the only reason he's here? Right." Mari waited for him to turn off the bike, and when he reached the kitchen stoop, she pushed her way outside.

"Mornin'." He tried to peek over her shoulder, but she shifted to block his view. "Jude here?"

"Aren't you supposed to be working for my father?" Mari said.

"Just wanted to talk to Jude a second."

"Why?"

Emilio sighed. "I need a favor."

"Sorry, she's not here."

"She coming back today?" he asked.

"She's never coming back. She's totally gone."

"Yeah, all the way to the kitchen table," I called out. I scarfed down the last pastry and tried to get outside, but Mari wouldn't budge from the doorway.

"We need to clarify the terms of your employment," she told Emilio. "You think you can come in here with your . . . your dimples and . . . that bandanna and that bad attitude? I got news for you, *Vargas*." She crowded into his space, poking him in the chest with every syllable. "My baby sister was not put on this earth to do you any favors. She's off-limits for favors. My whole *family* is off-limits. In a hundred years I still wouldn't let our great-grandkids play with yours in the sandbox, so why don't you turn around and march yourself into the barn and stop worrying about my sister."

Jeez. If Mari wasn't being such a melodramatic asshole, I would've been highly entertained. Maybe even impressed. But the fact remained. . . .

"Mari, you're being a—"

"Go back inside, Juju. I'll handle this."

"But—"

"Emilio!" Papi appeared behind me, his face bright and warm, shirt dotted with crumbs. "Thank God you're here. These women are driving me crazy." Papi grabbed his favorite flannel from the back of his kitchen chair and followed Emilio out to the barn. Pancake stumbled out the doggy door after them, DOOR FOR PANCAKE ONLY—DO NOT USE.

Clearly, Papi wanted some male-bonding time with Emilio, so I grabbed my tackle box and pole and caught up with Pancake to go scare away some fish. He was really good at it—stuck his snout in the water like he could sniff them out, and then he'd come up sneezing and shaking like, *Blasted! Dogs can't breathe underwater—how could I forget? We don't have gills and we can't . . . Hey, what's this? Water? Oh boy oh boy I wonder if I can sniff out fish?*

I was pretty sure the fish saw us coming a mile away.

When we were both sufficiently wet and bored, I gathered up the gear and hiked back to the barn. Pancake trotted in first, straight to Papi with a big shake. *I brought this river back for you! Do you like it? Do you? Do you? Do you?*

I went to check on the bike. When Emilio saw me, he held out what looked like a balled-up paper bag.

"Hornets' nest," he said. "It was in the tailpipe."

I backed away, but he laughed and stuck it inside his shirt like a single lopsided boob. A sliver of tan skin peeked out above his jeans, and my eyes followed it across that long, rough scar on his abdomen.

"Don't worry," he said. "Ain't any hornets left."

"You okay, Juju?" Papi came out from behind the work-bench with Pancake and a four-way wrench. "You look a little flushed, *queridita*."

"I was just . . ." *Accidentally imagining Emilio with his shirt off again . . .* "Emilio showed me the hornets."

"It's old," Papi said. "They can't get you now."

"I know but . . ." I took another step back. "I should go. I need to do . . . something. Else."

"I thought you were spending time with your sister today?" Papi said. "Why is your hair wet?"

I tugged at my ponytail. No offense to Pancake, but I couldn't rock the wet dog look like he could. "Pancake and I went to the river. Anyway, um, bye."

"Wait, *querida*, listen," Papi said. "Tomorrow you're going to Emilio's house to help with something. Okay? Okay."

Um . . . What?

I narrowed my eyes, scrutinizing him for signs of another meltdown. "Papi, Emilio works *here*. Are you sure that's—"

"Yeah." Emilio dropped the hornets' nest and dusted off his hands. "I need a favor. *El jefe* kind of agreed on your behalf."

My eyes were still on Papi, and now I tried to make them shoot lasers like that guy on X-Men. "What did you sign me up for, old man?"

"Baking cookies," he said. "You love baking, Juju."

"That's Celi," I said.

"It's for my ma." Emilio ran a hand over his bandanna. "Her school's doing a fund-raiser for this summer trip thing. She has to bake, like, a thousand cookies. She roped Samuel and me into helping—he never says no to her."

"I can't tomorrow," I said. "I have to stay here with Papi."

Papi swatted the air. "I'll stay with Mari. You go with Emilio."

"His mom doesn't want a bunch of strangers over," I said. *Especially the ones related to the girl who almost became her daughter-in-law . . .*

"Obviously you don't know Ma," Emilio said.

I glared at him. Still no luck with those eye lasers. "Was this the favor you mentioned to Mari?"

Emilio was all smiles and dimples again. *God.* Where was Clint Eastwood, rescue cowboy, when I needed him?

"It'll be a big help," he said. "If we get done early, I can still put in time on the bike."

I sighed loudly through my nose, but Papi kept on grinning like this was the best idea ever.

"You're really racking up the debt with me," I said to Emilio. "Picking up the bike lift, baking cookies . . ."

Emilio laughed. "That a yes?"

I nodded, but it was only to buy Emilio more time with Valentina. It had nothing to do with his eyes or his wavy black hair or the thin white scars on his arms or anything else. Just to be clear.

"But now you *really* owe me," I said. I gave him my *own* sexy raised eyebrow, because unlike Emilio, I knew how to do that shit correct, and Papi's eyes were on Emilio, and that boy couldn't say one more flirty, charming, inappropriate thing.

Papi turned to me with an approving nod, and I dropped the eyebrow and went strictly business. *Cookies, yes. I accept the challenge and promise to deliver on time and under budget.*

"*Está bien, queridita*," Papi said. "You need to get out of the house once in a while. You're turning into a hermit."

"What are you reading?" I *fwumped* on the couch next to Mari, careful not to mix up the papers that surrounded her. I picked up the closest stack.

"It's the one I sent you." She assembled another stack and handed it over, each page scrawled with red notes. "The love interest was totally inspired by Tim Riggins."

"Why didn't you say so? I would've read it last week!"

Mari smacked my leg with her pen. "Read it tonight if you can. I have a call with the author tomorrow—you can sit in, let her know what you thought."

I jumped off the couch, scattering half the stack in the process. "Seriously? That would be awesome! I could totally . . ."

All the fun died on my lips. I flopped back onto the couch and closed my eyes. "Papi volunteered me to help Emilio's mom tomorrow with some bake sale thing."

Silence flooded the space between us.

I opened my eyes, and Mari was totally catching flies.

"I tried to get out of it," I said. "You know how Papi is."

More silence.

"After that we're coming right back here so he can work on the bike," I said.

Crickets. Birds. Ticking clock. I swear I heard my own hair growing.

"It's just cookies," I said.

Mari returned to her papers, scribbling down some notes. After a few more awkward seconds, she set down her pen. "Question: Why is Tim Riggins so hot?"

I pounced on the subject change. "You're too old for him."

"I am not! He's eighteen. Right? Besides, it's research. I make my living evaluating the romantic potential of fictional boys."

"I'm sure the judge will believe you," I said.

"It's true."

"Welcome to cougar town. Population: you."

"Shut *up*! I'm not that old!"

"Shh! Let me read." I flipped the page and we settled down, our bare feet finding their way back to each other on the couch as I tried to lose myself in the fictional hotness.

A few paragraphs in, I was already loving the book, panting as expected over this new Riggins-esque bad boy.

But no matter how cute he was, no matter how infuriatingly sexy, he couldn't distract me from the spark behind my belly button. The *non*fictional hotness that had unexpectedly invaded my summer was getting brighter and harder to ignore.

I peeked at Mari over the top of the manuscript and studied her face, the tiny wrinkles around her eyes. They were clever eyes, smart ones. All my sisters had that look, that *we know what's best, we're wizened from experience and heartbreak*.

Emilio's stupid dimples broke into my thoughts, and I closed my eyes and allowed myself to consider the possibility that my sisters, crazy as they were, might've actually known what they were doing when they made me sign that oath.

"Keep reading," Mari said, mistaking my sudden cloudiness for a good old book-boy swoon. "Things are about to get seriously hot."

CHAPTER 13

Papi had sent me straight into the wolves' den: Casa de Vargas.

According to Mari, this adorable brick bungalow was the hearth and home of destruction, the birthplace of pure evil. So what if the front walk was edged with pink and white roses. So what if a Puerto Rican flag wind sock swayed proudly in the breeze. So what if there was a stone cherub in the garden, outstretched hands full of birdseed for the magpies.

Evil!

I steeled my nerves and rang the bell, and the youngest member of the Vargas bad boy dynasty opened the door in a lime-green apron with a big white daisy embroidered on the front.

"Is that . . ." I squinted at Emilio's face. "How did you get cookie dough in your eyebrow?"

Emilio swiped a hand across his forehead. "A better question is, why aren't you barefoot? You *are* a girl. And we *are* workin' in a kitchen, and—*ow*!" Emilio ducked away from the dark-haired woman who'd backhanded him.

"Watch your mouth, *mijo*," she said. "That's not how you talk to guests."

"Just a joke, Ma. Chill." Emilio kissed her cheek and she smiled, then she swatted him on the butt with a dish towel and shooed him back into the kitchen.

"Pay no attention to him." She held open the door and ushered me inside. "I'm Susana. You must be Jude."

Susana didn't wait for a response; she just embraced me. She planted a kiss on each cheek, then pulled away and looked me over, hands firm on my shoulders. "*Ay, corazón de melón*, so much like your sister. So beautiful, this family!"

Susana should talk—she was stunning. That was the only word for it. Glossy black hair pulled into a low ponytail, tanned skin, brilliant eyes like her son's. She was probably a hearbreaker too.

Evil!

"Come. We'll show those boys how it's done now that I'm not outnumbered." She took my hand and led me into the kitchen, and though my face was hot with embarrassment, the touch of her soft hand in mine felt like the most natural thing in the world.

"Division of labor," I was telling Emilio. "Your mom and I mix; you handle the baking and cooling. Samuel can box them up at the end."

Susana and I had been trying to instill order for twenty minutes, but so far, Emilio was wearing and eating more dough than he was baking, and Samuel was playing a zombie game on his phone.

"Ooh, I like this girl, Emilio." Susana laughed as she rearranged the kitchen to accommodate the new plan. "She's smart. Knows you need discipline."

He flopped into a chair next to Samuel at the kitchen table. Towering stacks of white bakery boxes dwarfed them both. "If you two are doing all the work and we're sittin' pretty over here, who's smarter?"

Samuel high-fived him, but before they finished snickering, Susana was looming over them. "Back to work, *charlatánitos. Ahora!*" She held up a wooden spoon like a threat, and the two "little clowns" scattered into place.

"Trust me," Samuel said when we'd finally lined up at our stations. "You gotta add grated chocolate. It's the secret ingredient."

"Grated chocolate?" Susana said. "This one thinks he's high society over here!"

I laughed and dumped a bag of chips into the bowl. "Like we trust a guy wearing a pink Kiss the Cook apron anyway."

"If it helps get me some sugar, I'll wear it." Samuel tugged at the ruffles running along his chest. "Takes a real man to rock pink, *mama*."

"He givin' you his 'real man' speech again?" Emilio tossed a pot holder at Samuel's head. "Takes a real man to shut up and work."

Eventually we found our groove. Susana had the radio on

low, some kind of salsa, and she hummed and shook her hips as she mixed the batter, pausing during commercial breaks to tell me about the fund-raiser.

"My summer school kids don't get as much opportunity for trips like the kids do during the year," she said. "So this time I ask the district, if I raise the money, can I take them?"

"Notice she didn't ask me to go," Emilio said. "I just got volunteered to do all the work."

She shot him a mom-glare. "I already said you're coming with us, *mijo*."

"Yeah, to babysit."

She reached behind me and swatted him with the dish towel again, all without missing a beat at the mixing bowl. "Anyway, if we sell all these cookies, the school will give us the bus and driver. I'm taking them to the Georgia O'Keeffe Museum in Santa Fe. I think it'll be good for them. For this one, too, spending all day in that garage." She nodded toward Emilio. "Señor Motocicleta could use some culture in his life, no?"

At that moment Mr. Motorcycle had his mouth open, catching gobs of dough that Samuel flung from the other side of the kitchen.

"Definitely," I said, but Emilio was too busy goofing around to hear us, and as soon as the music returned, Susana was dancing and humming again.

"Update," Samuel said through a mouthful of cookies. "Five hundred down, five hundred to go. Uh, not counting the ones I ate."

"*Ay*, we'll be here for three days," Susana said. "Back to work, *niños*."

"What are you guys making? It smells so awesome!"

We'd just started on cleanup when the girl appeared. She must've let herself in the front door, and now she flung herself at Emilio with glittery arms around his neck and a big glossy smooch right next to his lips.

"*Hola*, Rosette." Susana didn't make any moves to hug the girl. Instead, she stuck her dry hands back into the soapy sink water.

"We're baking cookies for Ma's school," Emilio said. "Just finished."

"Ooh, I want one!" She made puppy eyes and opened her mouth seductively. *Dios mío*. She was already prancing around the kitchen with her ginormous long hair and a handkerchief for a shirt. Now she was panting over our goods?

This girl was a walking health code violation!

Emilio handed her a plate with a few extras. "Help yourself."

She hopped up on the counter and nibbled on the edges of a cookie, feet dangling and kicking the cupboards underneath. Her eyes finally locked on me. "*¿Quién es esta chica?*"

"*Soy Jude*," I said.

"*Esta es la novia de Emilio*," Susana said through a polite smile. She gave me a wink that only I could see, and I knew she'd called me Emilio's girlfriend on purpose.

Rosette's eyebrows rose. I'd made an enemy for sure.

She looked me up and down again, then hopped off the counter. "I have to get home," she told Emilio. "We hanging out tonight?"

He made a noncommittal grunt, but she leaned in for a hug anyway, fake-whispering in his ear. "See you later, *chillo*."

Once the dishes were done, I rinsed the soap from my hands and asked Emilio to point me to the restroom.

I made my way down the long hall that joined the living room to the bathroom and back bedrooms. The walls were covered in photos, a monument to the lives of Susana's sons, babies to teenagers to men.

I'd never *really* known Johnny or Miguel; I had only vague memories of their comings and goings, picking up my sisters for dates and dropping them off again. It was strange to see them on the wall now, growing up before my eyes: teddy bears, school pictures, fishing the Animas, graduations, dirt bikes, surfing off the coast of what was probably Puerto Rico.

I stopped short when I found a pair of familiar eyes gazing back at me from the past.

Lourdes, smiling in her yellow prom dress. Her arm was linked in Miguel's.

My throat tightened. A few hours after the photo was taken, Miguel left her on the dance floor, crying and bewildered.

There were no pictures of Celi, and I was grateful. Maybe Susana removed them when she heard I was coming over today. Maybe she removed them five years ago.

Just like at home, there weren't many pictures of the siblings together. But Emilio looked a lot like his brothers. They all had that same flirty attitude, the dimpled smile that was more like a dare than a greeting. There was no denying their charm.

The bathroom was the last door on the left. There were four other open doors on the way, and I poked my head into the first—Susana's bedroom. It was immaculate and covered in flowers—on the bedspread, on the curtains, in a vase on the dresser. The walls were yellow and looked recently painted, and I remembered the matching paint splotches on Emilio's shorts, the ones he'd picked at after our driving lesson. In the far corner, a glass saint candle flickered on a short bookshelf. The rest of the shelves were covered with dried flowers, framed pictures, and toys—cars and planes, LEGO blocks. It looked like a shrine, and suddenly I felt like a trespasser. I moved onto the next room.

It was definitely a boy's room—two, maybe, because there were bunk beds—but there wasn't much to it. A few swimsuit models tacked to the walls, textbooks on the shelves. An old computer and cables collected dust on the desk, and a model airplane hung from the ceiling, but that was about it.

The next room was a cache for all the stuff that didn't have a place anymore: sewing machine table, bolts of fabric, arts and crafts supplies, books, stacks of CDs and videos, tubes of wrapping paper and ribbons, dresses in dry cleaner bags, cardboard boxes of who knows what. It was a lot like our storage barn.

In other words, normal. Homey. Regular, nonevil people stuff.

I inched into the last room, knowing it had to be Emilio's. My stomach got fizzy at the idea of seeing his personal space, where he slept at night, where he woke each morning. I hoped he hadn't left anything gross—e.g., Rosette's lacy underwear—on the floor.

His scent enveloped me—the leather jacket draped over the desk chair, the fabric softener his mother must've used on all his clothes. His room was messy but in a totally cute way—blankets thrown haphazardly on the bed, a stack of folded T-shirts toppling sideways from the desk. His shelves held old motorcycle manuals, and the walls—instead of the babes on bikes I'd imagined—were covered with maps. All different colors, different styles, some laminated, some with folds and staples from magazines. The one over his desk had a series of red thumbtacks that stretched from Blackfeather to California, looping in and out of towns and cities from the mountains to the sea.

His road trip route. It had to be.

I crept in for a closer look and imagined what it would be like to ride on the back of his bike, see the road with him. It was a silly fantasy, one that would never leave this room, but for a moment my arms and legs buzzed with anticipation, and I swear I felt the wind in my hair.

Below the map in a silver frame on the desk, a photograph caught my eye. Two boys, both around ten or eleven, maybe. They had their arms around each other, and there was a huge lizard thing—one of them dangled it by the tail. The other one was Emilio—those dimples were a dead giveaway.

They were covered in mud, totally soaked. It reminded me of summers near the river, all the trouble Zoe and I would get into digging for worms and letting the ground squirrels eat our trail mix.

"That's Emilio and his cousin."

I jumped at Susana's voice. "Sorry. I didn't . . . I was looking for the bathroom and I just . . . I saw the maps and the picture."

Susana came into the room and took the frame from my hands. She rubbed the glass with her apron and stared at it a moment before she spoke again, her fingers lightly stroking their faces.

"They were supposed to be raking leaves," she said. "I promised them ten dollars each just so I could have some time alone in the house. Imagine my surprise when they came back with this little dragon. And they look like they got into a mud wrestling match." She laughed. "*¡Ay Bendito!* I almost had a heart attack."

"Did you let them keep it?"

"Only to take the picture. It jumped out of their hands and ran away. I said, good riddance! Did they listen to me? No.

They chased it down again. I had to tell them it was poisonous. Just a little white lie, right?"

I smiled. "How old are they here?"

"Emilio is ten and Danny is twelve." She shook her head. "They were always wild, those boys. Emilio was the worst—that kid hated being told what to do. He was packing his own lunch and walking to school by himself in the first grade, and he dragged Danny around everywhere he went, *pobrecito*. Always getting him into trouble." She set the frame back on Emilio's desk, adjusting it until it was exactly where it belonged. "Don't tell him this, but I used to follow them in the car to make sure they got there safe."

"Sounds like Emilio," I said. "He's so stubborn. Oh—he's really good with the bikes, though. I just mean that he's . . . you know. Independent."

"*Sí*. Can't tie that one down for more than five minutes, that's for sure. Always had one foot out the door, just like his Papi. Ah, but we love them anyway. It would be easier if we didn't, but what can you do?"

All Emilio had ever said about his father was that he lived in Puerto Rico, that it was kind of a weird situation. I'd never heard anything about Danny, either, and I wondered if they were still close, or if Danny had moved away like Emilio's father and brothers. I wanted to ask Susana, but she seemed lost in her own memories. I held my tongue. No family was immune to heartbreak, and it wasn't my business to go mucking around in someone else's.

Susana tugged playfully on my ponytail. "Okay, *cariño*. Let's go check on them before they eat all our hard work."

"Sure you don't need a ride home on the bike?" Emilio asked. We were outside again, and he was totally smiling at me, like, all dimples all the time.

I thumbed toward the blue pickup in the driveway, not that he could miss it. "I'll follow you up there."

"I could bring you back later to get the truck." He dangled the bike keys in front of me, and my mind flashed back to the map in his room, the parade of thumbtacks marching to the sea. "You might actually like it."

"I seriously doubt—"

"Jude, wait!" Susana burst through the front door with a Tupperware container full of cookies. "These are for you. Take them home for your family, okay? Especially your mom. You tell her I'm always thinking of her."

I took the container and she kissed me, her hand smoothing my hair, fingers slipping under my chin.

"Come back and see me again, okay? You're welcome anytime, *cariño*. With or without this brute." She leaned over and ruffled Emilio's hair.

"*Te quiero*," he told her, and her whole face lit up, and seeing them together, joking around and just being . . . well, a mom and her kid . . . I don't know. It was hard to reconcile what my sisters had said about this family. How could someone so dark-hearted love his mother so much? How could they have pictures of cousins and maps and flowers and candles? How could they be so sweet to me?

After Susana went back inside, Emilio squeezed my hand, then let it go. "Thanks for your help. Ma's practically glowing. She really likes you."

"Yeah?" I looked away to hide my inevitable blush. "Guess you're not the only one who's a charmer with the parents."

Emilio laughed. "You know, *princesa*, I think this boyfriend/girlfriend thing might actually work."

"Not if Rosette has anything to say about it, *chillo*." I hopped into the truck. "You know that's a fish, right, *chillo*?"

Emilio shrugged and started up his bike. "Nah." He revved the engine, shouted over the rumble. "We say *chillo* for lover."

CHAPTER 14

"Of course your mother fell in love with me. Look at me!" Papi pointed to an old group shot of Las Arañas Blancas. He was the front-runner of the gang, a motley collection of black-haired and ripped-jeaned bad boys on even badder bikes. Valentina shone like a jewel among the others, and I tried to imagine being a young girl in Argentina, coming upon this wild bunch, all chrome and leather and heat.

Every last one of those boys should've come with a warning sign.

Danger: Serious heartbreak ahead!

"It wasn't hard to meet girls." Papi's eyes glinted. "But your mother . . . tough, that one. Every time we'd ride up to the diner where she worked, I'd order the same thing: chicken milanese with a side of *ensalada rusa* and a Coke. She'd bring the food, set the bill on the table before I took one bite. She never said hello, nothing! The guys used to call her *coco*, like a coconut. They bet money I wouldn't get her to crack and talk to me."

"What happened?" I'd never heard the story. Across the kitchen by the coffeepot, Mari shrugged like she hadn't either.

"It took me all summer, but I made a bunch of pesos." Papi flipped to the next picture, a shot of him and one of the other guys kneeling in front of a black motorcycle. It reminded me of Emilio and his friends at Duchess.

"I went back on the road again, took another long trip. But your mother couldn't resist my charms forever," Papi said. "Two years later we got married. All these guys did. Most stopped riding too." Papi went quiet as he thumbed through the rest of his album. I wondered if he regretted it, if he thought he'd missed out on a more exciting life, and a tingly mix of sadness and guilt crept down my spine. Sadness that he'd left his old crew and stopped riding Valentina. Guilt that it was our fault. That maybe if he'd never stopped riding, if he'd never taken the path from the open road back to here, to Blackfeather, to the wife and the house and four daughters, things would've turned out okay for him. If he'd stayed there, he'd probably still be riding now, and he'd keep on living the life he was supposed to live, no wrong turns, no dead ends. No idle time or empty space for El Demonio to sneak in and set the whole thing ablaze.

"Don't look so serious, *queridita*. It's only a picture." Papi patted my hand across the table, bringing me back to the moment. His other hand rested on a photo of a bike partly wrapped around a tree. One of the guys stood next to it, totally bamboozled.

"Who's that?" I asked.

"Benny was our daredevil. Lucky dumb bastard," Papi said. "That's what we called him. He jumped off before the crash here. Not a scratch on him. But he lost the bike, went back to riding a Honda after this."

"You guys were all crazy," Mari said.

"Crazy times, yes. Great times." Papi shook his head, the ghost of a smile on his lips. For a second I thought he might tear up, but when he looked at me, his eyes were full of life. "Wouldn't trade my girls for anything, though."

He leaned in and kissed my forehead, and when he disappeared upstairs to put the album away, Mari poured two fresh cups of my Dark Moon blend and joined me at the table.

"He remembers everything about his biker days, huh?" she said, reaching for a cookie from the stash I brought home the other day.

"It's completely . . . unfair." I took a chug of coffee to keep the emotion in check, but it was pointless. "He'll probably always remember that story about Mom. But one day he won't remember that the Mom who lives here now is the same woman. He'll think she's someone else. Like the one he loves is still some nineteen-year-old waitress in Argentina."

"I know it's unfair, Juju," she said. "All of it. Unfair he's sick. Unfair there's no cure. Unfair you're giving up your last summer as a kid. You're missing out on everything, and Mom is working crazy hours, and it's just . . . it sucks."

I tugged at a loose thread on one of Mom's woven place

mats. Yeah, maybe I'd given up part of my summer, but it was already the Fourth of July, and what had I really missed? Ogling stupid boys at Witch's Brew, golden summer boys none of us ever had the nerve to talk to? Trying to force some last great summer just because we were heading to college in the fall, and this was the end, our last chance to be kids? What did that mean, anyway? Like if Papi wasn't sick, I'd be outside in my Mr. Turtle pool, catching fireflies in a mason jar and chasing down the ice cream truck with a dollar in my hand?

"I didn't give up the *whole* summer," I said. "I'm still going to the Dunes next month. I'm just . . . I'm trying, okay?"

Mari shoved in another cookie, gulped it down with a swig of coffee. "I've been kind of a hard-ass since I got here, huh?"

"We're all worried about him. I get it."

Mari shook her head. "I was pissed at you. You knew I was coming, and you never even mentioned Emilio. Maybe you don't remember what that family put us through, but I do. I was totally blindsided. Not to mention hurt."

Okay. Maybe I should've told her. Warned her, prepared her, something. I'd kept my mouth shut, lied to my favorite sister. But we both knew where the honest road would've led; the bike project would've been canceled the moment she arrived. She probably would've gotten my other sisters involved, gotten everyone to remind me what a bad guy Emilio Vargas was.

The thing is, she would've been wrong. They all would've been wrong. They *were* wrong.

"Emilio's different," I said. "It's not like that with him."

Mari traced the rim of her coffee mug. "When I saw you guys, the way he looks at you . . . it was like going back in time with Celi and Johnny. I saw the same thing happening to you, and I freaked."

I nabbed a cookie and thought of Susana, her bright smile, the way she laughed at Emilio's jokes and scolded him for trying to lick the beaters before we were done. Maybe Johnny and Miguel had hurt my sisters, maybe they deserved to be on our blacklist for all eternity. But Mari didn't know Emilio or his mother or anyone else in that family. How could she punish Emilio for his brothers' past?

"I met Emilio's mother yesterday," I said. "I guess she and Mom were friends before?"

Mari nodded as if she were remembering, maybe imagining how things could've been if Johnny hadn't staked Celi through the heart. But then she downed the last of her coffee and rose from the table, swept her cookie crumbs into the empty mug. "How much have you told Emilio about Papi's condition?"

"We don't talk about it. But he's seen Papi's mood swings." I didn't tell her that Emilio was the one who'd talked Papi down during the Great Tampon Incident, or that he was pretty much the only person outside the family who hadn't gotten totally scared off. "I'm sure he can put it together."

"He doesn't need all the details, okay? That's family stuff. *Our* family stuff." Her eyes glazed with emotion, but she blinked it away. "Lourdes and Celi still aren't sold on this bike idea."

"You *told* them?" My stomach twisted just imagining Celi's

reaction. Last year when I visited her in New York, she'd left her Facebook open, and she was totally creeping on Johnny. And she still had the ring, tucked away in a velvet box in her top dresser drawer. "It was five years ago, Mari. You guys made me cut my hands and sign that stupid paper, and it had nothing to do with Emilio. I just wanted to be, like, included for once. I was twelve!"

"I told them about the bike, not Emilio. We're Skyping tonight. I told them to dial in before the fireworks."

I jammed in another cookie.

"Papi and I are having lunch in town," she said, "but I need you to pick him up at two so I can do a phone meeting. I'm setting up at Witch's Brew."

"You have a meeting on the Fourth of July?"

"New York doesn't sleep." Mari slung her computer bag over her shoulder and bent down to nuzzle Pancake. She didn't offer additional insights, big sister advice about how she was going to fix everything.

She'd stopped telling me not to worry after the first day, and in her short time here, she'd already aged another year.

So had I.

CHAPTER 15

Mari had been right about a lot of things in our seventeen-years-and-counting relationship: which books would hit the bestseller lists. The culinary masterpiece that is french fries dipped in *dulce de leche*. The swoonworthiness of Dillon Panthers fullback number thirty-three, Tim Riggins.

But she was wrong about the Vargas family. Wrong about Emilio. She'd mistrusted him before he'd ever set foot on our property, pegged him as a heartbreaker the moment we cut our hands and spoke the words five years ago.

I'd misjudged him too. Maybe he'd never know it. Maybe he'd never care. Maybe he'd ride on out of here at the end of summer with his final check and a bag full of clothes and bandannas, hit the road, and never look back, just like he'd been saying all along.

In a whole string of maybes, there was one thing I knew with absolute certainty. Emilio Vargas didn't deserve a page in the *Book of Broken Hearts*. We'd put him there anyway. I had to make things right.

"Gimme ten minutes," Emilio said when I found him at Duchess. "Hang out awhile?"

I staked out a bench along the back wall. Emilio was shirtless again, so watching him work wasn't exactly punishment. I'd just settled in for the show when the rest of the boys kicked off their predictable red-hot hazing.

"Hey, Jude . . ." One of them—Marcus, I think his name was—started singing the old Beatles song and laughed like it was the most original idea in the world, like I hadn't been hearing it my entire life. His voice wasn't bad, but he screwed up most of the words, and by the time he got to the second verse, Paul McCartney was probably ready to get on a plane, fly on over here, and smack him.

"You should stop," I said. "You've got a good thing going with the bikes. Maybe stick to that."

"No, here comes the good part." He cleared his throat and started again, one hand over his heart. The whole thing was kind of endearing, if you liked that sort of thing, which I didn't. Not coming from him, anyway. "Hey, Jude, don't be a fool. Don't go out with . . . that bum E-mee-lee-o. The minute . . . you let him into your—"

"Better be the end of your song, bro." Emilio clapped him on the shoulder, and Marcus winked at me and turned his attention back to the Harley he'd been working on. A knucklehead, I remembered from Emilio's lesson.

"He's a dumb ass," Emilio said to me. "I'm almost finished."

The second he was out of earshot, Marcus sauntered back up to the bench with stiff, rehearsed swag. Definitely a mirror practicer, that one.

"Why you messin' with Emilio? What's up with you and me?" He wiped his hand on his black tank top and held it out, presumably for me to take, at which point we'd presumably climb aboard his moped and ride off into the sunset. Before I could shatter his dreams, Samuel smacked his hand away.

"Keep it movin'," Samuel said. He nudged him back toward the bikes, but the guy was unfazed.

"She likes me."

"She thinks you *stupid*," Samuel said. "And she right."

Marcus cocked an eyebrow and licked his lips, more dazzling mirror work, and leaned in for another proposition. "When you're ready to graduate from a boy to a man, you call me."

"How about I call when *you're* ready to graduate from a boy to a man?"

The other guys howled, and just when I decided this game might be kind of fun, Emilio was at the bench, tugging a shirt over his head. *"Vamos, princesa."*

He led me out a small door in the back, one I'd seen him use before. I'd always assumed it led to a break room or smoking area, but it opened onto a sidewalk with a crooked, sun-splashed path that forked into the woods behind Fifth Street, and I followed him, eyes on the white bandanna dangling from his back pocket. I wondered what happened to the blue one.

Not that I was launching a police investigation of his backside or anything. I mean, that bandanna was like a beacon. *Look! Look! Look!*

"No bodyguard today?" he asked as we hit the path. He turned and waited for me to catch up, obscuring the view of his butt. Bandanna. Whatever.

"She's at lunch with my father, so you're okay for now."

His dimples vanished. "What's up with her? I get that she's worried about your pops, but damn."

"You're kidding, right?" I'd been tiptoeing around it since we met, but there's no way he didn't know, and I was sick of pretending otherwise. "Araceli . . . Johnny totally dicked her over!"

His face changed, forehead crinkling beneath that mop of hair. It clearly wasn't new information for him, but it was like he'd never considered it, never imagined it would affect the present day.

"Shit's got nothing to do with me," he said, continuing up the path. "And it was a million years ago. That's seriously why she hates me?"

"She doesn't hate you. She just . . . extremely dislikes you. Distrusts you. No, dislikes. Maybe both."

"Because of my douche of an older brother?"

"Technically, there were two douches."

"A douchette?"

I laughed, but only for a second. "Miguel dumped our sister Lourdes at their prom a few years before that. There's a picture of them in your house."

"Hold up." Emilio stopped in his tracks and grabbed my arm. "How many sisters do you have, and please tell me the story ends there."

"That's it. Three, plus me. And two of them got their hearts broken by your family. Obviously Johnny was the big one." I thought again of the wedding, the lilac dresses. I'd already had one fitting, and it was my favorite dress ever. I felt like a princess in it. A real one. I probably would've had to dance with Emilio during the bridal party song since we were closest in age. "Think about it. They were supposed to get *married*. Imagine?"

"Yeah, I know." Emilio kicked a bleach-blond tumbleweed that had lodged itself on the path. "My mother was so pissed at him when she found out."

"After that . . . Okay, this might sound crazy—"

"You? Sound crazy? No way. Better call the news copter." Emilio grinned. "Okay, hit me with the crazy."

I took a deep breath, let it out slow. "That night, after Celi and Johnny broke up, I made a promise that I'd never get involved . . . like, I wouldn't hang around a guy in your family. Ever."

"We're not ax murderers."

"Just heartbreakers." I smiled, but Emilio was shaking his head, and I rushed to explain the rest. "I took an oath. A real one." I told him the whole sordid tale.

Emilio turned to me at the end of the story, eyes fiery and intense. "Lemme get this straight. You and your sisters burned a bunch of my brother's shit, stabbed yourselves with a knife, and swore an oath against my family over a Saint Michael candle?"

"He was an archangel, not a saint. And it was just against your brothers. All the males, actually. Your mom is probably fine." I kicked the ground, dust swirling on the path. "Actually, I'd have to read it again to be sure."

"Did you put a curse on us?"

"No."

"What about future kids? Or my uncles? Anything I need to warn my aunts in Puerto Rico about?"

I shook my head.

"What if I see a black cat or a ladder? Do I have to watch my back on Friday the thirteenth?"

"Yeah, okay, but I was twelve. They were looking out for me."

Emilio shook his head. "You stabbed yourself with a knife and burned your hair in a church candle. Where I come from, we got a word for that: *loca*. You were right. You *are* crazy."

"But your brothers—"

"You think I'm like them." It wasn't a question. His voice lost its playfulness; he was suddenly edgy and cool. When I looked into his eyes, I saw something else there too. Hurt.

"Not anymore," I said. "Not after getting to know you this summer. And being at your house, seeing you with your mom . . . I just . . . you're not what I expected."

He started on the path again, silence chilling the air between us.

"I'm sorry. All I remembered was seeing you at BHS," I

said. "All those girls following you around, hanging on your every word. 'Oh, *Emilio*! You're so cute! We love you, *Emilio*!'" I'd meant it teasingly, but the words floated on a current of jealousy, and I silently cursed them. My cheeks flamed.

Emilio was laughing though, and the hurt I'd seen in his eyes vanished. "Can't help it if everyone falls for me. I'm charming, what can I say?"

"You're annoying, that's what you can say." I tried to punch him in the arm, but he caught my hand and held it. Heat crept slowly up my arm.

"I'm not, you know." He took a step closer.

"Not . . . annoying?" It was only a whisper, but it shook like the aspen leaves overhead.

Quaked, that's what it's called. Quaking aspens.

"Not like my brothers." He took another half step. His dimples deepened as the space evaporated between us.

I looked at the path again, focused on a shiny black beetle making its way across. It stopped when it reached Emilio's foot. "I'm . . . I came here to say sorry for the weirdness. I didn't want you to think it was your fault. Or to stop coming around—"

"Why would I stop coming around?"

A little blue flame flickered in my stomach, but I snuffed it out. "All the craziness with my family. I figured you'd bail."

"Not a chance, *princesa*." He smiled, eyes lingering on my mouth. "You're paying me."

I tried to laugh, but it got twisted into a nervous hiccup, so I tugged out of his grasp and started back toward the garage.

Immediately I felt his hand again, warm skin against warm skin. He stepped in front of me and grabbed my other hand too, all his fingers lacing through mine.

"Do you trust me?" he asked. "I need to know if you trust me."

He was dead serious, and the question lingered, binding us with invisible thread. For that one moment we were both vulnerable, both achingly honest. Even the trees seemed to hold their collective breath, waiting to see who would speak first.

"My father has Alzheimer's."

There it was, a whispered confession floating into outer space, where it would live on for eternity. Unlike us.

"When they first diagnosed him," I said, "I didn't think it was a big deal. I figured he'd forget stuff. Stupid stuff like when you space and put the milk in the cupboard or your socks don't match."

Emilio was speechless, still holding my hands, still looking into my eyes.

"Mom and I used to tease him. I mean, before we knew. He'd go to the kitchen to microwave popcorn for movie night, and we'd find him making omelets or pie or some crazy thing." My voice cracked, but I pressed on. "We called him Señor Olvidadizo, Mr. Birdbrain. Mom teased him that he used up his smarts at work every day so there wasn't any left for us when he got home. We had no idea. . . . He's not that old."

"Fifty?"

"Fifty-two," I said. "But looking back, we remembered him doing other weird things even a few years ago. Stuff that we thought was, like, midlife crisis. One time, totally out of the blue, he used some of their retirement savings on a Caribbean time-share, and he couldn't understand why Mom was upset that he didn't discuss it with her. He thought she was being ridiculous. But later that month he broke some stupid generic wineglass, and he cried like he'd ruined this family heirloom or something. He was apologizing for days. It made no sense."

"How did you finally find out he was sick?" Emilio asked.

"One night he called me from his office, totally panicked." I let go of Emilio's hands and we sat down in the grass. "He babbled on and on, and I was like, 'Papi, are you drunk?' He was stuttering. He finally made this coughing sound, then he said real fast, 'I don't know the way home.'"

"You serious?"

I yanked out a clump of grass, sprinkled it over my bare legs. "He'd been sitting in the parking lot for twenty minutes. I thought he was messing with me, but then he got super serious. Mad. Even then, he sounded so . . . freaked out, I guess."

"What happened?"

"My neighbor drove me down to get him—I made something up about Papi getting the flu, so they dropped me in the parking lot. Papi had the truck. That's when I learned how to drive stick. Crash course." I yanked up more grass, dropped it again on my legs. "When we got home, he wouldn't look at me. All he said was, 'Jude. Not a word to anyone.' And I knew he meant it, because he never calls me Jude. Always Juju or *querida*.

"I was scared and I kept my mouth shut, but it happened

again the next day, and I had to tell Mom. She took him to different doctors, months of appointments. They gave him antidepressants and told him to cut back at work. Didn't help." My stomach twisted as I remembered the frustration, the lack of answers. "It felt like forever, not knowing anything. Finally they got him to see a dementia specialist. They did tests and scans to rule out other stuff. Early onset Alzheimer's, they told us. I never heard of it before."

"How do they treat it?"

"Medications, healthy eating." I shrugged. "They say they're trying to slow the progress, but there's no cure. Mari says he's supposed to do puzzles and exercises. Who knows. They can't predict shit. It feels like a guessing game."

"Is that why you take pictures of me and *el jefe* all the time? Like, memories or something?"

"Yeah. I'm really *not* trying to launch your modeling career."

"I don't need you for that." Emilio nudged my knee with his. "But . . . working on the bike is good for him, right? Keeps his mind busy?"

"That's the weird part. The Harley . . . sometimes he can't remember what he had for breakfast, or where his shirts are, or that it's summer. But ask him anything about the bike, and it's like he's back in Argentina with his crew. He remembers everything about his old life. It's insane."

"Definitely not insane." Emilio brushed the grass off my knee. "Your pops is mad cool."

"Seriously?"

"Jude. He was in a motorcycle gang. He biked around South America. He has a 1961 panhead, for chrissake. Dude's a living legend." Emilio laughed, and when I saw his face, open and genuine, unchanged from the moments before I'd confessed the family secret, I knew I'd made the right call in telling him. He must've known Papi had something like that—Alzheimer's, dementia, memory loss. But it felt important to say it out loud, to trust him with the fragile, eggshell words.

Warmth spread throughout my insides. I had an ally again, a friend. A real one who knew the truth and wouldn't freak out, wouldn't bail.

I wanted to thank him, to tell him how much that laugh meant, how all the stuff he'd said about Papi made me feel safe and happy and somehow okay. Instead, I slipped my hand in his and squeezed it once, and he squeezed back, and pretty much everything about that moment rocked my grass-covered socks until I realized, with utter dread, I was late for meeting Mari.

CHAPTER 16

Araceli smiled at me through the split screen of Mari's laptop. On the other side, Lourdes watched on from her kitchen in Mendoza. Occasionally her husband passed through, Alejandro, a blur of light blue and white in his lucky *fútbol* jersey. It was tournament season, and Argentina was kicking butt.

Mari still hadn't said a word about me being twenty minutes late this afternoon. I'd brought Papi home for a nap—he'd been snoozing ever since—and the moment Mari got back from Witch's Brew, we Skyped my sisters. Now we were updating them on Papi's medications and his daily regimen and everything Mari had read in the literature.

Lourdes nodded solemnly. "What did we decide about the test?"

"Papi does a hundred tests every time he goes to the doctor," I said. "Which one?"

Lourdes shook her head. "The—"

"We're still getting information," Mari said. "Mom's in touch with the doctors. We don't have any details yet, but I'll let you know." Mari's eyes widened and Lourdes clamped her mouth shut. A strange look passed between them, almost like a warning. Mari was used to running the show, despite Lourdes being the oldest, and one little family tragedy wouldn't change that.

I waited for the conversation to turn to Transitions, for someone to finally let me in on Mom's plan, but no one mentioned it, and I didn't have the heart to ask.

Thirty-seven minutes in, according to the Skype countdown, Celi finally said the *M* word: *motorcycle.*

"Papi's pretty into it," Mari said. "They're out there almost every day working on it."

"What about the chemicals?" Lourdes asked. She'd been in Mendoza for more than a decade, and she spoke with a faint accent that made her sound both familiar and strange. Familiar, like my mother. Strange, because she wasn't Mom, but she was getting closer. It showed in her voice, the lines around her mouth, the firm set of her shoulders. "Isn't it bad for him to be exposed to that stuff?"

"Right now they're just taking it apart and seeing what it needs," I said. "No chemicals."

Celi raised her eyebrows. "Who's they?"

"Papi and the mechanic."

"Who?" Celi asked again. "Wait, is that the cute boy Mom told us about?"

In the background Alejandro whistled. "Juju has a boyfriend?" he asked.

"No," I said. "He's just a guy from Duchess."

"Duchess is the motorcycle shop," Mari said. "Juju and Papi hired him."

Thanks for being helpful! I shot her a look, and she shrugged, like, *What?*

I realized then, if for no other reason than protecting Celi's heart, Mari wouldn't say Emilio's name. It was up to me, but I couldn't reveal it either. Secrecy had been my plan all along: Keep Emilio's identity in the background, let him finish up the bike and disappear as if he'd never been here. As if I'd never broken the oath.

But I remembered our conversation this afternoon, his hands warm in mine, eyes soft and encouraging, and suddenly it felt unfair. Wrong.

I wanted to spill it. I wanted to tell them that Emilio, more than any of my old friends, continued to show up when he said he would. He listened when I felt like talking, didn't push when I wanted to stop. He showed me stuff about motorcycles and made sure I understood what he and Papi were doing. He didn't freak out at Papi's episodes, and he didn't treat him like a kid in need of a babysitter.

I wanted to tell them how amazing he was with Valentina, how he seemed to know her on some deep level, more than you could learn from the manuals.

I wanted to tell them how Papi's eyes sparked whenever

Emilio showed up, how Emilio loved to hear about Papi's travels and all the people he met and the miles he covered.

I wanted to tell them how Emilio was becoming a good friend, someone I was warned against my whole life but who'd taken better care of my heart than anyone.

But when I saw Celi's hopeful face, her lips curved in a shy smile, all the right words evaporated.

"How do you know the kid really works there? What if he's trying to rip you off?" Lourdes's brow furrowed with concern; even Alejandro pulled up a chair to offer his two *pesos*.

"Juju, Mari," he said. "Be careful with these people. They could be taking advantage. How do you know you can trust him? Why didn't you go to the dealer?"

"Harley-Davidson was way expensive," I said. "Three times as much."

"So you found some random kid?" Celi raised her shoulders, like, *What the hell?*

"Harley referred us to Duchess. Papi and I met the owner, got his opinion, saw all the guys working there, and hired—him." I stopped short of saying his name. Lourdes probably wouldn't remember, but Celi would. She'd spent enough time at Johnny's house to know his little brother, and it's not like there were tons of other families in Blackfeather with kids named Emilio.

"Sounds suspect," Lourdes said.

"Papi's happy," I said. "He loves working on it; it's like he's back in Argentina. Did you guys know he biked all around South America?"

"Really?" Celi said. "That's so cool! And romantic! Like Che."

"Before all the killing," Mari said.

"Don't be morbid, Mari." Lourdes rolled her eyes.

"Anyway, back to Papi," I said. *Che. Really!*

"What does Mom think?" Lourdes asked.

I'd been spending my days with Papi, *giving up my last summer* like Mari'd said, but maybe that was the easy part. So far, other than a few meltdowns and confusing moments, our days were filled with laughter and sunshine and the memories he shared from his biker days. I'd been writing them down, tagging all the pictures I'd taken, scanning his old albums. I was collecting them for him on my computer, curator of his memories.

But Mom worked all day. And she came home and cooked and took Papi to appointments and asked the big questions. *What if? When? What next?* She was the one who had to deal with the paperwork and social workers and Big Future Contingencies. She knew Emilio was there to restore the bike, but once the project got under way, she hadn't said much about it.

I had no idea *what* Mom thought.

My sisters' faces were etched with worry. I wanted to reach through the screen, slip my arms around them like I used to. I wanted them to be here. I wanted them to promise me they'd figure something out, that all of us would be just fine.

Go back to bed, Juju. . . .

"Mom's got more important things to worry about now,"

Mari said. "I'd really like to get him on a stricter exercise program, but . . . I don't know. He loves the Harley. He's . . ." She looked at me and smiled. It was a small smile, but a real one. "He's happy when they're working on it."

"You sure you trust this mechanic?" Celi said.

Lourdes and Alejandro leaned forward, filling their half of the screen with kind, concerned faces. I looked at Mari and held my breath. Here in Colorado, she had seniority. A shadow of doubt from her could shut the whole thing down.

After a million years Mari nodded. "He knows his way around the bike, and he's not put off by Papi's mood swings. He's a good kid."

"Super good," I said. My heart lifted at her unexpected praise.

"Keep an eye on things," Lourdes said. "But as long as you trust this kid, I don't see a problem with letting Papi work on the bike."

"Me neither," Celi said. "Sounds like it might actually be good for him. Juju, what's wrong? Why do you look so emotional?"

"I don't know." I spoke through the sudden tightness in my throat. "I just . . . I figured you guys would do the united front thing. I thought we'd have to stop working on the bike."

Celi ran her hands through her chocolate-brown hair and sighed. "We're just worried. It's hard being so far away. We want to be there too."

"We can manage," I said. "Mari's here and—"

"I know," Celi said. "We miss you guys."

"I'm trying to find a cheap ticket," Lourdes said. She was totally tearing up. We all were. Family tragedies had a way of smashing everything apart and then gluing it all back together.

The problem was no one ever knew how long the glue would hold.

Celi's apartment echoed with the sudden cannon boom of fireworks from New York City, two hours ahead of us.

"Happy Independence Day, Americanos!" Lourdes said.

"I'm going up to the roof to watch," Celi said. "I love fireworks."

"Do you guys have everything you need over there?" Lourdes asked. "Can I send anything?"

"Dulce de leche," I said. "The real stuff."

We exchanged a round of *besos* and promised to check in again soon. The screen went blank, and Mari shut her laptop and stared at me.

"Sorry I was late today," I said, hoping to preempt a lecture. I lost track of time and—"

"I got the author."

"What?"

"The call today. I'd offered representation to an author along with four other agents last week, and today was D-day. She picked me. I can't even tell you how excited I am about this book."

"Mari, that's awesome!"

"I know! I can't wait to show it to you!" She beamed. "Mom said she'd meet us at the Bowl straight from work. Let's get Papi ready and pack up the cooler."

I wanted to throw my arms around her, but something held me back. Mari was so *not* gung ho about the bike project. The sudden change of heart didn't make any sense—it felt like a trap.

"Why are you looking at me like that?" Mari asked. She was already hunting for leftovers to bring to the fireworks.

"Emilio." I shrugged. "You were kind of . . . I don't know. Defending him."

Mari set a stack of Tupperware on the counter and sighed. "It was all Papi could talk about at lunch today. He remembers so much about it, Juju—you were totally right."

Hey, Jude? Your old pal Devil-Jude here. The boss just called—wants to know why it's so cold down here. We're freezing!

"For some bizarre reason, he loves that Vargas boy," Mari said. "He went on about him forever—I almost got jealous. Like, hello, you don't need a son! Four awesome daughters over here!"

I laughed at Mari's indignant huff, and I was relieved she'd softened up, but my chest ached with the effort of keeping quiet. I had all this stuff in me to say, things I wanted to tell her about Emilio. About how I couldn't stop thinking about him. About his dimples and how the smell of his leather jacket made my stomach flip. How sweet he was at the garage today. But I couldn't; her understanding had limitations. Expirations. Once the clock on our project struck twelve, Emilio would be gone, and that was how Mari wanted it.

But that wasn't how *I* wanted it. Not now. Not anymore. Not ever.

CHAPTER 17

The Bowl was Canyon Rock Bowl, a natural amphitheater carved into the red sandstone that sloped toward the river valley. Across the swoop from the very top, it was a smooth terra-cotta bowl dotted with rock-slab benches and patches of yellow-green scrub grass.

"Watch your step, Papi," Mari said as we navigated the terrain. "Juju, help him."

I reached for Papi's elbow, but he shook me off, the silver Alzheimer's Association bracelet glinting in the setting sun. "I'm fine, *queridita*. You two keep grabbing at me like little monkeys, that's the problem."

"I could use some help," Mom said. "I wore the wrong shoes for this adventure." She finally slipped out of her wedges and went barefoot, picking her way along the rocks.

The freaks were definitely out tonight, and by freaks I mean everyone in town plus a good number of tourists, not to mention all the dogs, but we found a spot close to the exits.

We had enough *ensalada rusa*, pressed red pepper *sandwiches de miga*, and *medialunas* to feed everyone here.

I tied Pancake's leash to a screw drilled into the rock and headed down to the vending area for drinks, which we'd forgotten to pack.

"Jude!"

I almost didn't recognize her voice, but the wild red curls clued me in fast. Zoe was hanging out at the lemonade stand, pink-filled cups spiked with lemon slices in each hand. She was tan and glowy, and a hot streak of jealousy raced through me when I pictured her and Christina splashing around the Animas, beach towels side by side on the riverbank.

"You have new freckles," I said when I got close enough for a hug. "Like, a thousand more at least."

Zoe giggled. "I didn't know you were coming tonight. You should've texted!"

So should've you. . . .

"Mari's in town. Family-bonding time." I rolled my eyes like I'd rather be anywhere else.

"Your sister's here?"

"She came to help with my dad."

Zoe swirled her pink lemonade. "How's . . . everything?"

*Glad you asked, because it's capital-*A *Awesome!*

"Okay," I said. "Considering." I'd reached the front of the line, and Zoe waited off to the side while they handed over my lemonades and change.

"How's the play stuff going?" I asked.

"Rockin' it. I was basically born to be the Queen of Hearts." Zoe's mouth curled into a wicked, Queenly grin, but it faded fast. "Alice kind of sucks, though. She's not from Blackfeather. Animas High, I think. Everyone misses you."

I smiled. It was a nice sentiment, but for all that missing, I hadn't heard a peep from anyone but Zoe and Christina since the BHS picnic, and even *their* peeps were getting shorter and less frequent, more like chirps than peeps.

"We're doing a sneak preview on the eleventh. Like, a special screening for friends and family. I have extra tickets if you and Mari want to come. Oh, Christina's here too. Come say hi."

I peered into the crowd to find my family, but everything was a blur. "I should get back—"

"Just for a minute," she said. "I brought some of the guys from the Crow too—Mad Hatter and Tweedledum. We got a good spot." A fresh grin lit her face, warm and hopeful and nothing like the Queen's. "Come on. You're totally sitting with us."

I didn't know the Crow guys—they must've been from Animas High like Alice—but Christina wasn't wasting any time. She'd draped herself over the blond one like a sheet. A wet sheet. A super-clingy one.

The dark-haired guy—Mad Hatter—was loud and brutish, going on about some party happening later that night, but

Zoe seemed into him, so I just sipped my lemonade and waited for the punch line that never came. Christina wasn't saying much either—too busy flirting with Tweedledum.

At least the lemonade was fresh squeezed and super good and . . . *tart!* Theme of the night.

I turned toward Christina and tried to wedge myself into the conversation. "Have you been watching the rehearsals?"

"Yeah, Zoe is so good!" she said. "You *have* to see her do the Queen. It's intense. Zoe, show her."

Zoe cleared her throat and sat up straight. She made eye contact with each of us, seemed to be counting in her head. Her lips twitched. And then . . .

"Off with her head!"

Everyone within a twenty-foot radius turned to stare, and Zoe drank up the attention. Her eyes were wild and convincing, and the boys clapped, and Zoe bowed, and the whole scene morphed into a bunch of Crow inside jokes, most of which Christina was in on too.

Note to self: Exit, stage left.

"I have to get back to my family." I rose from the blanket. "They're probably wondering where I went."

"Can't you call them?" Zoe asked.

"I need to be there before fireworks start. For Papi, you know? Just in case?"

Zoe's eyes flickered with disappointment, but that was it. She didn't go off on another "normal teenage summer" monologue or tug me back to the blanket or offer to come with me to see my family, to hug my sister that was practically a big sister to her, too. There was a sigh, a shrug, and then Mad Hatter offered her a can of Pringles but not me and that was that.

"See you next week, right?" I said. "For the sneak preview?"

Zoe nodded half-heartedly, elbows-deep in Pringles, and Christina was hung up on some dramatic story about Tweedledum's broken leg in tenth grade, so I left without saying anything else. I looked back only once, after I'd put a good amount of bodies between us, and Zoe was curled up against the Mad Hatter, laughing it up. I squinted at the image of my best friend until she dissolved, curly red hair blending into the rocks behind her.

I picked up fresh lemonades for my family, and on the way back to Camp Hernandez, I was so far into outer space missing Zoe that I didn't see Emilio until I practically tripped over him. He and his friends had staked out a spot near the grills just outside the main area.

Emilio's eyes shone with summer, like the whole season was made for him. He flipped a burger with a metal spatula, and when he saw me he smiled. "You brought me empanadas? I knew it."

"You wish."

"I want cheese on mine." Some skankalicious skank draped her arms around Emilio's neck, really working the pout. "Please?"

Rosette.

I waited for her to remove herself, but she just stood there watching Emilio at the grill, one hand lingering on his shoulder.

What a parasite!

"Hey, Rosette," I said.

She looked over as if she'd just noticed me, even though she'd been eyeing me up the whole time.

"It's Jude," I reminded her. "Cookies?"

"I know who you are, Jude Cookies." She flashed a freshly glossed smirk, twirled her long black hair. Right near the meat and everything. Seriously, was she always trying to contaminate cooking surfaces?

"Leave them alone, Ro," another girl said. On an adjacent blanket, she and Samuel and Marcus were going to town on a bag of Combos, and Rosette plopped down next to them with a ginormous sigh.

"Hey, Jude," Marcus sang. "Don't be a—"

"Shut it." Samuel elbowed him in the ribs before he could continue, and then he offered me the Combos in Spanish, which I gladly accepted.

My phone buzzed with a Where r u?? Thirsty over here! text from Mari, totally foiling my master plan to infuriate Rosette while chowing down on Combos all night.

"I gotta get back to my parents," I said.

"You're here with your parents? How sweet." Rosette stifled a laugh, and the other girl smacked her arm.

"Hold up, I'll walk with you." Emilio turned to Samuel and held out the spatula. "Off your lazy ass and handle this, *cabrón*. I'll be back."

Emilio palmed my lemonade tray and put his other hand on the small of my back as we walked. We took the long way around the back of the Bowl, past a high sandstone wall that rose from the ground like a flame.

"I used to walk back here and wish I'd see a dinosaur," I said. "They excavated some bones a while back." I ran my hand along the rock face, grit scratching my fingertips. The feeling brought me right back to those dinosaur days. Three years ago? Five? Ten?

"This one time," I continued, "Zoe and I got into a huge fight over Trevor Fluke. She crushed on him for five years straight, but in eighth grade, he and I got the leads in *Romeo and Juliet*, so we had to kiss." I laughed at the memory—it felt like a story from someone else's life.

"You had to kiss Trev?" Emilio gave a fake shudder. "Nasty."

"It wasn't a big deal at first. Just acting. But on the last night of the show, Trevor got, like, *way* into it. Weird, you know? But I couldn't show it onstage, so I rolled with it."

"Sick little bastard." Emilio cracked his knuckles. "I know where he lives. His dad comes into Duchess sometimes."

"Stop."

"Hey. No one kisses my fake girlfriend but me."

"Anyway." I tried to ignore the heat that shot across my

neck. "Zoe didn't speak to me for two weeks. Like, ten years in girl time. I'd come out here and draw her name in hearts on the wall with rocks. Finally she forgave me and got a new crush."

"Argentinean voodoo magic?"

"Something like that." I stopped on the path and squinted at the rock face, wondering if the trick would still work.

Emilio slipped his free hand into mine. He traced his thumb over my skin and it sent shivers up and down my back, and we continued on the path, side by side as the sun sank before us, walking where the dinosaurs walked, millions of years before we were even a blip on the radar.

Maybe we *still* weren't a blip.

We'd stopped walking again, and the red walls behind Emilio blurred as I focused on his eyes.

He nodded toward the pink silk flower clipped in my hair. "I like it."

"Yeah? What's the story with Rosette?"

His eyebrows rose. "Just some crazy Catholic school girl from the neighborhood. Known her forever."

"A crazy girl with a crush," I said. "Obviously."

"Yo, that ain't a crush. Girl's been in love with me her whole damn life."

"And?"

He shook his head and laughed. "Come on. I wanna say hi to *el jefe*, then I have to get back."

"To Rosette?"

"You know how it is." Emilio shrugged. "Samuel will forget her cheese and it'll be this whole drama and I'll have to comfort her. Loss of cheese is a real difficult thing. Try to be more compassionate, Jude."

When we found my family, Papi insisted that Emilio join us, and Mom chimed in too, always jumping on a chance to feed someone, anyone, anywhere. When Emilio declined, Mom portioned out containers of potato salad and sandwich halves so he could take it to go.

Mari sighed. "He's not going on a three-day trek."

"Hush, Mari." Mom gave Emilio the food, and for one millisecond I let myself pretend that he really was my boyfriend. That this was a normal night for us, hanging out together, eating, waiting for fireworks. That someday—maybe not tomorrow or next year or the one after that, but someday—he'd be welcome in our family, expected even, the legacy of bad boyfriends finally forgotten.

"*Muchas gracias*, Mrs. Hernandez." Emilio smiled at all the goodies. And then he leaned toward me and my heart ran up into my throat. . . .

"See you soon, *princesa*," he whispered. His lips brushed my cheek for a second too long, and his fingers grazed the flower in my hair, and then he was gone.

The fireworks exploded in bright green starbursts. I kept my eyes on Papi, and though he flinched each time the sky split, he clapped and pointed out his favorites to Mom, and I took a few pictures in the twilight without a flash, hoping they'd turn out okay.

Mari looked up occasionally, but she was glued to her iPad, probably reading submissions about monsters that fall in love with humans and the dangers of having a deadly, immortal boyfriend. I didn't know how those girls managed—I could barely handle a few flirty innuendos from a nonmonster who *wasn't* out to kill me.

"Anyone want more sandwiches?" Mom was digging into the cooler as if we hadn't been eating all night. "There are two red peppers and a bunch of asparagus. Mari, *querida*?"

"No thanks." Mari smiled at me in solidarity. "Stop trying to fatten us up."

"*Ay*, I don't want the food to go bad. Bear? You want?" She held one out to Papi. "No?"

"Papi, you're not hungry, right?" I asked. Another round of fireworks cracked open the sky, and he flinched.

I raised my voice. "You're not hungry, right?"

"What, *queridita*?"

Pop . . . pop . . . boom!

"Never mind," I said.

"*¿Que?*" He cupped his hand over his ear.

"Food," Mom said. "Do you want more food?"

Pop-pop-pop!

"Put it back. We're fine." Mari waved away the sandwiches.

"Your father is hungry."

"He isn't. Papi, tell her," Mari said.

"I don't . . . know." He glanced up at the sky. "What is . . . what time . . ." He trailed off.

"Should I put these away?" Mom held up the sandwiches, her last ditch attempt to stuff our faces. "Or do you—"

BOOM!

All of us jumped at that one, especially Pancake, and Papi covered his ears, his mouth pulling into a grimace.

"We need to go," I whispered to Mom. She glanced at Papi and nodded. She remembered the BHS picnic scene as clearly as I did and needed no further explanation.

We packed up quickly, and I kept my hand on Papi's arm as we crept along the rocks in the dark. Each time the sky lit up, his bones jumped beneath my hand. When we finally reached the bottom, I saw Emilio in the lemonade line with Rosette the Succubus, and I waved. Like, really big. Could've-landed-an-airplane big. It totally worked, because he said something to her and then jogged over to us.

Mom smiled at Emilio, then turned to me. "You go with your friends, Juju. Don't worry about us."

"Mom, it's fine. I'm tired anyway."

"She's tired," Mari said.

Mom fished the keys from her purse and handed them over. "You can take my car home, yes?"

"I don't—"

"It's the Fourth of July. Stay out, enjoy yourself. Here, take the sandwiches for your friends, okay?"

I took the food and nodded, clearly unprepared to battle

the force of Mom. And, okay, maybe *slightly* intrigued by the sudden change of plans. Not that anyone in my family needed to know about that. "Guess I'll see you guys at home later," I said.

Mari shot me a warning glance. "Not too late, Juju."

CHAPTER 18

Everything looked different in the morning. The dusty barn, scattered with boxes and bike parts and tools, held none of the forest's magic. Emilio and Papi worked diligently on the exhaust system while I dug through a box of old mugs from Celi's paint-your-own-pottery phase, just another glamorous day at Casa de Hernandez.

Papi went inside for more coffee, and Emilio called me over to show me something. When he held up a chrome pipe and started talking about dual exhaust something or other, my heart sagged.

Who cares about dual exhaust when I couldn't stop thinking about you last night?

His turn: *You were thinking about me last night?*

Me: *I hardly slept.*

Him: *I thought about you too. Matter of fact, I'm* still *thinking about you. Here's another killer smile with a side of dimples. All yours . . .*

"Don't you think?" Emilio was saying.

"Yes! Wait, what am I thinking?"

Emilio set down the pipe. "I could totally take advantage of this situation. You know that, right?"

My breath caught in my throat as I laughed. Last night at the Bowl, Emilio had looked at me with that same fire in his eyes, and something inside me swirled, and I saw the whole terrible ending right there. It didn't matter what I wanted, what I thought was possible, what I thought my sisters had misjudged. If I let it continue, if I let it cross the line we almost crossed last night . . . whether he'd meant it or not, come next month, Emilio Vargas would flash his dimples one more time, ride that black motorcycle out of town, and break my heart.

Now he reached for my hair, and I flinched.

"Sorry," I whispered. "I didn't mean . . . sorry. Papi will be back any second. And my sisters are finally okay with the whole motorcycle thing, you know? If Mari saw . . ."

I met his eyes, and the regret there twisted my stomach, but almost instantly it was gone, replaced with his usual teasing.

He stretched out his arms and took a step backward, like, *Look at this fine specimen before you!* "Okay, *princesa*. If you think you can keep your hands off, be my guest."

He started singing "Be Our Guest" from *Beauty and the Beast*, and when he looked at me and smiled again, all of last night crashed into my head. He picked up the pipe and got back to work attaching it, still singing, and though I'd ordered myself not to, I replayed the movie for the hundredth time. . . .

After my family left the Bowl, Emilio and I walked back to the lemonade stand to collect Rosette, who spent the entire march back to their blanket hissing like a viper. When we hooked up with the rest of their friends, Samuel took one look at us and then he was all, *Look at the time!*, and he and Marcus and the other girl packed up their stuff, including Mom's sandwiches and one extremely irritable Rosette, who finally agreed to leave but not before pasting herself onto Emilio for a good-bye hug.

Most of the crowd had funneled out after the grand finale; only a handful of stargazers remained. Emilio waved for me to follow him along a narrow dirt trail on the other side of the Bowl, close to the woods.

"I wanna show you something," he said.

"This totally sounds like a stranger danger video."

"I'll give you some candy if that's what it takes."

I raised my eyebrows. "What kind?"

"You'll see." He held out his hand and I took it, and together we strolled along the path, the sounds of car doors and laughter and cell phones fading behind us. The trees thickened as we walked, and soon there was only us and the woods and a metal sign nailed to a charred stump.

PRIVATE PROPERTY. TRAIL ACCESS—

CROSS AT YOUR OWN RISK.

SNOWMOBILING, CAMPING, HUNTING FORBIDDEN.

"Should we keep going?" I whispered. I didn't want to alert whoever had hung the sign.

"Says cross at your own risk," Emilio said. "That's what we're doing."

He held back a pine branch so it wouldn't whip me in the face, and as I stepped past, I caught a whiff of his leather and softener scent.

"It's risky for me to be here with you?" I was only half kidding; my heart sped up and my body was electrified with nervous energy. Emilio was still his flirty, jokester self, but in the shadow of our conversation behind Duchess today, all words had more meaning.

He put his arm around my shoulders and leaned in close. "Scared?"

My skin zinged from the current that passed between us. It was all I could do to keep one foot in front of the other on the moonlit path. Somewhere from the distant past, a little voice called out . . . *never, ever, under any circumstances . . .*

I shook off his arm and stepped ahead as if I knew the way, but he reached for my hand and I let him take it, lacing our fingers together. He'd stopped walking, and I had no choice but to do the same.

I turned to face him, bodies and lips and skin and scent closer than they'd ever been. I forced myself to hold his gaze, stared at a tiny freckle beneath his eye, hidden behind a fan of soft black lashes.

"Close your eyes." His breath grazed my lips, teased every hair on my scalp to attention.

I did as instructed, my other senses heightening in the sudden absence of sight. Emilio released my fingers and wrapped his hands around my shoulders, giving me a gentle nudge.

The ground, cushioned by old leaves and moss and things that time forgot, gave slightly. We'd stepped off the hard-packed dirt path and now headed deeper into the woods. A jolt of exhilaration raced up my spine.

"Keep 'em closed," he said softly. "No matter what."

It was so still and silent. I'd lost track of the frogs and crickets whose songs usually flooded the summer night. The air sweetened and thickened, and it felt like an eternity passed, no sounds but our breathing, opposite and out of sync, and the heartbeat in my ears, and maybe the trees growing cell by cell.

Emilio's hands slid to my neck. He gathered my long hair and held it behind me. I fought not to shiver, not to shudder.

"Lean forward," he said. "Take a deep breath through your nose."

"Seriously?"

"Would I joke about something like this?" Even through the softness of his moonlight voice, a playful taunting rang out.

I leaned in and inhaled.

A cloud of sweetness. It wasn't sugary or syrupy. It wasn't a flower. It was softer, yet more potent, underlined with something woodsy and ancient. Here in the dark, alone in the woods with Emilio Vargas, everything had taken on a new intensity, a surreal magic that didn't exist in the daylight.

It was intoxicating. The scent. The feeling. The simultaneous hope and fear.

"It's like . . . vanilla bean?" I said.

"Butterscotch."

I thought he'd finally produced that promised candy, and I was about to give him some serious credit for building up the suspense. My heart was still hammering behind my ribs.

I opened my eyes. I was standing a half inch away from a giant tree trunk.

"Ponderosa pine," he said. "The bark smells like butterscotch."

"When did you become a tree sniffer?" I took another whiff. "I've lived here my whole life and I never knew we had butterscotch trees."

"My cousin Danny taught me. He was a hobbit or something. Serious. When we were kids, right, we'd go out in the woods for hide-and-seek or Dungeon Defender, and hours later everyone would be, like, where the hell's Danny? We'd find him off in the woods, looking at leaves and bugs and shit, doing his thing. He always told me stuff about trees. Thought I wasn't listening." Emilio shook his head. "Crazy nature boy bastard."

I remembered the picture on Emilio's desk, the lizard one, but if I mentioned it, he'd know I'd been in his room. "Where is he now?"

"He's . . ." Emilio didn't answer right away, like he was trying to remember an address. "In Puerto Rico. Hopefully surfing some gorgeous-ass beach. There's more. Come on."

He edged deeper into the forest, and I followed in silence. I wanted to ask about Danny, about his brothers, about the maps in his room. I wanted to tell him how that thing with the ponderosa pine was so small and special and how I knew, in that moment even more than at his house baking cookies, that my sisters were wrong about his family, that he could never come from cruelty, that he could never hurt me the way his brothers had hurt them. That it was okay to want this—being alone in the moonlit woods, talking about trees while the smoke of fireworks still hung faint and blue in the air.

Automatically I thought of Celi again, crying in her bed, and Mom's face in the weeks that followed as she tried to get their money back for the wedding flowers and catering and everything they were once so sure about. I thought of Mari, washing Celi's hair in the sink because she didn't have the strength to do it herself, and how Mari had flatironed it and all Celi did was go back to bed. I thought back to Lourdes, too, the morning I'd found her prom corsage in the trash. I'd assumed it was a mistake at first—it was so pretty—so I retrieved it and left it on the edge of the sink, and later it disappeared and no one said anything about it.

Lourdes had cried a lot too, and after that, Miguel got his eyes scratched out in all the pictures that had once been so lovingly arranged in her bedroom mirror. They all met the same fate in the black book.

But Emilio wasn't his brothers. He was different. He was kindhearted and funny. He was sweet. He was . . .

Always wild . . . one foot out the door . . .

Leaving.

And that, more than his family legacy and the oath and all the warnings, was Emilio Vargas's fatal flaw.

"It's right up here," Emilio said, and I followed the white glow of his T-shirt deeper into the trees until we stepped into a clearing encircled by tall, silver-barked aspens. It was a sacred place, some impossibly perfect creation that none of us was meant to see.

"Did you come here with your cousin?" I asked.

He shook his head. "I never came here with anybody but me."

I met his eyes and braced for a jab about Rosette or some other girl but there was none, and then he stepped close and reached for my chin and gently tilted it to the sky.

"Orion," I whispered. The constellation, like everything else, had taken on some kind of magic intensity. "Araceli had a telescope when we were kids—I remember him. The three bright stars are his belt."

"I never remember their names," Emilio said. "This one . . . Orion? He follows me everywhere. I gotta try to outrun him on the road. I mean, not for real. I get this feeling when I look up and he's always there, like . . . hey! I'm watching you! I don't know. . . . It's hard to explain."

He was stammering in the wake of my silence, maybe mistaking it for confusion or boredom or judgment, but when I looked at him again, my eyes were watery and I knew he'd noticed and he finally stopped babbling.

Something passed between us then, and my heart kick-started and I smiled.

"Not worried about the risks anymore?" He slipped a finger through one of my belt loops and pulled me close. Our legs were almost touching, everything hot and charged.

"This is the second time today you dragged me alone into the woods," I said. "No one knows we're here, and I still haven't seen any candy."

He slipped his arms around my waist and looked deep into my eyes, his own unblinking.

"So." My voice was shaky. "You don't have any candy, do you?"

He traced his fingers over the flower clip in my hair, brushed a lock behind my ear. Now our legs were touching. Everything was touching, fabric on fabric and skin on skin, all the space between us erased. "Nope."

Moments passed like eons, and his hands were in my hair. All around us crickets and frogs started up their night songs again. The entire forest seemed to open up and bloom in the dark.

"Your heart's pounding like mad," he whispered. Fingers brushed my collarbone, tapped gently. "Ba-*bom*. Ba-*bom*."

His breath fell against my skin, soft as a breeze, and my lips could already taste him. My mouth watered, and something swirled from a deep place inside me and my heart continued its mad dash beneath his fingertips and my whole body ached with the desire to touch him, to feel him against me.

I'd never been so exhilarated in my life.

I'd never been so scared.

"We should go," I said. The trees rustled overhead, the aspens quaking, and despite the warmth between us, I shivered. "It's late, and . . . Mari's waiting up."

Emilio smoothed my hair, calming the strands that had gone wild under his touch. He held my gaze a moment longer, and I thought he might say something else, but he just smiled and took my hand and led us out of that magic, beautiful place, back through the woods, and I looked up at Orion one last time and sighed.

"Looking good, looking good!" Papi clapped his hands and I jumped, yanked back to the present, back to the dusty barn and the bike parts and the bright yellow sun outside.

"Think she's ready to make some noise?" Emilio straddled the Harley frame. He'd rolled it off the lift, and it looked like something out of *The Terminator*, all metal bones and bolts, naked without its seat and fenders.

"She's ready." Papi was alive with excitement: eyes sparkling, cheeks pink and healthy, all evidence of last night's fireworks overload gone.

Emilio turned the key to open the ignition switch. "Drumroll, please."

Papi and I rolled our tongues and tapped our thighs. Not exactly the Colorado Symphony percussionists, and Papi's attempt was more of a sputter than a roll, but Emilio smiled. He looked up at the ceiling, said a little prayer, and jumped with all his weight on the kickstart. The bike coughed and shuddered, and then . . .

Nothing.

Emilio jumped again.

Another cough, another nothing.

Papi and I cut the sound effects. After two more failed attempts, Emilio hopped off. He knelt beside it, poked and rattled a few pipes, squinted, scratched his head.

Papi hadn't heard the growl of that engine in more than three decades, and the anticipation crackled around him like mountain lightning. I laced my fingers through his and squeezed, nodding for Emilio to give it another go.

"Come on, baby." He patted the engine gently as he threw his leg across the frame again. "Here we go."

Papi crushed my fingers.

Emilio jumped.

Hit the kickstart.

The bike coughed.

The engine sputtered.

Everything shuddered and shook.

And after thirty years of silence, Papi's Valentina roared to life.

I squealed and flung myself into Papi's arms. He couldn't

speak, just kept opening and closing his mouth like a fish, his eyes glossy with emotion.

Emilio slid off the bike and leaned it on the kickstand, still rumbling.

"Welcome back, old girl." Papi pressed his hand to the engine. Valentina, finicky old girl, returned his tender greeting with a cough and a sputter and a final gasp.

The day was silent once again.

"No worries, *jefe*," Emilio said. "First breath in thirty years? You'd probably cough a little too."

"Do I look worried?" Papi waved him off. "No way, José. You know how many times she tested me like that on the road? More than I can remember, even if I *could* remember."

"Papi!" I rolled my eyes.

"It's true, *querida*. One time I *do* recall, we got caught in a rainstorm near Mendoza, you know?"

"*Sí.*" We'd visited the region a few summers ago for Lourdes and Alejandro's wedding.

"Lots of mountains, like here," he told Emilio. "And the storms? Boy. I was pushing Valentina to get us off the hill, but she wouldn't have it. I got caught up there. Lucky I found some nice people to take me in, and they had a daughter about my age, so . . . it was a fun visit."

"I thought you met Mom at the diner?" I asked.

"*¿Que?*" Papi knocked on his head, ears suddenly red. "You know, I think maybe I got the story mixed up."

"It *wasn't* Mom?"

"It was a long time ago, *querida*. Let's leave it at that."

He laughed and Emilio returned to the bike, but I was still forcing images of Papi and another girl out of my mind. It was hard to remember he had a whole other life before he married Mom, before he had us.

I wonder who he'll forget last.

"Don't be sad, Jujube." Papi pulled me into a side hug. "She's fine. Needs a little time is all. She'll come around."

"Who?" Mari trotted in through the barn doors with Pancake at her side. They'd been out hiking most of the day.

"Emilio got the bike running," Papi said.

"Almost," Emilio said.

"That's great!" Mari said. "I met someone on the trail today. A biker."

"When's the wedding?"

"Hilarious." Mari turned to Papi. "I told him about the bike. He's interested in looking at it, maybe making an offer."

"Who says it's for sale?" I asked. "It's not even running yet."

"I know, but . . . Have you guys thought about it?" Mari's eyes flashed to Emilio, then back to me. "Can't hurt to let him check it out, right? He said he'd consider it as is. You might get to take your road trip early, Vargas. How's that?"

She grabbed Pancake and headed back to the house before I could find the words to talk her out of it, to come up with some logical, financially sound reason why we should keep a vintage motorcycle that Papi would never be allowed to ride. I didn't know how to tell her I *felt* it more than I knew it, way down in my bones and my heart, where medical research and doctors' opinions didn't matter: Getting rid of that bike meant surrendering to the demon. The end of Papi's last chance. The end of everything.

I sagged against the workbench, wishing I could disintegrate and blow away with the dust, and across the barn, Papi and Emilio looked at me with the same wounded faces.

"Say something." I was alone with Emilio after Mari had called Papi into the house for a nap. Or a snack. Or a drink or a pill or a crossword puzzle—I didn't know anymore. And now I stood dumbly before Emilio, the bike between us like unhideable evidence of some heinous crime.

"You're so different when she's around." He wouldn't look at me, just gathered up his tools and assembled them back in the box. "You give me shit all the time. You stand up to those guys at the garage, dish it right back. You make Rosette crazy jealous. You put me in my place every five minutes. But Mari? You never say jack."

I kicked the dirt floor. "She's my sister."

"So she gets to make the decisions, tell you what to do? How to live?" He ran a hand over his bandanna and shook his head. "Who to be with?"

His questions jabbed my chest. I wanted to defend myself, to defend Mari, to tell him how she'd always looked out for me. How she'd given me my first cigarette when I was in sixth grade because she knew it would make me sick and I'd never want another. How she'd comforted Celi after Johnny broke her heart. How she'd read books about Papi's illness so she could figure out the best ways to help him. How she'd kept her promise not to tell my sisters about Emilio.

Why can't he see it?

When I opened my mouth, the words wouldn't come. I saw a snapshot of how things had always been between my sisters and me, just as they had that night in Celi's room five years ago. Lourdes, the oldest, picking up the pieces for everyone else. Celi, soft and romantic with a giant, open heart. Mari, the baby of the three, full of fire and impulse.

But that's where everything got screwed up, because Lourdes should've been here helping with Papi—she'd know exactly what to do. And technically I was the baby, not Mari, and I'd spent most of my life living like the child of my three older siblings, wearing the clothes they'd given me, reading their books, listening to their advice.

Following their rules about boys.

I looked down at my body, clothed in an old tank top from Celi's closet, faded olive cargo shorts from Mari's summer stash. Even the flip-flops were hand-me-downs, some faded old pair with missing sequins I'd found in an unlabeled box of toys.

Emilio thought I let Mari make my decisions, tell me how to live. And maybe he was right.

Maybe I didn't know how to do it myself.

"You let your pops think this meant something to you,"

he said. "I seen him watchin' you. His face lights up like Christmas when you're around. Now you're gonna let your sister sell it out from under him? Before I'm even done? I thought we had a deal."

A deal. He was more concerned about the bike than anything else. About his job. His money. Heat boiled inside, sputtering into my throat. "Worried you won't have enough cash for your trip now? Relax, Emilio Vargas. I'm sure my father will pay you in full."

Emilio's eyes widened, lips curling into a pained smirk. There was no more laughter in his eyes. Only disappointment, the dull ache of it spreading and blooming in my chest as he left without another word, half his tools still scattered on the floor.

CHAPTER 19

"Another lovers' quarrel?" Mari held a cigarette to the electric burner and sucked until it caught fire. It was a miracle the girl still had eyebrows.

"It's not a lovers' quarrel," I said. Emilio had been working with Papi every day since our fight, five and counting, and so far we'd managed to totally avoid each other. Mari's biker friend had stopped by yesterday, but other than eavesdropping on his enthusiastic visit, I'd spent my time indoors, putting the finishing touches on a scrapbook I was supposed to make months ago for Zoe's birthday. "I just don't want to talk to him."

"So your big plan is to stare at him out the window all week?"

I backed away from the screen door and sat at the kitchen table. "I was looking for Pancake."

Who, me? Me? Was it me, Jude? Me? Or do you have actual pancakes to share? The dog, who'd been in the kitchen the whole time, trotted over and nuzzled my hand.

"Juju . . ." Mari leveled me with one of her no-nonsense stares. "Are you falling for him?"

I rolled my eyes. "Okay, first of all, you need to go on the patch. Second of all, you're crazy."

She blew a dragon plume out the window over the sink. "I read enough books about teenagers in love to recognize the signs."

"Yeah, well. Emilio and I aren't werewolves or fallen angels, so there's that."

"I'm just saying—"

"And where's the other guy? Shouldn't there be a love triangle of impossibly hot boys or vampires pining after me?"

"I'm worried about you, that's all." Her voice was soft, almost protective. "This is what Vargas boys do, Jujube. Things get heated, they bail."

Emilio's words echoed in my skull. *She gets to make the decisions, tell you what to do? How to live? Who to be with?*

"Things aren't heated," I said. "He's not bailing. He's working."

"You need to stop this before—"

"You smell like an ashtray from all the way over here. Papi's gonna bust you."

Mari narrowed her eyes, a warning shot that grazed my head. She crushed the butt in the sink, blowing out a last puff of smoke, and ransacked the cupboards and drawers like a psycho.

She emerged with matches and one of Mom's old Virgin

Mary candles and sat down across from me, flame sputtering as she lit the dusty wick. I hadn't seen the knife at first, but now she held it out over the fire. "Give me your palm."

I sat on my hands. "I'm not getting stabbed again."

"No one *stabbed* you. It was a blood oath. And obviously it didn't work the first time. Palm."

"I never should've signed that thing. It's a relic, Mari. Nothing to do with me or Emilio. He's not like Johnny." I hated that I was crying in front of her, five years old again.

"What do you think will happen when things get bad with Papi? I don't mean mood swings. I'm talking when he can't go to the bathroom by himself. When he can't remember your name. When he freaks because he thinks we're strangers, that we're trying to hurt him."

I rubbed my hands on my shorts, my fingers tightening. Sadness rose inside me like bubbling tar. It coated my thoughts, my words, my heart, made them all heavy and black. "I don't know."

"Do you really think Emilio will stick around for that? And what about after that? After Papi's gone and—"

"Don't say that."

"Juju . . ." Mari's voice finally broke. "This is bigger than the oath, okay? And it's not just about Papi and the next few months or years. There's stuff we haven't even considered yet."

Her face held its familiar stubbornness, the know-it-all confidence that had settled into her eyes in childhood. But there was something new there too, hiding in the shadows. Something powerful and dangerous that left in its wake a girl even younger than me.

Fear.

"What stuff?" I asked.

Mari held my gaze for only a moment, then it was gone, the fear I'd seen no more than a ghost in her watery eyes. "I'm just saying we can't predict the future, and getting tangled up with a Vargas now will only make things harder later." She scraped an old splotch of oatmeal on the place mat like it was no big deal, but her voice had betrayed her, cracked and uncertain. The Virgin candle fizzled out, smoke coiling like a serpent between us, and in that moment the fear I'd seen in her eyes filled my chest.

What stuff? She hadn't said, and I couldn't cough out the words to ask again.

Mari returned the unused knife to the drawer. She filled a glass with ice water, and once she'd chugged it, everything bad was erased, and she turned to me with a bright smile.

"The guy e-mailed about the bike. His wife is cool with it. He's interested in making an offer. Papi doesn't really know what it's worth, but I checked around. I think we can get a nice chunk of change."

She stood there with her jutting hip and her smoky "essence of Mari" and rambled on about the specs and collectors' editions and Blue Book values until the bubbling black tar inside me finally boiled over.

"A nice chunk of change? Are you serious?" I shouted. "I've been here all summer, all year, and you swoop in for a few weeks and suddenly you know what's best, right? Did you even ask Papi if he wanted to sell Valentina?"

Her eyes widened, but I plowed on. "Your way or no way. My whole life it's been like that. You're—"

"I can't believe you." She slammed her glass on the counter. "You act like you know something, but *you're* a spoiled little—"

"At least I'm not—"

"Mariposa *y* Jude Hernandez!" Papi's voice boomed through the kitchen. He pushed open the screen door and loomed in the doorway, filling up the space in a way he hadn't since the diagnosis. He towered over everything in sight. Even Pancake scampered under the table.

"Enough is enough is enough!" Papi let the door slam behind him and squinted at the Virgin candle. "I don't know what kind of séance you're doing in here, *mi brujitas*, but this bickering has to stop. And don't let your mother catch you using her church candles. *Dios mío.*"

"*Sí*, Papi," we said simultaneously.

"Emilio is done for the day. I'm going upstairs," Papi said. "And you two will work this out like adults. *Ay*, it's like the Wild West in here. You're sisters, *queriditas*. No more fighting."

"*Sí*, Papi," Mari said again.

"And another thing." He looked from Mari to me and back to Mari again, the air as thick as gravy. This was usually the part in the conversation where the demon woke up and gave him a good zap, reminding him he had no business having a rational adult discussion, playing the authority figure.

But Papi's eyes were clear, his directive focused. "E-mail your friend and tell him thanks but no thanks on the bike. I've made my decision. Until I start wearing diapers and drooling, Valentina is *not* for sale."

"Don't talk like that, Papi." Mari's voice was faint and frail.

Papi swatted her words out of the air. "Don't be so sensitive, little butterfly. Just remember, *soy tu padre todavía.*"

I'm still your father.

"We need to talk." Mom swept the hair away from my face and frowned, her body sagging next to mine on the bed. Behind her, Mari stood in the doorway, eyes red and exhausted.

I'd been hiding out for the past two hours, paging through the black book, and I didn't hear Mom come in from work. Mari probably ratted me out for refusing to accept her apologies, a stance that took epic willpower because her last round of *I'm so super sorry* involved peanut butter cookie dough. The warm sweetness of it still wafted through the hallway.

My stomach grumbled. *Traitor.*

"Come in, *mi amor*," Mom said to Mari. "Close the door."

I shoved the book under my pillow as Mari collapsed into my desk chair, facing me and Mom on the bed. The slump of their shoulders was identical, the air around them heavy and sad.

I bolted up straight. "Did something happen with Papi?"

Mom shook her head. "Just some things . . . We need to get things out in the open."

Vargas. She knows.

"Emilio's just . . . he's helping us. You know, to get the bike running," I stammered. "He's not—"

"It's not about the bike." Mari flashed a warning look, a silent signal meant for me alone: *Don't say another word.* I exhaled with temporary relief.

What is this about?

"We need to start making some decisions about your father's care, *mi querida*. Long term."

"For when you're back in Argentina?"

Mom bit her lower lip, tears welling in her eyes.

Mari scooted the desk chair close to the bed and rested her hand on my knee. "Papi could get really disoriented if we interrupt his routine now. The doctors agree it's better for them to stay. Permanently."

"The doctors just want our insurance money. We're practically putting their kids through college." I said it like it was the most obvious thing in the world, but even I heard the desperation in my words.

"It's not that simple," Mom said.

"What about Transitions?" I'd meant it as a challenge, but my voice was so small, it came out sounding like a good idea, like, *Hey! Have you guys thought of this awesome place, Transitions? I think Papi would capital-*L *Love it.*

Mom didn't flinch. Maybe she'd meant to tell me about it all along. Maybe she thought she already had. Obviously Mari was in the loop—she didn't ask any questions.

"That's one option for the table, yes," Mom said.

"*On* the table," I said.

"*Sí.* But there are other considerations. Things you and your sisters have to . . . more decisions." Mom shook her head and mumbled something under her breath. I barely understood her through the accent. "The doctors . . . you explain, Mariposa."

"I don't know how much you know about the illness," Mari said, "but early onset isn't exactly the same as regular Alzheimer's. There's often a genetic component."

"What do you mean?" I asked.

"They can test EOA patients to see if they have these gene mutations." She clenched her fist, then opened it, traced her fingers over my knee. "Papi has them."

"So . . . they can fix the genes? Like, alter them? Radiate them or something?" The questions tasted stupid on my tongue, but if there was a fraction of a chance . . .

"It's just to help them look for the probable cause," Mari said. "The doctors said that with the mutations, Papi likely has familial early onset Alzheimer's. Inherited."

My brain struggled to put the pieces together. "Papi's parents had it, then?"

"One of them most likely did," Mari said.

We didn't know much about our paternal grandparents.

Papi's mother left when he was in preschool, and his father died in his forties from lung cancer. Papi was already out of the house by then, and when they tried to locate his mother to tell her about her husband's death, they found out she'd died early too. Something to do with alcohol. Liver failure maybe?

When I'd first heard the story as a kid, I thought they were so stupid, so selfish. Smoked and drank themselves to death, leaving my father and uncle before their time, depriving us of ever knowing our grandparents. But now, as I watched Mom fidget with my fleece blanket, felt Mari's hand on my knee, I wondered if my grandparents somehow knew what their future held. If they'd gotten a glimpse and taken another way out before the demon could get a foothold, set up his evil lair.

I shivered at the thought. "What about Uncle Sebastian?"

"He's getting tested," Mom said.

Last I'd heard, they hadn't told Papi's brother about the diagnosis. He lived in Buenos Aires, and they spoke only every four or five months, if that. We weren't close with my uncle, and neither was Papi. They hadn't wanted to bother him with it before.

"*Querida*, you and your sisters . . . the way the disease works . . ." Mom pulled at a thread on my blanket. "I'm sorry. I feel like it's our fault. Like I should've been able to . . . I didn't understand how it worked."

"We have a fifty-fifty chance of getting it, Juju," Mari said, and then her face crumpled. Fear was back in her eyes, and in that moment my big tough sister looked small and weak, shoulders hunched over her chest, sweater hanging on her frame like a shirt on a wire hanger. "There's a test. They can tell us if we have the mutations too. If we do . . ."

Her words faded away, leaving a sharp black gash on my heart. Everything felt hot and sticky, breath rushing in and out in gulps. "Are you . . . and the . . . What did Papi say?"

"We agreed not to tell him," Mom whispered. "Worrying about you . . . he'd blame himself. It would only make it harder on him."

"We need to be prepared." Mari's eyelashes were dark with tears. "If we get early treatment, maybe . . ."

"Maybe what?" My hands shook. "We know about it sooner? So we can look forward to forgetting everything? No way. I'm not getting tested."

"I get it," Mari said. "You think I'm not scared shitless? But the benefits—"

"This is what Lourdes meant, right? On the call? She asked about a test, and then you guys got all quiet and weird and—"

"Not weird," Mari said. "We're trying to figure out the best way through this."

"And?"

Any second now Mari would leap out of her chair, punch a pillow, come up with some way to beat the whole thing, and laugh about it later. And I'd go along with it. *Tell me what to do. Tell me how to fix this. . . .*

"Celi and Lourdes are coordinating flights in a few weeks," she said. "They want to be here so we can all get tested together.

We can talk to the counselors first. It's better if we're together. We can . . . It's just better." She sank deeper into the desk chair. My knee went cold in the absence of her touch.

There was nothing left to say, and after a few moments of uncomfortable silence, Mom kissed my forehead and they retreated to their separate bedrooms, leaving me alone with the big white elephant in the room sucking up all the air.

I slipped the *Book of Broken Hearts* from beneath my pillow and flipped through the pages again. There were the Vargas boys, and all the other breakups my sisters had endured, decades of collective heartache immortalized. Other stuff too—Duffer, the dog they'd had before I was born, buried behind the barn. A boy from Lourdes's class who'd committed suicide. Mari's best friend who moved to France their senior year. Other friends who'd graduated early or cut ties after some stupid girl fight.

My parents were barely mentioned though, not even in the background of the diary-style entries. It truly was a time capsule of the Hernandez Sisterhood; it was as if my parents never existed. Important back then was falling in love, passing a test, getting into college. It was unfulfilled crushes and secret dreams, first drinks, first kisses, the best way to the river in the dark, the sneaking out that had sparked some of the very entanglements that later ended in tears. They didn't have to consider my parents in their possibilities of broken hearts. It never occurred to them that there might come a day when Papi wouldn't remember them, a day when they'd long for a way back through the tangle of memories, back to all the little things, back before they'd ever thought about saying the long good-bye.

The long good-bye. That's what they called Alzheimer's on the message boards, the websites I'd scoured in the weeks after his diagnosis looking for a loophole, a way out for us. Maybe not today or tomorrow or even next month, but one day, they said, one day we'd wake up, and Papi wouldn't know what day it was. He'd forget my name maybe, forget we had a dog, or maybe instead of Pancake he'd call him Waffles or Window or Shoelace. And every day it would start again, us scrutinizing the lines in his face, the arch of his brows, wondering if today was familiar or new.

Maybe it *was* the long good-bye, the longest one ever. But it was worse than that, too. Because in that good-bye were a hundred hellos, every day brand-new, as if we were meeting for the very first time.

The demon would ensure that. There wasn't a cure. Only the destruction. The aftermath.

And now, a 50 percent chance it would live on in us.

CHAPTER 20

The sun wove pink-orange webs in the dawn sky, and Pancake yawned and smacked his jowls at my feet, like, *Please can we go back to sleep now, puh-lease?*

He'd stayed with me all night, and as he gazed longingly at my bed in the morning light, I wanted so badly to crawl under the blanket with him, to curl up and pretend everything Mari and Mom had told me was just another nightmare, some worse-than-worst-case scenario invented by my subconscious.

But every time I closed my eyes, the number flashed before them. The big five-oh. Fifty percent.

Half.

Half a chance at living a normal life, growing up and falling in love and getting married and having kids, or maybe not getting married, maybe just collecting a few broken hearts for the book, but either way living to tell the tale.

Half a chance at death. A slow and painful fading away. The long good-bye.

I looked at my feet sticking out of the blanket, toes glowing in the sun that streamed through the window. My nails were painted bright green and blue, and they looked like the little mint candies that came with the check at restaurants. I wriggled them, curled and uncurled them, felt every one, and in that moment it was all decided.

No. I wouldn't go out with a long good-bye, turn into some pale and tattered paper moon. If Papi's demon was my legacy, I'd fight that bastard all the way, breath for breath, memory for memory, fire with fire.

I sat up fast, put my feet on the floor. *Starting now, Juju.*

Tonight was the *Alice in Wonderland* preview. I plucked the tickets Zoe'd given me from my bulletin board and rubbed my thumbs along the edges.

If things had gone according to plan, I would've tried out for Alice. I would've spent the past few weeks rehearsing with Zoe and the other cast members, practicing lines with Christina at Witch's Brew, reading monologues to Pancake as I wolfed down breakfast before dashing to the theater.

Instead, the demon reared its ugly head, sank its venomous fangs into our lives. And I'd spent most of those weeks in the barn learning how to rebuild a Harley, all my fragile hope pinned on that machine.

On Emilio Vargas.

On my father.

I would've made a perfect Alice, tumbling ass over teakettle down the rabbit hole, drugged and dreaming and wondering what—if anything—was real.

Real. Here was real. I still knew my name and I could still paint my toes and wriggle them in the sun and hug my dog, and no matter what some genetic test might say about the end of days, that's what I had.

I grabbed my phone and scrolled to Emilio's number, pressed the device to my ear. *Please pick up . . .*

"I knew you couldn't resist seeing me again," Emilio said. He'd accepted my apology easily, no grudge attached, and now he was standing by his bike in my driveway, all dimples and clean-soap smell, and for once I didn't argue. He was right—I couldn't resist.

"I'll drive," he said.

I looked down at my denim skirt and the pink wedges Mari had lent me. I was pretty sure she still felt bad about how we'd left things yesterday—the fight, and then all the bad news—because all she said as I was blow-drying my hair in the bathroom was that the shoes would look really cute on me and to tell Zoe to break a leg tonight.

No warnings about Emilio, no cautions against the perils of love. Just a pair of pink shoes and a smile. And after that, a headband, because I'd lost my silk flower clip at the Bowl that night, which totally sucked because it was my favorite and it would've gone perfect with Mari's pink shoes and Emilio liked it.

"I'm not getting on a bike in this," I said now. "I'll drive."

"I meant—" Emilio plucked the keys from my hand and jangled them in front of my face. "You promised me another lesson."

I rubbed my neck in protest, but he was already climbing into the driver's side of the truck. I climbed in, buckled up, and took a deep breath. "Okay. Push in the—"

"Clutch. Got it." He started the engine smoothly and shifted us into reverse, backing us all the way down the driveway after only one stall.

"You've been practicing," I said.

"Samuel let me drive his Jeep. Which he never does. I had to drop your name a few times." Emilio laughed, and despite one more stall at an uphill stop sign, he got us to town in one piece.

We found our seats easily. A handful of people from school dotted the auditorium, but the audience was mostly parents and grandparents. I was grateful Emilio had accepted my invitation, and I smiled and thanked him again and then the lights dimmed and the curtain rose and everyone cheered as the show began.

The play was amazing. Zoe shone as the maniacal Queen, and my heart swelled with pride and admiration, and I took about five hundred pictures. She'd obviously worked really hard this year; her acting and singing skills had grown exponentially. The girl who played Alice could've been better, not that I was biased or anything, but Zoe's friends from the Bowl—Tweedledum and the Mad Hatter—rocked the stage too.

After the curtain closed, Emilio and I wove through the crowd in search of Zoe. I found her near the dressing room with the other cast members collecting roses and kisses and accolades, which was perfect, since I'd finally brought her the birthday scrapbook. I stood on tiptoe and called over the sea of heads and shoulders that separated us, and soon she was right in front of me, one of her arms wrapped around a bouquet of red and white roses. The sugar-sweet smell made my throat itch.

Zoe was glowing beneath her stage makeup, her shoulders high and proud as I snapped a few more pictures.

"Thanks for coming! Did you bring Mari?" When she noticed Emilio leaning against the opposite wall, her eyebrows rose.

"We're together," I said. "I mean, we came together. Mari's home playing Scrabble with my parents. Oh, she said break a leg, which you obviously did. Not literally—"

"Are you and Emilio, like, a thing now? Even after that stuff with Celi and Lourdes?"

A chill rose between us. "We're . . . friends."

"Dark hearts, every one," she said, just like that day at my house when she'd first seen Emilio. Just like we used to whisper to each other in the dark, flashlights throwing shadows on the tent wall as we pondered the otherworldly origins of the Vargas brothers. Zoe was smiling now, but I couldn't tell whether she was joking or being cruel. Her pinched red lips were painted on, her eyebrows blackened into severe arches.

I almost laughed at the memory of our childhood campouts, all that elaborate speculation. The Vargas brothers weren't vampires or angels or dark things that went bump in the night.

It was a lot more complicated and frightening than that.

"We're friends," I said again.

"I saw you with him at the Bowl. After you ditched us."

"I didn't ditch you, I just . . . I ran into him there. We hung out after my family left."

"Hey, Jude!" Christina waved from across the hall. She was draped around Tweedledum, and the two of them whooshed by and melded into a crowd of parents before I could return the greeting. Clearly, Christina had been fully adopted by the play people.

Zoe watched me a moment longer, maybe waiting for me to offer up a few more details about Emilio, some explanation for tonight's date.

"You did awesome out there," I said.

"Thanks." Her red-paint smile didn't falter. "It was *so* fun. There's great new people at the Crow this year. Christina's been a big help too. She did a lot of the backdrop paintings."

I wondered again whether she'd meant it as a jab or just a fact, and with a rush of sadness I realized that one day I might not care what she meant. I might not remember this night, all the times I'd counted her freckles, the fact that we'd ever been friends at all.

My chest hurt and I wanted to hug her, to spill all the details about this summer, to tell her I missed her already and didn't want things to change between us. But it was too late. Things *had* changed, and here in the hallway where everyone else cheered and hugged, silence enveloped my best friend and me in a suffocating bubble. It wasn't the time to admit what I'd learned last night; it wasn't the place to talk about Emilio. I couldn't think of anything else to say about her performance. She didn't ask about my parents, Papi's health, the motorcycle.

After years of friendship, sleepovers, study sessions, clothes swapping, shopping trips, summers, winters, crushes and french fries and movies and plays, we'd run out of things to say. In a flash I saw us hand in hand on the dinosaur path behind the Bowl, walking barefoot through the red dust, and then we let go. She went left, I went right. Neither of us looked back.

"Happy birthday," I finally said, handing over the gift bag. "Sorry it's so late. It's a scrapbook." I fumbled to explain, to fill up the awkward silence with words I no longer had. "I made it from some of our old pictures. Mostly plays and summer—"

"Off with their heads!" A crowd of still-costumed heart cards cheered from the doorway to the parking lot.

"Off with their heads!" she roared back, jabbing her finger in the air like the Queen. The handle on my gift bag tore. It hit the ground with a thud, and she was still waving to her friends as if she hadn't noticed. I picked up the bag and waited.

"Sorry," she said. "Play stuff. What were you saying?"

Play stuff! Like I didn't know what that meant. Like I hadn't been a part of it for her last play and every single one before it.

For the second time, I passed her the bag. "Happy belated birthday."

"Zoe, come on!" The white rabbit waved from the doorway. "We're late! We're late! And we're totally leaving without you, dude."

"Be right out." She flashed them a fake gang sign that I was pretty sure didn't exist in Wonderland and turned back to me, her forced smile creasing the white paint around her mouth. From our seats in the auditorium, she was treacherous and beautiful, a perfect Queen of Hearts. But up close her lips were clownish and uneven, black hair dye bleeding onto her forehead.

"Jude?" I'd lost track of Emilio, and now he was right there, right behind me. He slipped his hand beneath my hair and squeezed my neck, leaned in and kissed my cheek. "Ready to head out?"

I glared at him. "Five minutes."

He retreated to the wall he'd been holding up. When I turned back to Zoe, she was staring at me in disbelief.

"Looks like 'just friends' to me," she said. "Right."

Another pack of cards interrupted, four boisterous club- and diamond-boys, all of them urging Zoe to jet over to the party.

"Are you guys going to Emma's?" I asked. Emma Scully

always had the Crow parties because she had a pool with a swim-up bar and her land overlooked the whole river valley. Her parents were pretty don't-ask-don't-tell about the whole thing too.

It seemed stupid and inconsequential now—the post-play giddiness, all of us squealing and dunking one another in the pool like kids and then acting grown up with our syrupy rum drinks, little paper umbrellas sticking out of the cups.

"You could come if . . . I mean, I guess you're with Emilio tonight, so . . ."

"Thanks," I said. "I should probably . . . I should head home."

"Yeah. Okay." Zoe was already inching toward the exit. Something flickered in her eyes—Regret? Discomfort? Sadness?—and I wondered if we were sharing the same memories. Was it even possible that a year ago I would've been the first name on that party list? The first one in the pool, jumping in before any of the boys got a chance to toss me over the edge? I looked to the floor and back up again, and it was gone, that look in her eyes, and after another silent moment she leaned in for a one-armed hug that barely reached around my shoulders.

"Thanks for coming," she said. "And for the books."

"Scrapbook," I said, but too much time had passed and she was already halfway down the hall, my gift bag buried in the crook of her arm with her backpack and the too-sweet roses and a brand-new zip-up hoodie from the Crow.

"Why did you do that?" I asked Emilio. We were back in my driveway, the truck ticking and cooling with the windows down, crickets and frogs singing their hearts out.

"I thought you needed a wingman," he said. "Look, you were totally edgy, and Zoe was bein' a bitch. Sorry, I know she's your best friend, but she *was*."

I didn't know if that last part meant she *was* being a bitch or she *was*—past tense—my best friend. I turned toward him to say he was right on both counts, but as the last bit of sunlight leaked into the earth, the dusk cast a spell on everything it touched, and silence grew between us again. Outside, the crickets buzzed and sang, drowning the TV-track laughter that wafted through the open windows of the house. I looked to the living room, the blue-white flicker throwing rickety shadows on the grass.

"Well, you can't just go around kissing people whenever you feel like it." I turned to face him again, but he was staring out the windshield, quiet and still, hands gripping the steering wheel like we were on some vast gray road to nowhere.

"Why are you so nice to me?" I whispered. Another moment of silence passed, and I turned to open my door, but then his hand was on my arm, my name passing delicately from his lips. I thought of the breeze, the quaking silver aspens in the woods, and I turned back expecting to see the playful dimples I'd grown so used to this summer.

Instead, there was fire. Fire on his breath, suddenly shallow. Fire in his touch, warming my skin by degrees. Fire in his eyes, where it burned with an intensity so fierce it sent my heart into a somersault.

"You ask me why I'm nice to you," he said. "Why, why, why. But you don't ask me stuff that matters. Who I am or where I been. What I see when I look at you. What I want." His fingers brushed my jaw and stopped at my chin, tilting my face toward his. His breath was hot, the words urgent. "I promise you this, Jude Hernandez. You think you know something about me? *Lo siento, mi princesa.* You don't know shit."

Everything inside me begged for his kiss. I wanted it, no matter who might be watching from inside the house, no matter which sister might find out, no matter how many oaths I was breaking or when he was leaving. . . .

But I knew he wouldn't kiss me. Not tonight. Not like this. There was too much between us now, all the words and near misses. All the potential, the alternate futures that would stretch out before us in an unending spiral, all built on what happened in this moment. I held his fiery gaze and remembered the five-oh, the half-and-half, the promises I'd whispered to myself in the dawn light.

I might lose all my memories one day, but that wouldn't keep me from making them.

Think you can take me without a fight, Demonio? Bring it.

Adrenaline shot through my veins, electrified every nerve and blood vessel and cell. With a rush of desire I wanted to experience everything at once, all of it, life and death and sex and love and every crazy, reckless, ferocious dream my heart could imagine.

Emilio was still breathless, half smiling, dimples flashing in the dark like a dare. I took it.

"So what do you want, Emilio Vargas? Will you tell me?" I leaned in close, rested my hand on his thigh. His skin was warm through his shorts, and when I pressed my lips to his earlobe, he gasped. "Or do I have to force you to talk?"

Emilio swallowed hard. I was still so close, and he'd run out of things to say.

"I know what you want," I whispered. "Take me out on your motorcycle."

"Take . . . I . . . what?" His voice came out all wobbly, but I didn't respond, and we sat like that for seconds, minutes maybe, neither of us speaking, neither of us calling the other out.

"Good night, Jude," Emilio finally said. I couldn't keep the disappointment from my face. He slipped out of the truck soundlessly, but seconds later he was outside my passenger door, fingers on the frame.

"Tomorrow morning," he said. His flirty grin was back. "Ten o'clock, outside, dressed for the road."

CHAPTER 21

"Swing your leg up and over," Emilio said.

I stared at the rumbling machine in our driveway as if it were some wild, living thing.

"Like a horse?" I asked. It was ten in the morning, the helmet felt like a bowling ball on my head, and sweat trickled down my back.

"More like a pony. With wheels." Emilio grinned from his perch on the black beast. "You don't have to do this, *princesa*. If you're scared—"

"Don't play reverse psychology on me."

He cocked an eyebrow, a trick he was getting a lot better at since we'd started hanging out.

"I'm *not* scared," I said. "I've never done this before. It's like when you drove the truck that first time."

"I was trying to impress you," Emilio said. "It was our first date."

"You normally impress girls by trying to break their necks?"

"Ah, no. You were my one and only at that." He winked and stuck out his arm. "Use me to balance and get on. We're burnin' daylight, girl."

"*Dios mío.* You totally stole that line from one of Papi's movies!"

"What? No way. I don't watch westerns."

"If the Duke was alive, he'd kick your ass for swiping his line."

"Duke's alive. Saw him this morning."

"Not that Duke. *The* Duke. John—"

"Jude?"

"I'm just saying—"

"Quit stallin' and get on this horse before I change my mind."

I threw myself at the bike. That's how it felt, a great helpless flinging of arms and legs. Luckily, Emilio kept her steady and didn't try any funny stuff as I adjusted my limbs and torso and other seemingly disconnected body parts behind him. He'd started her up before I got on, and beneath my legs, everything shook.

I tried holding on to the seat, but I couldn't get a grip. Nothing behind me either. I crossed my arms over my chest and hoped for the best.

Emilio laughed. "Better hold on."

"There's nowhere—"

"To me." Emilio looked at me over his shoulder. "Put your arms around me and hold on or you'll face plant on the first turn."

I slipped my arms around his waist. It wouldn't do me any

good if I died before we'd even gotten this beast up to speed. That wouldn't show El Demonio a damn thing.

"You okay back there?"

I gave him the thumbs-up. Only one, though. Double thumbs would immediately disqualify me as authentic biker-babe material. It was bad enough I was wearing a pair of Mom's old button-fly jeans from the nineties. *And* a bra. Two strikes against my motorcycle street cred already.

"Pay attention to my body," he said, raising his voice over the engine so I wouldn't miss any important details. "When I lean in for the turns, move with me. Straighten up when I straighten up. And when we stop, put your feet on the ground like I do. Basically, on the bike, we're one person. It'll help keep us balanced."

"Balanced is good." I let out shaky breath and leaned in closer, tighter.

Embrace the oneness.

"Hey. I won't let anything happen to you." Emilio grabbed my hand and gave it a squeeze, then he pressed it to his stomach, right over the ridge of his scar. His body was hard beneath his shirt. "Do you trust me?"

It wasn't the first time he'd asked, but I'd never fully answered. I closed my eyes and focused on the feel of his hand over mine, safe and strong, and my stomach filled with butterflies. "I trust you, Emilio."

He squeezed my hand once more, then shifted forward, fingers curling over the handgrips as he lifted his feet from the ground. He rolled us into a slow turn, guiding us down the driveway and out into the street.

We rocketed over the pavement, rapidly picking up speed on the hot blacktop. The wind tornadoed my hair at the base of the helmet and snapped against my sunglasses. At first it was hard to catch my breath, but I didn't turn away. I faced it head on, gulped it up, tasted every moment.

Abandoned silver mines, sky-high rock walls, overhangs that dropped into oblivion—we passed them all. The wheat fields were a golden blur, the sky a vast blue possibility, everything and nothing all at once, and my legs trembled from the vibrations, the bike growling between them, eating up the road as we zoomed along.

Emilio hugged every curve. At times we tilted so low to the ground I was sure we'd wreck, sure we'd spin off into the canyon. But I trusted him, like I'd said, so I leaned in closer, mirroring his angles and moves, following the lines of his body and the bike as if we were one, a bullet cutting through the air.

We climbed the Million Dollar Highway, the sun streaming around us, and I tipped my head backward and stared at the sky, cloudless and perfect. I lost all perspective, all sense of time and place. I couldn't see what waited ahead, but one thing was certain.

Behind, there was nothing but memories and dust.

I'll outrun you, black demon. So hard and so fast, I'll be gone before you even know I was here.

An hour later we'd reached our destination and left the bike and helmets at a trailhead parking lot. I'd packed a bunch of empanadas and sodas and grapes into canvas bags, and Emilio took them out of the saddlebags and slung them over his shoulder. My legs still hummed and ticked like the engine, not quite steady on solid ground.

"You'll get used to it." Emilio beamed at me in the sun, his whole face shone. "You just had your first ride up the Million Dollar Highway. How do you feel?"

"Amazing." It was such a cheap word, the wrong word, but the right word to capture this feeling didn't exist. So I said nothing more, just grabbed his hand and hoped that was enough.

He led me along a rocky path away from the main trailhead, another secret passage through the woods. We hiked a short, steep climb, and just when I thought my legs would give out, we reached the last boulder.

"This used to be Danny's spot," he said from the top of the rock. He held out his hands to help me up, and then we walked into a thick cluster of aspens. "He kind of left it to me."

"Do you miss him?" I asked. "You guys were close, right?"

A breeze ruffled the trees, and we both stopped and turned our faces toward the sky. The canopy of yellow-green leaves shivered, scattering the light. It felt like they were sprinkling us with sunshine.

Emilio leaned sideways against a tree, still watching the leaves. "Danny and me were like brothers."

"Does he visit ever? Or does he pretty much stay on the island?"

"Ain't seen him in two years. I miss him. Hell yeah, I miss him." Emilio peeled a loose flake of bark from the tree and dropped it to the ground, and when another breeze laced its fingers through the leaves, my heart felt heavy. I didn't know the details of Emilio's family problems, and it was clear I'd said the wrong thing, asked too many questions.

"I'm sorry," I said. "I know family stuff is . . . I just thought . . . because you talk about him sometimes, and you said this was his spot, and—"

"It's not you. It's . . . complicated. His mother basically hates me and Ma, and . . ." Emilio smiled and held out his hand. "Damn. I should be the one sayin' sorry. Your first bike ride and I turn into a downer."

"You're not—"

"We ain't even there yet." Emilio put his arm around my waist and guided me through the grove, out the other side where the land opened up like a giant storybook.

Together we took it in, the infinite canyons below, rolling foothills of green and gray and purple in the distance. It seemed everything that had ever lived and died in this world had passed through here, had left its indelible imprint.

I walked to the edge, looked down into the dusty red canyon. The walls were smooth and rough all at once, great columns of weathered stone that rose out of the earth. The river here had dried up millions of years ago, but still the rocks weren't safe from the unstoppable effects of time. Now it was the wind rather than the rapids that hollowed their bellies. It whipped through the canyon as we watched, carrying dust and debris, particles that carved new pathways on their unending quest to exist. To change.

I pulled out my phone and snapped a few pictures, tried to get a panoramic shot I could stitch together later. My hands were fumbling and giant, and the strangest thought came to me as the wind peppered them with dust: I could approach the seemingly immovable rocks with my giant human hands and impossible human strength, beat on them with all I had, and cause not even a flicker of the destruction that these tiny, invisible forces would wreak, day by day, second by second, for thousands and millions of years after I'm no longer remembered by another living being.

It made me dizzy.

I sat down next to Emilio on a red-brown boulder. He set the food on the ground behind us, and as he looked back across the vast stretch, I picked up a shard of rock and carved beneath my legs.

I was here. . . .

The wind hurtled through the canyon below, moaning eerily as it clawed its way up to us. It lashed me, but by then it had lost some of its power. It vanished before I could catch my breath.

All of it—the wind, the dust, the rocks, the trees, the road—it was the most pointless and beautiful thing I'd ever seen.

Emilio opened his mouth to say something, but when he saw my eyes, his face twisted with concern. "What's wrong?"

"This place is amazing. It's . . . I can't . . ." I choked back a sob, and Emilio rubbed my back until the words found their way out. "My father's disease is genetic."

"What? What does that—"

"I have a fifty-fifty chance of ending up the same way."

I'd spent two days fighting off those words, locking them deep inside, because I knew the moment they passed my lips, they'd grow into something I couldn't ignore.

The truth.

Emilio confirmed it: the shock crossed his face like a visible current. "Okay, but you don't know if . . . Don't they have ways to . . . Are you sure? Like, *sure* sure?"

I nodded, the confession growing bitter on my lips. "Here's another way to crunch the numbers. Of me and my three sisters, two of us will lose our memories and fade into oblivion. And the other two will watch it happen."

Emilio twisted away from me. His jaw was tight, shoulders tense. "Can't they treat it? If you know early like this? There has to be something. . . . Medication? Surgery? Therapy? Something?"

The desperation in his voice was almost too much. I hated and loved it all at once, and the mix of emotions tightened my throat.

"There's a test," I said stiffly, "but all it does is give you the bad news early."

Emilio reached for a fist-size rock.

"My parents were supposed to go to Argentina." I was rambling now, but I had to get it out, and if I said it all here on this boulder, maybe the wind would carry the words away, take them someplace far, someplace I'd never have to hear them again. "Their dream was to move back with Lourdes. They wanted us all to go there eventually, but they were supposed to head out next summer. They were waiting for me to get settled in at college."

Emilio pitched his rock over the edge and listened for the sound that never came.

"Now it's too risky to move," I said. "Papi might remember stuff from back home, like his old neighborhood and friends, or he could get totally disoriented. Besides, with all the logistics involved . . . they can't. They're stuck. So when Lourdes shows up next month and looks at me like I'm not taking care of him . . . I mean, she'd never say it. She wouldn't even think it, really. It would all be me. They *should* be with her."

The wind smacked us again, filled my mouth with hair and dust until I coughed it out.

"Lourdes?" I said. "She's the calm one. She always took care of things before, and she never got all dramatic like Mari or freaked out like Araceli. She's just one of those people. Like the saying, she's good people. You know?"

Emilio wiped the tears from my cheeks. It was hard to tell whether it was the wind or the truth, but both were whaling on me.

"It's like this," he said. "I know you love your pops, and, yeah, this whole thing sucks, right? But you have him now, and you gotta enjoy it. You have your own life too. Don't sit around and . . . I don't know. Don't settle for stuff. That's pretty much the only thing I learned in life. You see something, some chance for something great, you take it. You grab your keys and jump on your bike and go, no regrets."

I looked back over the canyon, the endless cycle of death and rebirth below.

"Sorry." I wiped my eyes again and gave him a faint smile. "I guess I turned into my own downer now."

"Shh." Emilio slipped his arm around my shoulders. "Hey. Not to get all, like, religious. But this summer, workin' with you guys and hangin' out? It's the most at peace I been in a long-ass time." He met my eyes at the end, held them like he had more to say, but the words dropped off, and so did mine. I watched them march over the edge, right into the abyss below.

I leaned into Emilio, let him wrap around me like a blanket. My breath was on his neck, and he shivered in its wake. I closed my eyes and inhaled deeply, and I ordered my brain to be still, to catalog his scent and the haunting moan of the wind in the canyon and the grind of the ancient dust on my skin and the taste of him, so close to my lips.

I didn't want to forget any of it. I wouldn't forget it. Fight or no fight, that demon could hunt me down and smoke me out and take whatever he wanted. He could devour my favorite songs and the color of my bedroom and the sound of my own name on my tongue, but he'd never take today.

My heart thudded in my ears and I pressed myself closer, burying my face against his neck. His arms were so warm and strong around me, my insides were buzzing and light, and for once I was giving in. Letting him take care of me, take this one thing entirely for myself that no one—not from the past, not from the future—could touch.

I looked into his caramel eyes, closer than we'd ever been. He didn't look away, didn't smile, didn't breathe. I pressed my lips to the scar on his chin, tasted his skin, and he gasped. All we had left were sounds and tastes and looks and smells. He took my face in his hands and slid his thumb across my lips, and I closed my eyes. His mouth found mine, feather soft, and then we were kissing. My heart raced, the butterflies unfurling their tiny wings inside me, floating and fluttering, and his hands felt so good, fingers slipping across my skin like powder.

I shuddered as his tongue traced my bottom lip and slid into my mouth, setting everything inside me on fire. I pulled him on top of me as we leaned back onto the boulder, and I let my entire body go boneless, nothing but heart and spirit and maybe, way down underneath the shadows, a little hope that everything would be okay after all.

I wrapped my hands in his shirt and peeled it off, tugged it over his head. My fingertips traced the lines of his arms, his chest, the thin white scars, the mysterious gouge that snaked across his abdomen. I stopped there, lingered, looked into his eyes for an explanation I was too scared to ask for with words.

I thought he'd look away, but he held my gaze, his eyes full of a raw honesty I'd never seen in another person. There were nerves too, something uncertain and vulnerable. And in that moment I felt alive. Whole. Protected from the ravages of time and completely immune to its passing.

Nothing about this could ever end in tears.

He smiled, shy this time, and I smiled back, and then we were kissing again, pressing our mouths and bellies together while the rest of the world eroded around us, one pointless breath of wind, one insignificant grain of dust at a time.

We stayed tangled up on the boulder, pausing only for a late and hasty lunch, falling into each other again and again until the sun dipped behind the canyon and the rock cliffs blazed red-orange in the fading light. Emilio helped me onto the bike when it was time to go, pulling me into a long, deep kiss before navigating us along the winding road home.

As we rolled down the Million Dollar Highway, I closed my eyes and held him close around the waist, and he squeezed my hand like it was forever, like we'd really found a way to stop time, and I wanted so, so badly to believe it.

CHAPTER 22

Emilio and I stopped for mango shakes in town on the way back, but we hardly spoke—nerves, I guess, everything between us still hot to the touch—and the intense good-bye in my driveway was cut short by Mari's cigarette smoke puffing out the kitchen screen door.

"You were gone awhile," she said when I walked in. She gave me a hard stare, but a smile lit her face too, undeniable. "Papi said you guys went up the Million Dollar Highway? I've driven it before, but not on a bike. I've never been on a bike, actually."

"Seriously? You should," I said, and then her smile stretched, huge and bright. No warnings. No third degree about how I'd been out fraternizing with the enemy and how I'd come home with swollen lips and windblown helmet hair and guilt tattooed all over my face.

"I'm glad you had fun." She stared at me a few seconds, and I thought she might ask for more details, but she just smoothed my hair down, hands lingering. "You look happy, Juju."

Her voice broke at the end, but she turned to wash her hands at the sink, RIGHT FOR COLD/*FRÍO*. LEFT FOR HOT/*CALIENTE*, and I slipped away unnoticed.

My heart was still buzzing when I downloaded my photos later. But once I saw them up close, they didn't feel worthy.

That was the thing about pictures. No matter how beautiful, they couldn't capture the truly *felt* parts of a moment. Life was different looking through the lens, the colors less vibrant, the beauty less grand.

By the time you took the shot, the moment had already passed.

I sipped maté from one of Celi's hand-painted mugs, a big white one with sunflowers, and inhaled the tea's beer-bitter scent.

I certainly didn't need photographs to remember looking out across the canyon today, feeling small as we watched the dust erode the world. To remember being in Emilio's arms, his lips on my collarbone, my fingers tracing his map of scars. I didn't need photographs to believe in the story. To remember that I'd lived it, even if I was doomed to forget.

Pictures couldn't tell the whole story anyway. That was the other thing about them—they were always a carefully edited glimpse, a story out of context. My pictures of Papi and Emilio working on the bike showed the successes, the good days, but I didn't capture evidence of Papi's meltdown at Grant's Pharmacy. The doctor's appointments. The lines in Mom's face after all the bad news. Even the scrapbook I'd given Zoe was make-believe, a best-of-the-best highlights reel that fast-forwarded over the snags.

Through pictures, we cut reality in pieces. We selected only the choicest moments, discarding the rest as if they'd never happened.

So did El Demonio.

"You're up late, *queridita*." At the sound of Papi's voice, I looked up from my computer. He leaned against my door frame, an old Harley manual tucked under his arm with a hundred blue Post-it flags waving from the pages. "I couldn't sleep either. *Ay*, your mother snores like bears!"

"I think you woke yourself up, Papi. Mom doesn't snore."

He laughed. "You all do, *querida*. Trust me. How was your ride?"

"Pretty much awesome." My cheeks hurt from smiling so hard. "It was cool. Really great views."

Among other things.

The skin around Papi's eyes crinkled. "I'm sorry I never got to take you myself, Juju. When you're young, you think you have so much time, and then life comes and tomorrow turns into tomorrow, and before you know it . . ." He sighed and waved away the words. "Ah, don't listen to this cranky *viejito*."

I smiled and watched him watching me, and I wondered how much he really understood about what was happening to him. Every time that bastard demon devoured another of his memories, did he feel it? Was it like a scraping, a chipping away? An inexplicable, gnawing loss? Could he hear it? Did he know when it would happen, which thoughts or words or faces it would consume next? Which parts of his life story would end up on the cutting-room floor?

"I'm glad you had fun with Emilio," Papi said. "I knew he'd take good care of you. That boy knows what he's doing."

Yeah, no kidding. I shivered at the memories from the day, but Papi didn't seem to notice that my central nervous system had been replaced with a tangle of electric wires.

"Look at all the different parts, *queridita*. He knows all of them by heart." Papi laid the Harley manual on my desk and pointed to an illustration, charcoal-colored twists of metal and gears. He circled things with his finger, named them as if he were helping me study for a biology test.

He'd never actually helped me with homework—that task always fell to my sisters, and then I was too old for it, studying instead with Zoe and Christina at Witch's Brew. But Lourdes, he must have helped her. Celi, too. I imagined them huddled around the kitchen table, puzzling out one of those math problems about train speeds or some word association thing. He was probably really good at it, smart and patient.

Focus on the good memories you have with your loved one. Family members often find comfort in remembering the person how he was, not how the disease has changed him. Hold on to those precious moments. . . .

That's what one of the brochures said, something I'd repeated to myself in the early days after the diagnosis. It sounded like good advice, and I'm sure for many people, it worked. But what if all your memories of a person belonged to someone else?

God, my sisters had so many. I'd heard them, tried them on, borrowed them as my own. Playing backgammon by candlelight one night when the power went out. Camping at Rocky Mountain National Park, that hike up Twin Sisters with the bighorn sheep. Piling into the car for the *Jurassic Park* double feature at the Silver Gorge Drive-In. Even the stories of how my sisters had gotten their names were magical: Lourdes, after Mom's grandmother, who risked her life to fight for women's rights in Argentina. Mariposa, "butterfly," for the bright blue-and-orange butterflies that flooded my parents' garden the week before my sister's birth. Araceli, "altar of Heaven," who sent Mom into labor on an airplane and was born in an ambulance on the tarmac after an emergency landing. Their names had their own memories, so different from mine, which my sisters loved to tell me was hastily chosen after the first thing Mom had seen after delivery: the doctor's medallion.

Saint Jude, patron saint of lost causes.

My sisters got the good stuff first. All I had of their precious moments were imprints, shadows of the real thing cobbled together from the faded scraps of their reminiscing, bits and pieces that changed each time in the telling.

Like so many things in my life, the best memories of my father were a legacy, passed down to me like their hand-me-down clothes and toys and the Vargas oath.

Until I'd discovered the Harley, out in the storage barn under a blue tarp.

The motorcycle project was mine and Papi's, a real story that only he and I shared. Every time we talked about the bike, helped Emilio disassemble and reassemble parts, Papi told me about his life in Argentina—wild, impossible stories unearthed from places in his mind that had been buried under the landslide of marriage and parenthood and career. Stories that even my sisters and mother hadn't heard. Every one was like a gemstone I could keep in a box under the bed, something I could take out and hold up to the light whenever I longed again for its specialness.

Was that the reason I'd been so eager to help with the bike? So I could have something of Papi all my own?

Is that why Papi continued to work on it and read the manual and wear his leather jacket? For me?

Tomorrow turns into tomorrow, and before you know it . . .

"Papi?"

He jumped at my voice, eyes hazy from squinting at the manual. It took him a second to process; I could almost see the synapses firing behind his eyes, the slow passage of electricity along the nerves to and from the file cabinet of his central cortex, serving up my picture and my name and all the required information.

"I need to ask you something," I said. "It's important."

He closed the book and stared at the cover, tapped it with his finger. "Are you sure you don't want to talk to Mom? She's probably better for this kind of thing. Or your sister. I can get her if you—"

"No! It's nothing like . . . It's not a female issue or anything."

He let out an exaggerated sigh of relief and wiped a hand across his forehead. "In that case, your papi is at your service. But after this, we're watching *Ace High*. It has our friend Tuco from *The Good, the Bad and the Ugly*."

Papi cleared his throat, prepping for an inevitable Tuco impersonation. "There are two kinds of people in this world, Juju. Those who watch westerns in the middle of the night, and those who are disowned by their father."

"When you put it that way . . ." I looked him in the eyes, steeled myself for the worst. "Papi, do you *like* working on the motorcycle? Is it fun for you? It's not too much or anything?"

"Too much. Now that's a big question, isn't it?" Papi tapped the manual again. "What do you think, Panqueque? Do we like working on Valentina?"

At the mention of his Spanish name, the dog trotted over from his blanket on the floor at the end of my bed and nosed Papi's leg.

"There's nothing else I'd rather do than work on that Harley with you and Emilio. In fact . . ." He trailed off, his eyes seeming to focus on something in the distance, something out in the hallway.

"You okay?" I asked.

He squeezed his eyes shut, but when he opened them

again, they were as clear as the Animas. "*Sí.* I want to ride her again, *queridita.* That's what I decided. One more time, as soon as she's ready. What do you think?"

I started to protest, to remind him of the doctors' warnings about his heart, his head, staying safe. But the words turned to dust as I thought of my ride today, the rumble of the bike, the snap of the wind in my hair.

Don't settle. . . . You see something, some chance for something great, you take it. You grab your keys and jump on your bike and go, no regrets.

"I think there are two kinds of people in this world, Papi. Those who suck, and those who rock." I returned his broad smile and deleted my pictures from the Million Dollar Highway. "You rock."

CHAPTER 23

Don't be awkward don't be awkward don't be awkward. . . .

By the time Emilio showed up for work the next morning, I'd totally brainwashed myself—if such a thing was possible—to not be a freak show about everything that had happened between us. In fact, his lips were the furthest thing from my mind. Well, second furthest. Third? Fine. They were pretty much the main event, but I wasn't about to show it. Besides, I couldn't wait to tell him about Papi's plans—a safe, nonkissing topic we could agree on.

"So check it out." I sauntered up to the bike, smoothing out my hair as I went. It was raining today, a rare storm, and my locks were about five times bigger than normal. The moment Emilio saw me, he smiled, all dimples and dares, and my insides got a jolt.

"That an invitation?" he asked.

I tried to hide a grin behind my giant tumbleweed of hair, but Emilio's eyes were still on me.

Valentina was on the lift again, and Emilio stood up from behind it and stretched. He had on the blue bandanna today, and it made his eyes stand out against his brown skin. "How'd you sleep?"

"I didn't." *Just, you know, replaying everything that happened twenty-four hours ago and acting like a total spaz, and is it hot in here? I think it's hot in here.* "I had fun yesterday. Thanks for the ride. And the shake. And . . . everything."

"Everything, huh?" Stubble, dimples, scar. Mischief in his eyes again. And something more, something new. Understanding, maybe. Desire. I saw it, and he saw that I saw it, and when he smiled again, my stomach dropped to my toes.

"What am I checking out?" he asked.

"What?"

"You said—"

"Oh! Papi wants to ride Valentina," I said. "Later. After it's all fixed and Mari goes back to Denver."

"What'd you tell him?"

"Nothing. He already made up his mind."

Emilio grunted and returned to the bike. I peered through the metal bones, watched him sort through a pile of bolts until he found the right one.

Why doesn't he try to kiss me again?

"I know it's not registered yet," I said. "But maybe he could ride around here or something. You could get it set up for him, make sure the seat is level and everything. Right?"

He tightened a bolt, loosened it, took it off, scrubbed it

with a wire brush, put it back on, tightened it up with a wrench whose name I forgot. Not the Twizzler one.

"I mean, if you're not on your trip yet," I said.

The rain picked up, and the sudden metallic clang against the barn roof swallowed up all the sounds, muting the outside world into a dull blur and sharpening everything inside. If I closed my eyes, I was sure I'd taste the grit on the floor, smell the beat of my own heart as it crept into my throat.

I backed up toward the workbench, away from the bike, away from Emilio. Neither of us spoke for a while, just listened to the rain on the roof, to the click and clank of the tools. He didn't ask for help. He didn't narrate the repairs. He didn't ask about Papi.

He was officially being weird.

"What's up with you today?" I finally asked, forcing a lightness I didn't feel. "You're acting all, like, brooding and emo."

"Bike's leaking oil. One of the new seals must be busted." He stood up again, crept out from around Valentina. He walked toward me with slow, deliberate steps, eyes on me the entire time, black hair curling under the bandanna.

"Whatever, Emo Boy. You're not some kind of vampire, are you?" I attempted a flirtatious smile, but he couldn't have missed the tremor in my voice, the electric current still sizzling between us.

He leaned in close when he reached the bench, brushed his fingers below my earlobe, just over the pulse. He pressed his lips from ear to collarbone and back up again, and just before I burst into flames, he pulled away to meet my eyes. Something vulnerable seeped in, like when I'd touched his scar yesterday. I blinked and then it was gone and Emilio dropped his hand and took a step backward.

"Think you can stop fantasizing about vampires and find me an oil pan?" he asked. "Not one made of real silver?"

"Silver is werewolves. Totally different." I shuffled through the stuff beneath the bench until I found the pan. "And I don't fantasize about vampires. The whole blood-drinking thing . . . ick. My sisters made me watch this eighties vampire movie when I was little. *Lost Boys*? Totally scarred me."

Emilio slid the pan under the bike. "Me too. I hate that movie."

"Afraid of bats?"

"Girls."

"You. Afraid of girls." I thought about our overlapping years at Blackfeather High, the cushion of sparkly makeup and tight skirts that had always surrounded him. Rosette, draped over him at the Bowl. Me, up on the Million Dollar Highway. "Yeah, okay."

"Serious. Remember Star from the movie? I was so in love with her. I wrote her a letter asking her to marry me. After a month, when she didn't write back, I stopped eating for two days. Rejection hurts, *princesa*. I was wrecked." Emilio ran a hand over his bandanna and shook his head. "Shit. I can't believe I told you that."

Okay, I totally didn't mean to laugh. I tried to cough it out, but it was no use.

"Why do you mock my heartbreak?" Emilio held a hand over his heart and frowned, but the dimples were a dead giveaway. "No one else knows that story. Not Samuel, not even my own ma."

"Now I have to compete with Rosette *and* Star? Tough crowd."

I'd meant it as a joke—mostly—but Emilio didn't laugh or zing me with a comeback. He set down his wrench and met my eyes again. A smudge of oil streaked his chin, and I focused on the blackness, waiting for another wisecrack, hoping I hadn't said the wrong thing again.

Why is this so hard all of a sudden?

"Hey," I said. "I was just messing with—"

"Come with me," he whispered.

It was fast and blurry; I wasn't sure I'd heard him. I looked out the open barn doors. Outside, the rain pelted the dirt and the aspen leaves shook from its unrelenting attack. When I turned back, Emilio was right in front of me.

"I want you to come with me. See the road. Just . . . say yes."

"What road?"

"Jude." He tugged on the bottom of his shirt, smearing it with grease. "Are you serious with this? You know what road."

"Grand Canyon?" My voice was small and shaky. "The ocean?"

"Everything."

No smiles, no jokes, no dimples. His gaze didn't waver, and my heart thudded as I pictured us on his motorcycle again, the warmth of his body as we leaned into the turns, the smell of leather, the taste of summer air on the open highway. I closed my eyes. My skin tingled as if we were already there, standing on the rim of the canyon with the first rays of sun glowing through the mist. The rocks out there were redder, dustier, craggier, I imagined.

I could slip my arms around his waist and forget everything else I've ever known, look over my shoulder and watch the long gray ribbon of road disappear as we zoomed at once into the future and the distant past.

I opened my eyes and glanced around the barn, scanned the boxes of dust-covered heirlooms and long-forgotten memories.

I could leave all of this behind. I could be with him.

"Come with me," Emilio said again. He slid the keys from his pocket, dangled them in front of me like a ticking clock. A promise *and* a threat. His smile was once again playful and flirtatious, the disarming one that had infiltrated my dreams, but his eyes were serious. Fragile. Hopeful.

I reached for the keys and he grabbed my hand, pulled me close. His lips brushed mine and sent another hot streak up my spine.

"My sister is right inside!" I squirmed out of his grasp, but my protest was half baked.

He looped his fingers through my hair, brought the ends to his lips. "Don't even try it, *princesa*."

"Or else what?" I whispered.

His mouth twitched. A raised eyebrow. Flash of dimples. I closed my eyes and his lips were on mine, muting the downpour outside to a low, distant rumble.

He moved from my lips to my neck, then up to my ear. His tongue traced my earlobe, his teeth tugged it gently. His breath was hot, raising goose bumps on my scalp when he spoke again, deep and raspy. "You know you love riding that bike with me."

I pulled away so I could see his eyes.

"Say yes." Emilio ran his thumb across my lower lip.

"Finally!" Mari startled us both as she ducked through the doorway with Papi. The rain hadn't let up, and she pulled her fingers through her short hair to shake out the water. "I'm going stir-crazy in there."

"How's the game? Who won?" I shoved my hands in my pockets, hoping the evidence of my tangled hair and red mouth wasn't too damning. From the corner of my eye, I sensed Emilio at the workbench, pretending to look for tools while he willed his breathing back to normal.

Mari looped her arm through Papi's. "Me. Remind me never to play Scrabble with him again—what a cheater."

"*Perro* is a word," he said.

"Yeah, in Español."

Papi shrugged it off, but there was something sad in his eyes, something defeated.

She should've let him have *perro*.

"We're going for ice cream," Mari said. "Want us to bring anything back?"

"Black raspberry in a waffle cone," Emilio said.

"Wait." I stumbled awkwardly toward Mari. "I'm going with you guys."

CHAPTER 24

The rain finally stopped, but the streets of Old Town were slick and gray, and most of the tourists ducked into restaurants to wait for the sun. The line at Uncle Fuzzy's snaked around three times, and at each step I wanted to grab Mari and confess, tell her everything about the Million Dollar Highway, about all the things Emilio had said in the barn. He wanted me to ride with him, to see the Southwest, to see the ocean. To be with him.

Five times I opened my mouth. Five times I shut it. And then we were at the counter ordering our usuals—mint chocolate chip and hot fudge for Papi, Mari's strawberry shake, chocolate peanut butter cup sundae for me.

Papi watched the counter girl mix fresh berries and ice cream for Mari's drink. Over the whir of the blender, Mari told me about a witch and warlock series she'd recently sold, how she had to go to New York in a couple of days to meet with the author and publisher. Her face lit up as she talked.

Mari was so passionate about her work—about everything in her life, really—and for all our disagreements, I admired her.

"Your authors are lucky to have you." I had a hard time meeting her eyes, so I focused on a giant brownie poster tacked to the wall behind her. "Me too."

Of course, that was the moment the blender stopped, so it came out really loud, and Mari's smile turned into a giggle, and I laughed too, and Papi kept watching the counter girl as if the assembly of our ice creams was the most amazing feat anyone had ever accomplished.

Mari steered the conversation toward college, rehashing the plans we'd discussed months ago about helping me get set up at the dorms and showing me around the city. Honestly, I'd been so busy with the motorcycle and Papi, and then everything with Emilio . . . the University of Denver was a faraway voice at the end of a long tunnel. When I tried to picture myself walking around campus, meeting my roommate, ordering Thai food at the dorm, it seemed like someone else's life.

She asked about my major, asked whether I'd thought about getting into publishing, taking an internship with her agency. Of course I had, but what I really wanted to talk about was Emilio.

How I'd ignored all the warnings, stepped around the caution tape, fell right over the edge.

Never get involved with a Vargas? Please. I'd blown by

"involved" weeks ago. Wrapped up, enamored, entangled. Those were better words now, and my wrapped up, enamored, entangled heart thudded in my chest.

I just had to say it out loud.

Now or never.

"Mari, I think I might be—"

"What's this?" Papi's voice jackhammered into our conversation, and we snapped to attention. He'd taken his sundae from the counter—mint chocolate chip, the one he'd ordered ten minutes ago—and now he poked at it with his finger, scowling as if he'd discovered a cricket in the hot fudge sauce.

"That's your mint chip." Mari held out her hands, like, *What else?*

"This is not what I ordered, *querida*."

"Yes, it is, Papi." Mari kept her voice low, soothing, like she was talking to a sick child. She slipped her hand around his arm and nudged him toward a table that had just opened up. "It's your favorite, remember?"

A surge of anger crossed his face, all his features tightening and twisting.

"I'm sorry, sir," the counter girl said meekly. "Did you want something else?"

"I want you to get my order right, that's what I want, miss."

"It's just ice cream," Mari whispered. Her fingers turned white against Papi's arm.

"I understand that, Mariposa, but it's not what I ordered. If they can't get a simple order right, how do we know they're not ripping us off? How do we know they didn't overcharge? They're thieves." Papi slammed the ice cream down on the service counter. The red plastic spoon toppled to the floor, flinging hot fudge sauce in its wake. "You people are criminals. I want my money back."

"No problem, sir. I can do that." The counter girl plastered on a nervous smile. "If you'll just calm down, I'll get—"

"You want me to calm down? So you can trick me again?"

"Do you want something else?" Mari's voice trembled, her eyes darting around at the tourists in the ice cream shop. They were staring now, inching closer to the door.

I put my hand on Papi's arm like I'd just come into the middle of things. I held out my chocolate peanut butter cup sundae, my own favorite, the thing I'd ordered every time since before I could see over the counter. "I think you got mine by mistake, Papi."

Papi stuck his finger in the middle of my dish and scooped out some whipped cream. I held my breath as he popped it in his mouth.

A smile stretched across his face. "So *you're* the thief."

Relief spilled from Mari and me in a flood of goofy laughter. Papi watched us curiously, his head tilted like Pancake's when he's listening for the rabbits.

I apologized to the girl at the counter with all the usual excuses—he's tired, he's confused—and stuffed a twenty in the tip jar. I didn't have twenties for everyone though, and the tourists continued to watch us with a mixture of curiosity and embarrassment as we found our way to the table.

I made peace with Papi's mint chip sundae while he happily devoured my chocolate peanut butter bliss. Mari poked at her milk shake with a straw, but she hadn't taken a sip. When Papi shuffled across the room to toss out his trash, Mari looked at me, her face pale.

"How did you know . . . How did you get him to calm down like that?" she asked. "He doesn't even like peanut butter."

"Pick your battles." I scraped the last bits of chocolate from my sundae. "Sometimes it's easier to go along with it or try to distract him." I thought about the meltdown at Grant's Pharmacy, standing there in the tampon aisle with Emilio, singing that song from *Oklahoma!* It felt like years ago.

"Mint chip is his favorite," Mari said.

I shrugged. "Not today."

"Juju. I've never seen him eat another kind of ice cream our entire lives."

"Things change."

"I'm telling you—"

"Mari." I dropped my sundae cup on the table. "I know it's crazy. I know it sounds totally bat-shit impossible that he can remember every mile of his road trip thirty-some years ago but not a stupid ice cream flavor. Or that he can tell me what he was wearing the day he bought that bike, but he can't remember the way home from the river trail in the backyard. He helps Emilio take apart all those gears and knows exactly what they're called and where they go, but last week I caught him trying to call Lourdes through the TV remote. It's messed up and it's not fair and it's killing us, but it's the way things are."

Mari wiped her nose with a balled-up napkin. "I didn't know it was that bad. I knew he'd been wandering, forgetting stuff here and there. But I didn't . . . I'm sorry. I don't know how to make this better." It was only a whisper, faint and full of agony that pierced my heart. "You're amazing. You're so good with him and you did everything exactly right and I just . . . I don't know what to do. I'm scared, Jujube."

I'd never seen this Mari, a frightened version of the girl who'd once threatened to castrate an entire family, the girl we called Wrecking Ball, the one who smoked out the window and made six- and seven-figure book deals over the phone.

I squeezed her knee under the table. Papi had returned.

"I like this place." He glanced around, taking it all in again. "I wonder if they have mint chocolate chip?"

"I think they do." I scooped up the rest of our trash. "Next time you should get that."

The rain returned, and we helped Papi into Mari's car and headed back to the house, the sky crying huge, fat tears. It wasn't until we got all the way home that I realized we'd forgotten Emilio's black raspberry waffle cone.

He stood before us in the driveway, covered in grease and grime, rain running into his eyes as we tumbled out of the car.

"She works," he said. "She freaking works."

CHAPTER 25

Valentina leaned gallantly on her kickstand in the middle of the barn, the lift tucked away behind her. Emilio jumped on the kickstart and she caught, first try. He cranked the throttle and revved the engine, and when he climbed off, Valentina kept running, no sputtering.

"Told you." He beamed, proud as Valentina herself, and all the butterflies inside me simultaneously beat their wings.

Papi let out an earsplitting whoop. Emilio high-fived him, and when he turned to Mari, she threw her arms around him. Like, an actual hug.

"I can't believe you got that thing running!" she said. "Did you see Papi's face, Juju?"

I nodded, and in that moment it was like she suddenly realized she'd embraced a notorious Vargas boy. She released Emilio and took a step back. Her mouth still held the shape of a smile, but that was fading too, and she brushed her shirt absently.

Emilio stiffened, but I turned my eyes to Papi, walking around his motorcycle with an expression of pure glee. He stopped with one hand over his heart and rested the other on the engine. When he looked up, his eyes were glassy.

"This means the world to me, Juju. Emilio. You . . . I can't believe . . ."

The bike coughed and rattled, and Papi jumped, even though she didn't sputter out.

Please be okay, don't freak out, it's just a noise, you've had a long day. . . .

"She's just gettin' used to the air again." Emilio shut Valentina down. "Still needs some cleaning out, and we should get touch-up paint for the front and rear fenders. Needs a new seat, too. But once we get it all put back together, she'll be her old self again. Even got the rust off the chrome. Polish it up, she'll be good as new."

Mari took Papi inside, and we were alone again, me and Emilio and my racing heart. I couldn't stop thinking about Papi at the ice cream shop, how tired he looked, how he'd been spending less time in the barn, how he'd gone inside with Mari right after the bike spooked him.

Now, more than ever, Emilio had to finish the job. To get Valentina running perfectly—no more coughing, no more sputtering. To paint and polish her, good as new, like he'd said.

As long as it was ready before Papi got too sick to ride it.

"What else do you need?" I asked. He raised a flirty

eyebrow, but I shook my head. "For the bike. It has to be running, a hundred percent. Like, soon."

"Calm down, *princesa*. I'm almost there." He smiled teasingly, but there was a new hesitation in his eyes, a shadow across his face like clouds in the sky.

Silence stretched between us. I kicked the ground, looked at the ceiling, finally looked into his eyes. "How much longer, do you think? On the bike, I mean."

"I don't know, Jude. I'll keep you *appraised* of the *situation*." Emilio turned on his heel, reaching for his toolbox.

"I'm sorry. I'm being a crazy person. As usual. Come back."

His resistance only lasted a heartbeat before he turned to face me again. He rested his hands on my hips, touched his forehead to mine. "Answer my question. Yes or no. Will you come on the trip with me?"

Emilio was offering me a chance to cross state lines, to see the country, to watch the sun rise and set in dozens of different places, to zoom away on a motorcycle beneath Orion's unwavering gaze.

I never knew how badly I'd wanted it until he'd said the words. *I want you to come with me. . . . Say yes.*

It was the trip of a lifetime just waiting for me to take it.

But behind all those desires, all those daydreams, I saw Papi, a man who'd ridden thousands of miles and led a motorcycle gang and flirted with waitresses and fled from jaguars. After that, Valentina went into storage, slowly decaying under a tarp, and now that she was almost restored, it was too late.

He might never get another chance to ride. Again. Ever.

I took a deep breath, let it out slowly, watched it settle against Emilio's lips. He shivered and whispered my name, and in that moment I knew the whole truth.

I was falling in love.

I am losing my father.

With Emilio Vargas.

To smoke and shadow.

My heart fluttered.

My heart aches.

To feel it.

To deny it.

Life.

Death.

Possibilities.

Endings.

Stars swam before my eyes and the world tilted and Emilio breathed my name again and everything was all at once cruel and spectacular.

"Emilio, I want to go with you," I whispered.

He pulled me closer, wrapped his arms around me.

I rested my hand on his chest and felt his heartbeat through my fingertips. "But I can't answer yes or no. It depends on Papi, and then there's Mom, and my sisters, and the Valentina stuff. . . ." I closed my eyes. "I'm not saying no. Just . . . I need to think about it some. Not no, though."

"Not no. I'll take it for now." Emilio pulled my hand from

his chest and kissed my palm. His lips trailed to my wrist, lingered before moving gently to my shoulder. I kept my eyes closed as he kissed my neck, my chin . . . and then his mouth covered mine, and I gasped.

"Are you for real?" I whispered against his lips. "Yes or no."

"You're killing me, *princesa*." His words slid into my mouth as our bodies pressed together.

"Let's go for a ride." I spoke fast, desperate to say it without breaking our kiss. "Now. I don't care where. Just take me—"

"Jude." Mari's voice traveled straight into my skull. I twisted away from Emilio and turned to face her in the doorway, but it was too late—no way she missed us. The sudden lack of him felt so cold and wrong that I had to wrap my arms around myself to keep from shivering.

Mari fumed, hands on her hips. "You told Papi he could ride that thing?"

Emilio fidgeted on his feet beside me, and I knew he was waiting for me to take a stand. To stop letting her treat me like a kid, as if every important decision was already made, handed down like the toys and the stereo equipment.

"I didn't. . . . He said he wanted to," I said. "You know the bike is special. You've seen him—it's like he remembers it and something inside him connects. If he wants to ride, it's his choice."

"I can't even begin to tell you what a horrible, dangerous, stupid idea this is."

"It isn't. It's a great idea." I turned to Emilio. "Tell her."

Emilio looked at me with pleading eyes, and immediately I regretted dragging him into this, but still. He was my star witness. He knew Papi was made for the bike. He knew what this meant to him, even more than I did.

"It isn't my place to say." He ran a hand over his bandanna and his eyes held an unspoken apology and I knew it, knew he was sorry, knew he was right. It wasn't his place.

I pushed anyway.

"That bike means everything to Papi," I said. "You can at least say that much, right?"

"Jesus!" Mari threw up her hands. "What are you asking *him* for? You're only doing all this because you have a crush on Mr. Motorcycle here. Don't pretend this is about what's good for Papi."

"But it is! He wants—"

"It doesn't matter what he wants, Juju. He's not riding." Mari dragged her fingers through her white-blond hair, all bed-headed and mad. "You never should've gotten his hopes up. Both of you. He's totally crushed."

She stalked back into the house, shaking her head the entire way, and I crumpled onto the workbench.

"Here's what I think." Emilio sat next to me and took my hand. I met his gaze, expecting anger but finding only kindness, his endless patience. "Your father shouldn't ride. It's too dangerous. That's what I think, for real. He's not healthy. You gotta trust your sister on this one. She's right."

"But you know what this means to him and—"

"You have no idea." Emilio's voice was low and scratchy, and when he sighed, close to my ear, it was hard not to imagine waking up next to him, lying in his bedroom with all the maps, his shirt tossed carelessly over the desk chair, bare shoulders against the pillows.

"Why are you siding with Mari?"

"It's not siding. It's . . . yeah, I wish he could ride. Okay? I wish I could be there to see him do it. But I can't." Emilio's hands tightened around mine. "If anything happened to him . . ."

"Something *is* happening to him." I pulled out of Emilio's grasp and crossed over to the bike. "That's the point. And he can't fight it forever. It was stupid to try." I grabbed Valentina's handlebars as if they could grab me back, make the everything-will-be-fine promises my sisters couldn't. "The least we could do is let him ride his own motorcycle."

"What if he got hurt?"

"He'd live."

"What if he didn't?" Emilio clenched his fists, his voice rising as he stood from the bench. "What if he hit a tree? A house? A person? What if he died on the side of the road, alone, all because you didn't want to tell him no? What then, Jude? You get your way, and he dies."

His words hit me like sharp rocks. In all our time together, Emilio had never spoken about Papi's death, and now he was shouting, enraged. It erupted from nowhere; his chest and arms shook with it. I closed my eyes to shut out the pictures of

Papi lying in the road, helpless and still, but they kept coming anyway and my lungs ached and I wanted to scream. . . .

"It would kill you," Emilio said. "That guilt never leaves you. I'm telling you, for the rest of forever you have that thing haunting you." His voice cracked and dropped to a whisper, the rage suddenly gone. "I couldn't watch you go through that, *princesa*."

He reached for my hand, but my own rage took over. Rage at my sister, rage at the demon, rage at life's cruel jokes. My heart thudded in my ears and my mouth tasted like copper and I shoved him away, hard as I could, pushed until he stumbled backward and caught himself on the workbench.

His face crumpled. I hated myself for touching him that way, but I couldn't erase those pictures from my head.

Papi, dead. Papi, gone.

Because bike ride or not, I knew it was coming, and there was nothing I could do to change it, no one I could scream at loud enough, no one I could shove hard enough, no motorcycle fast enough to stop the inevitable slide toward Death's door.

"I'm sorry," Emilio whispered. The regret in his eyes matched the regret in my heart, black and heavy. "I didn't mean . . . I just . . . I don't want anything to happen to him. Or to you. I can't even—"

"Get out," I said softly.

"Jude . . ."

"Please go," I whispered. I couldn't face him anymore, couldn't breathe through the impossibly thick air, couldn't the weight of so much sorrow on my shoulders, and he left without another word, another touch.

I sat on the bench where he'd stumbled and covered my ears like a kid, trying unsuccessfully to ignore the rumble of his bike, ragged and low as it ferried him away.

CHAPTER 26

The battered orange Jeep bounced up our driveway two days later. Emilio was a no-show, and as I watched Samuel climb out of his truck, I knew he was here as a favor to his friend, to finish up the work Emilio had started.

"Hey, *mamí*," he said when I met him outside. "E sent me to—"

"*Unbelievable.* He can't finish the job himself?" I asked. "Sent you to do his dirty work? Where is he?"

Samuel put his hand up, shielding his eyes from the sun. Or maybe from me. "I look like his secretary or some shit?"

"When did you last see him?"

"We hung out last night."

"Did he say anything?" I asked.

"He said lots of things, Jude: *Hey, Samuel. Pass me the remote. You got any Doritos? I hate this show.*"

"Samuel." I rolled my eyes to the sky. If all boys insisted on being this dumb, I'd have to start my own book—*The Book of*

Broken Skulls. Because that's exactly what I was about to do to every last one of them. "I don't care about Doritos! What did he say about *me*?"

"What is going *on* here, girl?" Samuel laughed. "We at a slumber party? You wanna talk about boys and paint my nails?" He wriggled his fingers in my face.

Why do they all have such contagious smiles?

"Stop." I swiped his hands away. "I'm trying to be mad at boys right now. You're seriously messing up the flow."

"Sorry. How's this. Damn, *mamí*, that shirt makes you look kinda fat. Shorts ain't doin' you any favors either."

I flashed him a death stare. "They're my sister's clothes. They aren't even my regular size."

"Just trying to help."

"No more helping," I said. But he *had* helped, in his own sick little way, and I decided I kind of liked him, as far as boys went, but he was obviously here for the bike, and fangirl hour was over. I led him into the barn, back to Emilio's space.

"Valentina, *ooh*." He gave an impressed whistle. "This girl is *hot*. No wonder E loves working on her."

"Yep. Loves it *sooo* much that he bailed in the homestretch."

"What?" Samuel shook his head. "Has that boy ever bailed on you before?"

"No. But—"

"He didn't bail, you drama llama. He's in Santa Fe with his mom for that school thing. I'm just here for the lift."

"Santa Fe . . . the cookie project thing?" My face went hot.

I'd forgotten about their field trip once I'd polished off the last of the cookies, like, ages ago.

"Look at your face," Samuel said. "Jesus, I seen him mopin' around all night, and now you. . . . Oh, you two got it bad. It's kinda sick. Cute, but sick."

"I don't . . . wait. He was moping? Like, all night? How long was he moping? What was he doing exactly?"

Samuel held up his hands. "Sorry, I have to get to work. I'm sure you can find a shrink in the phone book, happy to listen to all your problems."

"You okay, *queridita*?" Papi strolled into the barn with Pancake and another Celi mug from the stash I'd found, this one with pink and silver hearts raining out of blue clouds. He was all happy-go-lucky-good-mornin' casual, and when he saw Samuel, he smiled. "You're from Duchess, right? You work with Emilio?"

My eyes stung at the mention of Emilio's name again, but I blinked it away and introduced them.

"¿Quieres un café?" Papi asked Samuel.

"No, gracias," he said. "I need to get this lift back to Duchess. We got two hogs comin' in today and we're short."

Papi set down his mug to help Samuel with the lift, and after they'd loaded it into the Jeep and Samuel took off, Papi found me right where he'd left me: sitting on the workbench in a puddle of sulk like the big fat drama llama I was.

Papi sat next to me and wrapped his arm around my shoulder. I leaned into him, soaked up the familiar strength, and my heart ached as I recalled a hundred scraped knees, all the forgotten lines onstage, the unexpected tumbles, monsters under the bed. Papi had chased them all away, comforted me after every pain, and now I closed my eyes and let myself pretend—just for a minute—that he'd get strong again. That he'd be there to dry my tears, to hang the moon and the stars when they fell down. That he'd always be the smart one, the one with all the right words and promises. That we'd never have to switch places on this bench.

But we would. In so many ways we already had. And no matter how close the inevitable got, I could never be ready for it, not in a year or five or ten or a hundred. So when he squeezed my arm and asked me what happened, why I looked so sad, I confessed as if it would always be this way between us. Old helping young. Wisdom guiding inexperience. Father loving daughter.

"Emilio and I got into a fight the other day," I said.

"Another one?" Papi said, an octave higher than normal. Even Pancake lifted his head at that one, like, *Jude, can't you keep your crazy shit together for five minutes? You have the attention span of a—look! Ohmigod! BUNNIES!*

Pancake shuffled off toward the yard, and I nodded. "Emilio's never talking to me again."

"*Que?* I doubt that. Why do you think?"

"I kind of flipped out on him. And then I told him to get out."

"Ah." Papi reached for his coffee and took a sip, his other

arm still strong over my shoulder. "That happens sometimes, *querida*. Especially with Hernandez women. Believe me, I know."

"Not helping, *viejito*."

"No?" Papi smiled. "I'm sorry, Juju. Tell me exactly what happened."

I took a shaky breath, trying to ignore the flashes of Papi lying on the road, Emilio's face after I'd pushed him away. "Basically, he said I should listen to Mari about not letting you ride, because it's dangerous and he's worried, and he doesn't want me to feel guilty if something happened . . . not that it would, but . . . he's wrong, Papi."

"He's not wrong about the risks. Motorcycles *are* dangerous, *querida*. But it's not his call—I made my decision. Emilio will finish the bike soon. Then I ride." Papi's sigh was heavy, but then he smiled again and tugged on my hair. "So you defended this *viejito*, eh?"

"I told him to get out. I mean, he kept going on and on . . . Forget it. He doesn't know what he's talking about."

I closed my mouth, suddenly feeling like I'd betrayed Emilio, ratted him out. But Papi just sipped his coffee like he wasn't surprised or mad or anything at all. I waited for him to dismiss it with a wave, to tell me I was being silly and promise it would all blow over. Instead, he rose from the bench, set down the mug, and held out his hand.

"Let's walk," he said. "I told Mari I'd make at least two trips to the river this week."

Mari had ducked out at dawn this morning, first to Denver, then on to meet her author in New York. She'd left a note under my door with strict orders, underlined three times, not to let Papi ride.

"How well do you know Emilio?" Papi asked as we made our way to the river, trailed as always by Pancake. He'd never miss out on a chance to spook those fish.

"Not *super* well or anything. We're . . . friends." My cheeks burned, but Papi was asking about history, not about how I'd been spending my summer, my forbidden dreams, the truth in my heart that remained, despite our argument. "He was ahead of me at BHS, and then he left early, so . . . just from this summer. Not a lot." The memories from that night in the woods by the Bowl, the motorcycle ride, the taste of his lips, the hurt in his eyes yesterday . . . all of them rose and fell.

"Did he tell you why he dropped out of Blackfeather High?" Papi asked.

"No. I asked him once, but I got a weird vibe. Like, he didn't want to talk about it. It's funny with him, Papi. When he's not cracking jokes or talking about motorcycles, he doesn't say too much. He's like that about his family, too. It's like deep down, he really doesn't want to talk."

But you don't ask me stuff that matters. Who I am or where I been. What I see when I look at you. What I want . . .

Echoes. Words from that night in my driveway after *Alice in Wonderland*. They lingered like smoke, and I yanked them from the sky and shoved them down deep with memories of all the good things.

We followed the path though the trees—ponderosa pines, I now knew—that led down to the Animas. The water was slow and lazy today, the opposite of everything inside me that churned and roiled, and we found a dry spot on the bank and took off our shoes and dipped our toes.

Papi kicked the water, watched the ripples float away. “A couple years ago, a boy got into a motorcycle accident on Phantom Canyon Road. There was fog on the mountain that night, low visibility. They figured he lost sight of the pavement and hit the shoulder, then lost control trying to swing back onto the road.”

I shivered. People wrecked on bikes, I knew that, but hearing about it now, I couldn’t help but picture Emilio. It hit me sharp and fast, cut even deeper than when I’d pictured Papi the other day because Emilio still rode his bike. All the time, everywhere.

Did he go out on Phantom Canyon Road at night? Had he heard this story? My heart sped up, and I held my breath as Papi continued.

“He hit a tree, got tangled in the wreckage . . . nineteen years old, like Emilio.”

Pancake paced the shore, sniffing out flowers and bugs and other living things, stepping over Papi’s feet when he needed to.

“I read about it when it happened.” Papi leaned forward to

scoop some rocks from the bank. "Obviously we knew of the family because of your sister . . . *ay, Dios.*" He poured his rocks from one hand to the other, back and forth, and when he finally looked at me, his eyes were glassy. "It was his cousin, *querida.* They were very, very close. He told me about him, a little."

Another shiver, cold and icy, ran from my skull to my toes. Papi didn't have to say whose cousin. I knew in my bones he was talking about Danny, and my heart sank as some of the pieces clicked into place. The picture in Emilio's bedroom, two boys splattered with mud. Susana's toys-and-candle shrine. All the time Emilio and Papi had spent alone in the barn, the bond they shared.

Papi tossed the rocks into the water and turned to face me. His eyes were wet with tears, but he didn't blink them away or cough like it was a tickle in his throat, a sneeze that didn't escape.

"Juju, Emilio was there. This Danny . . . he was ahead of him on the road about a half mile. Emilio didn't see the accident happen, but he heard it. When he got around the bend, he saw the wreck. He skidded to a stop and basically dropped his bike. . . ." Papi pinched the bridge of his nose, and when he spoke again the words were muffled by his hand.

"He dove at the tree, trying to haul the bike off Danny, but it was too heavy and mangled. All that twisted metal . . . Everything was sharp and hot. . . . *Ay*, what a mess. He hurt himself pretty bad trying to pull Danny out. But there wasn't . . . It was too late."

I buried my face against my knees as the rest of the pieces clicked together, the horrifying puzzle complete.

They were always wild, those boys. . . . dragged Danny around everywhere he went . . .

Ain't seen him in two years. I miss him. Hell yeah, I miss him.

His mother basically hates me. . . .

Emilio had said Danny was in Puerto Rico, but he wasn't. He was gone. Was his death the tragedy that tore apart Emilio's family? Or was it because Emilio chose to keep riding, to keep building the machines that killed his cousin? Did they blame him for that Phantom Canyon Road ride? Did they wish it were Emilio instead? Did they blame him for not being able to save—

"The scars." The words were so soft I wasn't sure if I'd spoken or thought them. I closed my eyes, remembering again the thin lines on Emilio's arms, the bone-white evidence of some long ago hurt seared across his abdomen. Though I'd finally touched them, I hadn't worked up the nerve to ask. I knew there had to be a dark story, maybe a bike-related thing.

But not like this.

Pancake lumbered over with some treasure he'd unearthed, a bundle of sticks and stones caked in river mud. He dropped it on the ground and buried his head in my lap as if he knew that's exactly what I needed.

"Emilio Vargas is a good kid." Papi's voice was thick with emotion. "He's not his brothers any more than you're Araceli or Mariposa or Lourdes. He's been through a lot. He's still a boy and he's already had his heart broken more than we can even imagine."

I sucked in a sharp breath as the final realization dawned. "You knew he was a Vargas?"

Papi's forehead was wrinkled with sadness, but he smiled at my question. "You girls think I'm already senile. I'm telling you, you can't sneak anything past me."

"The *whole* time?"

"No, no. Only since that day your sister met him. I kept thinking, what the hell got Mari so worked up? Every time I got close, this junker conked out." He knocked on his head. "But then I woke up in the middle of the night and it finally clicked. Emilio Vargas! Yes! Ah, what can you do?"

"Does Mom know?"

"Sure, she knows. I told her as soon as I figured it out. *Querida*, you're making a big deal for nothing."

"But . . . you guys weren't mad about the wedding and stuff?"

He shrugged. "That has nothing to do with Emilio, and nothing to do with you."

"But his family—"

"His family is lots of different people. Some of them made mistakes. Some of them are still making mistakes. But you can't judge everyone by their relatives. Look where that would get you." He tapped his head again and winked.

I laughed because he did, and because I was grateful for the momentary lightness, but laughing at his Alzheimer's jokes had the same effect on me as the disease did on him—it consumed a little piece of me every time, one I'd never get back.

Papi leaned over to scratch Pancake's ears. "Look in your heart, *querida*. Give it a chance."

When we got back to the house, Papi kissed me on the forehead and went inside, and I sat on the back porch with Pancake for the rest of the day. We watched the sun sink behind the Needles, and then it was gone, and Pancake put his head in my lap and we both sighed. Dogs knew the real deal.

Sometimes, a sigh was all the fight you had left.

CHAPTER 27

"Have you kids seen my big shovel?" Papi barreled into the barn in dust-covered jeans, work gloves black with dirt. He'd insisted on gardening this morning to give me and Emilio a chance to talk, even though he'd interrupted us five times already, searching for potting soil and trowels and tools. "Your mother had it out a few weeks ago."

I couldn't remember Mom ever doing yard work, and I wasn't even sure we *had* a big shovel, but Papi finally located it in the corner with the rakes. He dragged it back out into the yard, Pancake waddling behind him.

Emilio leaned against the workbench with his arms crossed over his chest. It was his first day back since the Santa Fe trip, and his eyes were dark and dim, red like he hadn't slept. I'd been trying to say the words in my heart all morning—how much I hated fighting with him. How much I missed his arms around me. How sorry I was about Danny, how I understood why he had to leave, why he was always chasing the next amazing thing. I even understood why he'd said those things about Papi and the kind of knife-edged guilt that never leaves you.

I knew why he didn't want to see me go through it. I hated seeing him carry it too.

I'm sorry about your broken heart.

All of it sounded right in my head, but I couldn't find my voice.

Emilio spoke instead. "I'm sorry for what I said. About your pops and the bike . . . I got pissed. I didn't mean it."

I nodded, waiting for him to continue. *My cousin died. I never got to say good-bye. I still feel guilty . . .*

But that was all he had, and he gave me a long sigh and got back to work. As he rummaged through a mason jar full of screws, I pretended to dig into a box of old Halloween costumes, fairies and frogs and clowns and Darth Vader, but my eyes lingered on his arms. I'd come to know his scars as mysterious but permanent, as much a part of him as his wavy black hair and soft brown eyes. But through my father's story, in an instant, they'd changed. Everything about Emilio had changed since I'd last seen him. It felt like years.

"Do you want a drink?" I chucked a yellow-blond Miss Piggy wig into the trash and headed toward the doors, but I nearly crashed into Papi. His face was twisted with panic, knuckles white around the shovel handle.

"I can't find it, Juju. I looked all over and it's not there."

"Papi. It's okay. You already found it. With the rakes, remember?"

He shook his head. "Someone stole it. They stole it, Juju. We should've been more careful!"

"You're holding it. Look." I reached for the shovel, but he snatched it away and ran back out to the yard.

It was obvious Papi was no longer talking about gardening. The familiar dread pooled in my stomach, and I counted to ten and waited for it to pass, to usher in the no-nonsense calm that would let me march outside and set things right, like I had at Uncle Fuzzy's.

But this time my nerves stayed tangled. My arms and legs felt old, the bones weak and stiff. Instead of calm, my body filled with utter exhaustion.

All I'd wanted to do today was fix the mess with Emilio, find a way back to the moments before our argument. But out in the yard, Papi was ranting again, louder by the second, and finally Emilio set down his tools to go investigate.

"I got this." He squeezed my shoulder as he passed, and a knot tightened my throat. I sagged against the barn's warped wood, wished on Celi's old fairy wand for all of it to stop.

"Jude," Emilio called from the yard. Through the wall, his voice was distorted but urgent, edged with panic. "Get out here."

"Papi, what . . . what did you do?" I stared openmouthed at the disaster formerly known as our yard. It was hacked apart, cratered with a dozen holes and corresponding mounds of grass and dirt.

"Help me find it, Juju!" Papi gave up the shovel, but when I laid it in the grass at my feet, he snatched it up and started another hole. "The treasure, *querida*."

Emilio tried to distract him with an update on Valentina, but Papi was undeterred. My so-called angelic singing voice bombed out too—"Thoroughly Modern Millie" fell on deaf ears. Mari was still in New York. Mom was at work. I was out of ideas.

"It's buried next to the grave," Papi said. "I know it is—he told me. But I can't find it. Someone must've moved it."

"Papi." I kept my voice low and steady, but inside the panic rose, pushing high into my throat. "There's no treasure. I promise."

He shook his head, wouldn't look at me as he jumped on the shovel head and speared the earth. "There are two kinds of people in this world."

I watched him closely, desperate for that punch line, the joke that would explain everything. "What are they?"

"Those with loaded guns, and those who dig. I dig."

"Papi, it's not—"

"He said it was buried under the grave of Arch—no, *next* to the grave of Arch Stanton. That's it. Help me find the headstone."

Realization pierced my heart. *Arch Stanton. The treasure.* It was a scene out of *The Good, the Bad and the Ugly*. He was looking at me with frantic eyes, desperate for that treasure, convinced it existed in our yard, that the characters existed in his life.

He thought it was real.

"No, the treasure was from your movie, remember?" I said. "With Tuco? Two kinds of people in this world?"

"Tuco wants the money for himself!" Papi wagged a finger in my face. "You better not be on his side. Are you working for Angel Eyes?" He squinted at me, scrutinized my face. Even Pancake was spooked, barking and barking despite Emilio trying to calm him, probably wondering how Papi could get away with this kind of property destruction when he always got sent to his doggy bed.

"I'm not working for anyone, Papi," I said. "I'm on your side. But maybe we should take a break, eat some lunch first?"

"I don't want to waste time." Papi leaned on the shovel and wiped his forehead, a yawn escaping his throat. "It's a lot of money, *queridita*. We could use it for Lourdes's college."

"You look tired, *viejito*."

He tried to wave me off, but he yawned again, and I seized the opportunity.

"Why don't you let us look for the treasure. Emilio's really strong—he can dig deeper."

"But—"

"Let's go inside," I said. "Emilio will find it. I promise."

Emilio rose when I returned to the barn, came out from behind the bike to meet me. Close. Super, crazy close. Warm breath brushed my lips, and a swirling vortex tugged behind my belly button, like falling, like delirium.

"Is *el jefe* okay alone in there?" he asked.

"I put him to bed." I closed my eyes and steadied my heart, forced out the words before anything else interrupted them, before Papi woke up wanting that treasure, before Emilio returned to Valentina, before I lost the nerve. "My father told me about Danny. The other day, after Samuel came for the lift."

He pulled back immediately.

I felt the cold between us and opened my eyes. "I'm sorry. I know why you said that stuff about Papi, why you're worried about us. And I'm so sorry Danny died, and I wish I could—"

"I don't wanna talk about it right now. Please, Jude. I can't."

I clamped my mouth shut. Of course he didn't want to talk—I'd blurted out the most insensitive thing ever, the thing I dreaded hearing whenever someone found out about Papi's diagnosis. *Sorry, so sorry.*

"I should probably . . ." Emilio nodded toward the bike. "I'm really close. Almost done."

"I didn't mean—"

"I know. I just—I'm not up for it today."

"But—"

"Why won't you let it go?" Emilio yanked a rag from his back pocket and wiped his hands. "You're, like, *obsessed* with the past. News flash, Jude: Not all of us wanna go back in time."

His harshness stung, but I pressed on. "I know you're—"

"You actually don't." He got in my face again, only this time the dimples were gone, the warmth in his eyes replaced with red-hot anger. "You don't know anything about it. And you never will. Know why? You can't handle it. You're the most scared person I know."

Tears pricked my eyes. I folded my arms across my chest and focused on Pancake, who'd wandered in from outside with a faded rawhide bone, probably unearthed by one of Papi's treasure holes.

"There's so much inside you," Emilio said. "But you won't let it out. It's like you need permission just to be *you*." He paced the dirt floor, running his hands through his hair. "You wait for your old friends to call you up out of nowhere, even though they bailed on your whole family. You wait for your sister to tell you what to do and how to do it—and I ain't talkin' about Valentina. I mean *your* stuff. I wish I could . . . *God*!"

He stammered and trailed his fingers over my heart, but then he pulled away and resumed pacing. "You sit there taking pictures and daydreaming about the way things used to be, like if you wish hard enough it'll all come back. The most alive and real I ever saw you was that day on the bike with me. It was like the bad news about the genetic thing woke you up for just long enough to realize that life is so short . . . but then you let it go again. It's like you're waitin' around for someone to invent a time machine instead of just livin' your life."

The words rang in my ears. Everything he said was right. True.

"Guess what?" His voice was quiet again, but heat radiated from his heart, out through his skin, rushing over me in waves. "The past ain't comin' back. It's done. No do-overs. You got what you got. We all do."

Dust floated in the light between us, and the breeze stilled outside, and Pancake quit chomping on his bone. It was like someone had hit the pause button.

"I get it," Emilio whispered. "Ever since Danny died, I been tryin' to leave too. 'Cause he left, and my pops left, and then my brothers. And it was like, when's my turn? Like, if I could just go fast enough, far enough, everything would be okay. But I'm tellin' you, things changed for me this summer. Everything changed. You . . ." He narrowed his eyes in the dusty air, his gaze sending white-hot sparks through my stomach. "You don't even know what I'm sayin', right?"

The sparks inside me collided and faded, fell like the July Fourth ashes at the Bowl. I shook my head, closed my eyes against the truth. The enormity of it was too heavy, too impossible.

"Open your eyes, Jude. Look at me. Say something."

I opened them. Looked at him. Said something. "Scared. You're right. I'm totally scared of everything."

Pancake yawned and laid his head against my foot, and just like that, this odd sense of peace floated over me. It was as if, all along, I'd only needed to say those words, to admit it out loud, and everything would turn out okay. I blinked away tears, and Emilio smiled. Real, whole, gentle.

We sat on the bench together. He put his arm around me and rubbed my back, and for a long time we stayed like that. Just breathing, just being okay.

"Danny Vargas," Emilio finally said. His voice was soft and low, full of reverence. "He was nineteen—same as I am now. He was a vegetarian, okay? Very unpopular in a Puerto Rican household. Couldn't spell for shit. Wore the same cologne since seventh grade. Loved comics. Never watched TV. He was always outside, any chance he got, smellin' trees or chasin' animals."

I smiled, remembering the photo from Emilio's room.

"He was waitin' for me to graduate," Emilio said. "We were gonna do the bike trip together right after. When he died, everyone wanted me to stop riding—everyone but Ma. She said that's not what Danny would want. She wouldn't let me sell the bike. Every time I put it out front with a sign, she dragged it back to the garage. I'm happy about it now, but you know . . . some people in my family don't talk to us because of it." He tightened his arm around me, his breath heavy in my hair.

"I made a promise at his funeral," he said. "I don't know if he heard me or what. But I promised him I'd still do the trip, see all the stuff we talked about. I told him I'd go as soon as I finished school and saved up the money. I had to take time off, you know, work out my shit. I finished high school online.

Picked up the gig at Duchess. I was finally gonna hit the road this summer, see everything."

Emilio shivered, and I took his hand in mine, pressed it to my lips. It was more than he'd ever said about his family. His life. I didn't want him to stop.

"You woulda loved him," Emilio said. "He was crazy. He always said that about me, but he was *loco* too. Always laughing at something, always making some crazy ass trouble or—"

"Wait. Hold on." I looked over at Pancake. He'd abandoned his bone and had crouched to the ground in a low growl, hackles raised from neck to tail. I'd only ever seen him like that once—we'd come up on a coyote in the woods, spooked it from behind.

"Pancake?" I took a step toward him, but he bolted out of the barn, shooting across the yard and into the house through his doggy door. A heartbeat later, he cannonballed back out the same way, barking and howling, zooming toward me as if I were a rabbit.

In the second it took for me to reach the barn doors, a horrible screech pierced the air, a deadly electronic vulture.

"Papi!" I shot toward the house, Pancake at my heels, Emilio close behind.

Smoke curled through the kitchen screen door, and we bolted through it without touching the handle, knocking it off the top hinge. The kitchen was gray with smoke and ash. Emilio coughed and shoved past me into the living room. I heard him thump up the stairs toward the bedrooms, calling for Papi.

Seconds later something popped and sizzled, and I followed the sounds to the stove. Heat rolled across my shoulders, my face, and in an instant I was on my knees, blindly groping around under the cupboard for the fire extinguisher.

We were out of immediate danger, Papi and I safe in the living room, Emilio on the phone with the fire department, but my legs still shook with leftover adrenaline. Papi stroked my hair as I hugged him, my face buried in his shirt.

"Didn't you hear the smoke detector?" I mumbled against his chest. The dreadful chirp still rang in my ears even though Emilio had disabled it.

"I thought . . . I don't know. The TV?" Papi pulled out of my embrace and looked at me with hazy, disoriented eyes. "I thought maybe you were watching. I put on my music." He pointed to the headphones around his neck, those big eighties kind with a jack the size of a screwdriver. We didn't even own anything they could plug into.

"We were outside," I said. "I thought you were sleeping."

He narrowed his eyes at the headphone jack, scratched his head like he was trying to piece together the mystery. "I was going to cook something, I think. But I don't . . . I guess I got hungry? I'm sorry, *querida*. I can't remember."

He shrugged like it was no big deal, just another funny story about him putting on mismatched socks or digging up the lawn or forgetting that he didn't have to drive to work anymore.

"They're on their way." Emilio slipped the cell back into his pocket. "I'll wait outside, flag them down."

Papi didn't remember anything else, and I didn't want to upset him, so we sat on the couch in silence. Six minutes later two trucks were in the driveway, sirens blaring, yellow-suited men stomping into the kitchen.

"Do you know how it started?" Fireman Jeff asked. I knew it was Fireman Jeff and not Bob or Larry or Ferdinand because I was at the honorary dinner the night Jeff finished his volunteer training and got his station assignment.

Jeff was Zoe's brother.

I'd hoped against the odds he wouldn't be on duty today, but of course he was, and now he looked at me with the same sadness and pity in his eyes that Zoe'd had after the BHS picnic.

"I was outside," I said. "I think my father turned the stove on and forgot about it. Something must've caught. Papi, do you remember anything else?"

Two firemen stomped past us to check the second floor. With every pound of their boots, every knock on the wall, Papi flinched.

"Mr. Hernandez?" Jeff's voice was soft but commanding, and still Papi didn't look up.

"It's okay. Tell them what you remember," I said. "They have to make sure everything's safe."

He returned his attention to the headphones, tugged on the cord, inspected the jack. Emilio had secured Pancake outside to keep him from spazzing out and Jeff was still looming over us and his red hair reminded me of Zoe and Papi wouldn't speak and everything smelled like campfire and from some deep, awful place inside, darkness seeped into my blood, welled up in a flood of tears and hatred.

For the disease.

For the summer.

For the future.

For him.

And for one flash of a moment, for one fraction of a heartbeat, I looked at my father and wished the unspeakable *what if*.

What if I'd just closed my eyes.

What if I'd just ignored the smoke alarm.

What if I'd just let him go.

"What is *wrong* with you!" I shouted, blinded by a rush of horrible guilt and grief. I didn't care that Jeff was still watching, that all those strangers were in our house, trampling our carpets, looking through the peephole on our lives. "You can't use the stove! You can't do that, okay?" I tapped his forehead with my finger. "It's broken in here. Don't you get that?"

Papi looked from the charred kitchen to the dangling screen door to my soot-smudged hands. He gasped as if he'd just realized the extent of the damage, how close he'd come to burning down the entire house. To killing himself. To disappearing forever.

"I'm sorry, *querida*. . . . I didn't . . ." He buried his head in his hands, and my heart shriveled inside, all the air escaping my lungs.

I'd lost my temper about the yard, the stupid treasure, Arch Stanton. I'd stashed him in the house to get him out of my way.

And then I'd wished him dead.

It was only a flicker, a barely formed thought, but it had been there, the evidence of it black and sooty behind my eyes. Now my throat burned with shame, my whole body trembled with sadness and fear.

I reached for Papi's hand. Even though I hadn't voiced the awful thought, I needed him to know that I didn't mean it. That I loved him. I needed to know that he loved me too.

That he'd remember me always.

"Papi?" I whispered.

The firemen continued to clomp and bang and shout all around us, upstairs and down. My hand curled up on his knee, and Papi closed his eyes, exhausted, his face colored with shame.

CHAPTER 28

I sat on the banks of the Animas trying desperately to do what Emilio had sent me to do: compose myself.

What a stupid saying. *Compose myself.* Like I could whip out a palette of paints and a brush, cover up all the mistakes.

She looks so real!

It felt wrong to dip my toes in the water while Emilio was home with Papi. It felt wrong to breathe the sweet summer air, knowing they were inhaling the acrid leftover haze.

But Emilio told me to try, and I couldn't handle the burden of another screw-up today, so here I was. Composing.

The water bubbled around my toes. I let myself get lost in the coolness, wondering if I could slip in, float down the river, come up on the banks of someone else's life.

All my fantasies ended with Emilio holding out his hand from the safety of shore.

I couldn't stop thinking about Papi, blank and confused, looking to me like I had the answers, like I knew what had caused the fire, like I'd lit the match myself just to watch it burn. And Emilio, charging up the stairs to find him. Calling the fire department. Staying in the middle of ground zero even now, making sure Papi was okay while the firemen finished up and we waited for Mom to drive home.

That was the thing about Emilio. He didn't come with a Before Alzheimer's and an After Alzheimer's version. He'd seen Papi at his worst from the start, yet his eyes hadn't judged. His conversation hadn't become guarded and full of sympathy, awkward and uncomfortable with the unsaid stuff. He took things as they came, every day. No matter what surprises Papi had up his flannel sleeve. No matter how Mari treated him. No matter how many times I screwed up, apologized, screwed up again.

Until Emilio, I'd almost forgotten what it was like to have a true friend. Someone I trusted completely, without reservation. He'd come into my life only because of the motorcycle, and I'd unearthed Valentina only because I thought she might keep the demon at bay.

I remembered something the doctor had said when we first got the diagnosis.

Alzheimer's is a terrible disease, but you never know who or what it may bring into your life.

With a sickening thud of my heart, I wondered now if I'd

always connect the two: Emilio Vargas and this illness, this horrible nightmare. The boy who gave my heart life and the evil faceless thing that stole my father.

El Demonio.

That was the name I'd write on my page in the black book, the old yellowed paper waiting patiently for the broken hearts I'd soon collect.

Emilio watched me through bleary eyes on the front stoop. "At least let me stay until your mom gets here."

"We're fine," I said. "You already . . . You did a lot."

I couldn't look at him without seeing the smoke billow out from the kitchen door, Emilio charging in after my father. The things I'd said to Papi . . . the things inside my head . . . a thousand times more reprehensible than letting my sisters boss me around or waiting for old friends to call.

Emilio had seen the absolute worst of me, and no amount of composure or fresh air would clear it out.

"I'm not leaving," he said.

"Thanks for . . ." It was an unfinished whisper, and I didn't meet his eyes. I couldn't. I shut the front door against his protests and turned back to Papi with an insincere smile.

"Still hungry? We could go get tacos or . . . ice cream maybe? Mom won't be here for a while yet." I sat next to Papi on the couch and rested my hand on his knee again, silently pleading that he'd say yes. That he'd make a joke about his failed cooking skills and I'd grab the keys and we'd zoom into Old Town, scarf down some sundaes, make a meal out of our dessert.

Share a few laughs about what a close call this was. *Phew!*

Because if he could laugh about this, if he could see the silver lining, I knew we'd be okay. That this would pass. That we could look back on the memory like a shared secret, our joint oversight, our near miss.

Please, Papi, I thought. *Please let's go for sundaes.*

"We'll deal with this mess later." I stood from the couch and waited for him to follow. "Ready?"

"No, *queridita*. I'm not hungry anymore."

"How about Scrabble? I haven't let you beat me in a while." I grabbed the game box from the shelf under the coffee table, but Papi didn't budge.

He wouldn't leave the couch, wouldn't look up from the floor.

"Western Channel?" I reached for the remote, but he shook his head.

"Okay. Let's go outside at least. We can peek in on Valentina," I said cheerfully. "Emilio says she's almost ready."

Papi squinted, his nose wrinkling. "Who's ready?"

"Valentina."

"Your sister lives in New York, *querida*."

"Not Araceli," I said. "The motorcycle. Valentina."

He waved me off and slumped back on the couch. "Valentina doesn't have a motorcycle. She's too young."

Our kitchen was a war zone to match our yard—black holes and gutted walls around the stove, broken dishes on the counter. I poked around the house and opened the rest of the windows, turned the fans to full blast, splashed my face with cold water at the bathroom sink. I wanted to crawl into bed, wake up later to the news that this whole thing was a dream.

But I knew it wasn't, and I couldn't leave Papi alone again.

"You want something to drink?" I asked when I got back to the living room. "Lemonade? Maté?"

He shook his head, but his eyes were fixed on the wall over the television, scanning the photos that had hung there for all eternity, now complete with labels.

DAUGHTER LOURDES, ROAD TEST.

DAUGHTER MARIPOSA, HIGH SCHOOL GRADUATION.

DAUGHTER ARACELI, COLLEGE GRADUATION.

DAUGHTER JUDE, SMILING.

Smiling. I was, too. It was summer; I was maybe ten. I'd just caught a fish, a rainbow trout, and I held it up to the camera with pride.

There was no real sound in our house now. Only the soft whir of the fans and a stack of magazines on the hall table fluttering in the breeze and the endlessly ticking grandfather clock. Even Pancake was subdued, curled up silently at Papi's feet.

I sat down next to Papi again and looped my pinkie finger in his. I wanted him so badly to joke about this. Or to freak out and yell at me to clean it up before Mom got home, or even to start ranting about that treasure again.

But he sagged on the couch and squinted at the wall, breathing heavy through his mouth, trying desperately to memorize the pictures of the girls he'd one day—soon—forget.

CHAPTER 29

For all Mom's dislike of strangers at the house, the place had seen more strangers in four days than it had in my entire life. Strange people. Strange voices. Strange boot prints. Strange mouths on our blue coffee mugs, strange hands on the cold empanadas and *medialunas*, strange fingers dipping pastries in the *dulce de leche* Lourdes had sent. Susana prepared a feast for us too, sent it over with Emilio, and now the Vargas and Hernandez family food mingled on the dining room table in foil-wrapped dishes.

You'd think we were having a party, a celebration, but it was nothing like that. It hardly felt like home anymore, and with every bang of the hammer and whirl of the drill on the kitchen walls, my heart fractured a little more.

Emilio and Samuel knew a guy, and the three of them had shown up this morning to put the kitchen back together, Emilio and Samuel working on the walls while the other guy handled the wiring and hooked up the new stove. Mom had left me cash for everything—labor, supplies. She didn't want to deal with it face-to-face.

After everything I'd said to Papi the other day, neither did I. Emilio tried to talk to me in his soft, gentle tone, as if we were at a funeral, as if I were made of glass. He was patient, he was amazing, but whenever I looked into his eyes I saw my own shame, and my mouth filled with dust and I couldn't speak.

Now I set out a fresh pot of Dark Moon blend with some of Celi's mugs—birds, these three had. A matched set. I fixed myself a plate of Susana's home-cooked favorites: fried plantains, some chicken thing, rice and beans, *pasteles*. I wasn't hungry, but I hadn't had a hot meal since the stove got destroyed, and everything smelled so good, so I heaped on as much as I could and slipped out the still-broken kitchen door with an overloaded plate and a hungry dog.

Please drop something, please oh please oh please, I love pasteles*! I love everything! This is better than bunnies! Wait, bunnies? BUNNIES!* And he was off, leaving me alone in the barn with a taste of the island and a view of the bike we'd worked on all summer.

Valentina gleamed as if she'd just rolled off the assembly line. Yesterday Emilio added a set of white leather saddlebags trimmed with fringe—Papi had covertly ordered them from Duke the day he'd wandered off to get ice cream. They were the final accessory, and after Emilio had finished putting them on, it was dark outside and Papi was asleep and I stood in the shadows of the barn, watching him polish the red Harley-Davidson logo on the gas tank with a soft cloth.

After all that, he packed up his tools. Valentina was completely restored.

Unlike my father.

I'd failed him, watched the light in his eyes go out after the fire. And now I sat in the barn looking at his prized possession, his Valentina, thinking about everything that had changed, everything that would end.

"What are you thinking about?" Emilio showed up a few minutes later with Pancake, both of them covered in sawdust, their eyes shining through the dirt.

I thought I'd wanted to be alone, but seeing him again in the barn, in the space that had somehow become ours, my heart rose.

"Endings. Life. Time machines." I smiled. As usual, there was no judgment in his tone, no scorn. There was no need to avoid him earlier, and now I was glad he'd found me. "You know, fun stuff."

"Can't be as fun as watching Samuel tell an electrician how to install an outlet. Talk about good times." Emilio sat next to me on the bench. "*El jefe* still lyin' low?"

"They drove to Denver yesterday. Mari's back from New York, and Lourdes and Celi flew into DIA this morning." I poked at the chicken on my plate. After the fire my sisters booked the first flights they could find, no more long-range planning or procrastinating. "Mom thought Papi could use a day away. They're all on their way back now."

Papi didn't want to be here for the kitchen work. He was mortified—Mom told me as much. He still didn't remember how the fire started, only that it was his fault. I was certain he remembered the aftermath though: the firemen. The smell. Emilio staying with him after I flipped out.

He hadn't looked me in the eyes since.

I tried to shovel in some food, but it was useless. I set the plate on the ground and let Pancake go to town.

"Valentina . . . she's perfect, you know? Like new. And I know it sounds stupid, and totally illogical, but part of me wished . . . I don't know." I looked into Emilio's caramel eyes for the first time in forever. "Papi remembered *so* much about that bike. I thought if we fixed it, somehow it would fix him, too."

I never wanted to believe them—my sisters, the doctors, Mom, all the research and the websites—but they were right. The bike couldn't fix Papi. It was blind hope, a daydream that never stood a chance anywhere but in the softest part of my heart. If motorcycles—or any object from a person's past—could cure this thing, it would no longer exist. People would unearth their family treasures, polish up the old jewels, bring their loved ones back from the moon.

"It's not stupid, Jude. You love him." Emilio leaned in closer, ran his hand over my hair. "You did so much for him this summer. You're not a doctor, okay? And I don't know your sisters. But anyone can see how happy you make him. Every single day, you make him smile."

I rested my head on his shoulder, admiring Valentina while Pancake scarfed down Susana's food. Far away and muffled, the drills and hammers continued their incessant march.

"We're almost done in there." Emilio tucked a loop of the hair behind my ear. "Just have to attach the new door frame. After that I'm not doing anything. You wanna go for a ride? Mango shakes or something?"

"I should wait for my sisters," I said. "Maybe in a few days when things settle down?"

"Jude . . ." Emilio brushed a layer of sawdust from his shorts. "I'm leaving tomorrow."

The words, soft as they were, dropped into my stomach like river stones. I knew it was coming, knew it was on the near horizon. He'd take the road and find some wild, beautiful place that time hadn't touched, and he'd leave this summer behind, our ride up the mountain pass, our lips pressed together under the sky. He'd ride all the way to the sea, like he'd planned, and by the time he heard the ocean, I'd be a memory.

It was another inevitable good-bye, and I thought I'd prepared for it. But now there was a giant hole inside me, a black space that already missed him, edging its way toward my heart.

"My offer still stands, *princesa*," he whispered. He stared at my face as if he were trying to memorize it, as if he already knew my answer. "I meant what I said. I want you to come with me."

I'd promised Emilio I'd think about his invitation, give it serious consideration. And I had, only now it felt more like pie-in-the-sky dreaming. Back then I still believed Papi might get his last ride. I still thought my sisters would postpone their visit and, by extension, the genetic test that would confirm which of us was bound to Papi's legacy. I thought I'd have time to outrun it, to slip away in the middle of the night while the demon looked the other way.

But now I knew the truth. None of us had time. Time had us.

"You took good care of Papi this summer," I said. "Me too. I'll never forget it." The last part was a whisper, a breeze. "I really wanted to go with you. I wanted to see all those places, all the thumbtacks on your map."

Emilio's eyebrow rose. He finally nailed it, perfect, and it sent a jolt right through my heart. "You were in my room, huh?"

I smiled despite the sadness. "Maybe."

"I knew you were a stalker."

"No," I said. "Just . . . okay. Kind of stalkerish. Your mother was in there with me. Um, part of the time."

"Like *that* makes it better." Emilio laughed, but soon his dimples faded and he reached for my hand, wrapped his fingers around mine. "You're gonna say no, aren't you?"

"I can't go with you."

His eyes clouded, dimples totally vanished. "You going to the Dunes, then? With Zoe and them?"

A ground squirrel scampered across a rafter. I turned my face toward the sound. He was fast, a little beige blur against the old wood.

"Christina," I said. "Zoe called me after the fire. That fireman, Jeff? He's her brother. He told her what happened. She said I needed to go with them, get my mind off everything."

Before the fire, Zoe and I hadn't spoken since the *Alice in Wonderland* preview, and she was worried about me, she'd said. Hated that we'd been apart all summer. She wanted us to make up for lost time on the road, put all the awkward stuff behind us before we left for college.

"Sand Dunes is a cool place." Emilio tried to keep the bitterness out of his voice, but I sensed it anyway, sharpening the edges of his words. He kicked at the dirt floor with the back of his work boot. "I been there once. You'll like it. Good for pictures."

I scanned his face, the full curve of his lips, the scar on his chin. "I told her no. I'm not going. It didn't feel right, not after everything this summer."

His eyes widened and he grabbed my hand. "So come with me. We could—"

"My sisters will be here tonight. I need to deal with all this family stuff. See what they decide about Papi."

"I don't have to leave this week," Emilio said. "We could let your sisters get settled, see how things look later this month?"

His smile was full of hope, but it was fragile and fleeting, not strong enough to climb over all the boulders in our path.

Later meant more discussions and arguments and painful choices about Papi's care, about the fate of the four Hernandez sisters, about Mom. Later meant me facing the reality of college, packing up my life, moving on, growing up, starting a new chapter.

Either way, Emilio and I would have to say good-bye.

I laced my fingers through his. "You can't wait on me forever. You have to go. For Danny, like you promised."

Emilio watched me with deep, intense eyes, full of fire, full of possibility. I waited for him to invite me again, to insist that I come with him, to tell me that nothing ever meant anything until he met me. I waited for him to grab me by the shoulders and push me against the wall, to smother my mouth with his, to swallow all the protests and doubts.

I wanted him to kiss me and make me believe it all again, to say that he wanted nothing if not to take me on his motorcycle, to ride all the way to the sea.

Maybe I would've said yes, if he'd asked one more time.

Maybe I would've left immediately, jumped on the back of that bike and never looked back.

But he didn't ask again, and when I wrapped my arms around him, he pressed his lips to my forehead, lingered for an eternity. When he finally pulled away, I looked into his eyes and smiled.

He squeezed my hand, whispered my name.

My heart fluttered.

My heart aches.

To feel it.

To deny it.

Life.

Death.

Possibilities.

Endings.

CHAPTER 30

The Holy Trinity had arrived. A blessing and a curse, as it had always been with my sisters.

I'd been hiding in the barn, waiting until they unloaded the luggage and cleared all the small talk. My heart was still raw from this afternoon, from watching Emilio test the kitchen door one last time, pack up his tools, start up his motorcycle. I'd memorized the smell of his leather jacket, the feel of his lips on my skin, the way the bike's deep rumble rattled through my chest. I'd archived it all, replayed it a hundred times to be sure, because he'd be gone tomorrow, a new life on the road.

I'd given him no reason to wait. I had to let him go.

Now, as I walked up toward the house, a dull ache throbbed with every step.

Lourdes, Celi, and Mari were in the dining room with my parents, chatter floating out through the window like little birds. They were playing the "everything's gonna be okay" game. In this round, they passed around Mom's empanadas, fresh from the new oven, and poured Malbec that Lourdes had brought from their winery in Mendoza.

I leaned against the side of the house and listened, let their laughter seep into my heart. This is how I wanted to remember us. Happy. Carefree. Together. Unbroken. I let it fill me up, imprint on my memories. If I was lucky, when the demon struck, it would let this one be.

I slipped inside. Tiptoed through the kitchen, air still scented with smoke and fresh sawdust, things ruined and rebuilt. I stopped in the dining room doorway before anyone noticed. They looked different in person than they had on Skype. Lourdes was tan and fresh faced, her dark hair gleaming. Celi looked more like her each year, and now they had the same hair, long and full like mine. Mari sat between my parents, and both of them looked happy too, eyes shining, the mood deceptively light.

"Welcome home," I said.

"Juju! Where were you?" My sisters squealed in unison and pulled me into a group hug, and I marveled again at the miracle.

For the first time in five years, all four Hernandez sisters were together under our Blackfeather roof. All four of us were home.

Dearly beloved, we are gathered here to say good-bye.

Mom sat across from me at the kitchen table after she'd tucked Papi into bed, her hands wrapped around one of Celi's bird mugs. She'd replaced her usual late night maté with coffee.

"Papi's not well," she said. "Juju, you have done wonders for him this summer, *mi amor*. But he's . . . Very soon he'll need professional care."

From the chair next to me, Mari reached under the table and found my hand.

"Home care is too expensive," Lourdes told me. That's how it felt, as if she were telling me, as if they'd already had this discussion without me. "It's not really an option for us."

I knew this conversation would happen, but now that I was in the middle of it, everything felt surreal and twisted, and beneath the table, my legs trembled. "So we let him get worse? Ignore him?"

"No, Juju," Celi said.

Mom pulled a letter from beneath her place mat. "We're not ignoring him, *querida*. Never."

I took the paper from her hands, but as soon as I saw the letterhead, I knew what it meant.

Transitions.

It was a welcome letter.

They'd already made the arrangements.

"It's a nice place, Juju," Mom said. "Top-notch. And they have excellent financial assistance. It's right near my hospital. I'll go every day on lunch hour, after work. You can see him too, whenever you want."

I squeezed Mari's hand, crushed it under the table, waiting for her to put up a fight. To jump up and knock over her chair and convince Mom and Lourdes we'd find some way to keep him home. But she just frowned at me, big and compassionate, and then it hit me.

"You knew," I whispered. "All this time . . ." The rest of the pieces clicked into place, a picture emerging from the broken haze. I pulled out of Mari's grasp. "All you guys knew."

"You're going off to college," Mom said. "It's not safe for Papi to stay here alone. Home care is too expensive."

"What about your retirement money?" I asked.

"I went over the statements." Lourdes thumbed through a pile of paperwork spread out on the table. "They can't dip into the retirement accounts without penalties since Papi's so young. Even if they liquidated some of their other investments, it wouldn't be enough. Not long term. And where would that leave Mom?"

"Use my college money," I said. "I can take out more loans."

Celi sighed. "No, Juju. Anyway, it's not enough."

"It's like, tens of thousands—"

"Celi's right," Lourdes said. "We'd burn through it fast. Transitions is the best option."

"But Papi—"

"Papi knows what's best too. It's what he wants." Mom tried to be firm, but her voice was weary, as if the weight of one more decision would break her. "The best thing we can do now is live. Live your life, Juju. Make your college plans. See your friends. *That's* your life, *querida*. It's important to Papi that you enjoy it."

"*This* is my life," I said. "You guys. And Papi."

"Don't be upset," Celi said, clearly upset. She kept blowing her nose on a napkin. "We still have time with him. This probably won't happen right away—we could be talking weeks. Months, more likely. The doctors can't predict—"

"Then why did you already sign the papers?" I asked.

"We had to be prepared," Mom said. "And now, after the fire . . . now we know it's happening sooner rather than later."

"It was an accident," I said. "It could've happened to anyone."

"But it didn't." Mom shook her head. "It happened to your father."

"It was my fault. I shouldn't have left him alone and—"

"He's sick, *mi amor*," Mom said. "He can't stay at home with you forever. We have to start making the transition."

Transition. If I never heard that word again, it would be too soon.

Mom had obviously made all the arrangements, and my sisters had known, and no one told me, and soon they'd ship Papi off to a new home, a strange place, a room without sharp corners and stoves and other dangerous objects.

My sisters looked at one another around the table with sad eyes and frowns and crinkled foreheads, and I opened my mouth to scream, to fight, to take a stand where Mari wouldn't. But I didn't make a sound.

Beneath all the anger at being edged out of the discussion, behind the embarrassment at not being able to look after Papi, a single emotion rose from the darkest part of my heart and sucked up my voice, my air, all the fight I had left. It was blacker than anything I'd ever felt, even the day of the fire.

Relief.

I closed my eyes and pressed my cheek to the place mat. It smelled like coffee, and Pancake shuffled across the kitchen and put his head on my lap.

Mari inched closer, ran her fingers through my hair. My nerves untangled, and I let myself be lulled by her touch.

"There's one more thing, Juju," she whispered, and I knew what was coming. It was in the gentleness of her hands, the softness of her voice. She didn't want to say it, but she had to, and I squeezed my eyes shut harder, focused on Pancake's warm breath on my legs, his fur tickling my knees.

They were selling the bike.

CHAPTER 31

Valentina was silent in the early morning, statuesque in the old barn. Sunlight filtered in through the gaps in the wood, and dust motes swirled before my eyes, but not a speck landed on the motorcycle. Back at the house my sisters flitted and buzzed, cooked breakfast, divided up the newspaper. But in honor of the day that officially started my summer, I'd put on the too-tight cutoffs and the ripped-up Van Halen shirt and snuck outside alone.

Now I sipped my coffee in the dusty barn, shared the solitude with Valentina.

A beige envelope poked out from between the speedometer and the handlebars. It was addressed to me.

After the family meeting with my sisters and Mom, I'd spent last night in my room, recording my long goodbyes on the final pages of the *Book of Broken Hearts*. Emilio. Papi. Valentina. I'd fallen asleep like that, the book a cold weight across my lap, my soul wandering through a shadowy dreamscape. It was dawn when I opened my eyes again. Something had tugged me from sleep, a gentle, familiar sound that enticed me to open my eyes, but it was gone by the time I'd fully awoken, a fading and irretrievable dream.

Only it wasn't a dream. It was Emilio, the growl of his motorcycle. He'd snuck in at dawn, left his final good-bye in an envelope scrawled with my name, underlined twice.

I set my coffee on the workbench and straddled the bike, turned the ignition key. It took me seven tries at the kickstart, pausing intermittently to de-wedge these impossible shorts, but I finally nailed it. Valentina thundered beneath me, anxious after her thirty-year idle to hit the road.

Papi was right—it was the sound of happiness.

No one heard it but me.

I couldn't argue with my sisters about selling it. Papi had more important things to focus on now, and the money would help, and it's not like Transitions had a motorcycle garage for all their ex-biker clientele, just in case one of the patients wanted to take the ol' girls out for a spin.

I tugged the envelope from the handlebars. It was heavier than I'd expected, thick with a letter and a trinket. I removed the note first, crumpled and soft as if had been written decades ago instead of hours. It looked like something from the book, which is exactly where it would end up, tacked at the end of all the heartbreaks. It was our legacy, the Hernandez sisters and those notorious Vargas boys. Mari'd been right all along, and now my heart was broken by a Vargas too, even though he hadn't done it on purpose. Even though he'd saved my heart first.

The end result was the same.

I unfolded the note.

J-

Hey. Everything should be set with the bike. Any problems, call Duke or Samuel. <u>NOT</u> Marcus—he's a little too excited to help you, if you know what I mean.

~~I wanted to see you one more time~~

I'm writing this because I know you'll still be snoring away when I get there. I hope you're at least having a few good dreams (about me—ha ha). Anyway, I prolly won't see you today before I hit the road—I'm leaving right after work. My last day at Duchess.

~~I don't I'm not No matter what happens with your family or anything else~~

~~Whatever happens~~

Sorry. I'm all over the place. I'm telling you something here, for real. Don't settle, okay? Not for anything. I mean it. You only get this one chance at life, far as I know. Take it. Even if it's not with me.

Man. If I keep philosophizing like this, Samuel's gonna kick my ass. Better keep it our little secret.

I'll be thinking of you. Always.

Love.

-E

P.S. I stole the flower from your hair that night at the Bowl (another thing you can't tell Samuel—goes without saying). Sorry, but I'm keeping it. I'm leaving you a fair trade. Something to remember me by.

P.P.S. No regrets, princesa.

I tipped the envelope into my hand and examined Emilio's fair trade, sparkling in the sunlight like it had the first time I'd seen it dangling from his fingers. The key chain, the Puerto Rican flag with the silver star, something to remember him by. I folded it into my hand and closed my eyes, felt the rumble of the bike deep in my bones.

No regrets . . .

Was that even possible? I had lots of regrets. Regrets that I wasn't with him on the road right now. Regrets that I didn't get to spend more time with Papi before he got sick or that I didn't ask my sisters to come home sooner so we could all be together. I even had regrets about how things had changed with Zoe and Christina.

But my biggest regret was that I never told Emilio how I really felt about him.

He was right—we only had this one life. We could wish for the past all day long. We could look at old pictures and tell ourselves the same old stories, but they were just that—stories. Memories. They happened. And maybe they were wonderful and amazing, and maybe they changed our lives in ways we'd never be changed again, but they no longer existed. By the time we stopped to reflect on one moment, it was gone, and another one was instantly upon us, also destined to pass.

I miss us, Jude. I miss the old days, the "us" in your scrapbook.

Zoe'd said it the other day as if the "us" in the scrapbook was somehow different from the "us" in reality, a better version we could jump back to at will. I missed her too, missed our carefree times together, but I'd spent my whole summer waiting on that time machine, and time just didn't work that way. The old days didn't exist. No matter how long you waited, no matter how hard you wished, no matter how much you missed the past, time marched forward. Everything ended eventually—storms, friendships, days, health, love, life. And Zoe and me, maybe our friendship didn't have to end this summer, but our past—the way things used to be between us—had to end. Those moments had already happened, had already ended. We were just too busy wishing otherwise to notice.

I was done wishing.

Done waiting.

Done being scared.

Done ignoring the fact that Papi wouldn't get better.

Done running from my feelings for Emilio, pretending I could say good-bye like it didn't kill me to see him go.

Done letting my sisters tell me how to live.

Done living in the past.

I turned off the engine and uncurled my fingers like a flower. I stared at the flag key chain, red and blue standing out against the silver, and it hit me all at once, like all the force of the wind and the river and the sun.

There was no going back to the way things *were*, because all you ever got was the way things *are*. One moment. Then another. What you did with that moment was up to you.

No regrets.

"We're not selling the bike!" I burst through the kitchen door panting like the dog, and Celi and Mari looked up from their newspapers and released a coordinated sigh, which Pancake helpfully mimicked.

"We talked about this," Celi said. She and Mari exchanged a glance, like, *Here we go again.* "What the hell are you wearing? Are those my shorts?"

"You guys don't understand. Where's Papi?" I peeked into the living room, but the television was silent.

"Lourdes is helping him sort clothes upstairs," Mari said. "Mom wants us to start paring down his stuff."

I tried not to think about what that meant. "We're keeping the bike."

Celi folded up the arts section and set it gently on the table, smoothed out the crease.

Mari shook her head. "Juju, sit down. It's—"

"I'm not letting you sell the bike. We worked really hard on it this summer. Papi never wanted to sell it."

Celi rolled her eyes. "Juju, you're being a little crazy. He can't ride it. Ever."

"He practically burned the house down!" Mari said.

"We don't even know if it's safe," Celi said. "Just because you hired some guy—"

"He's not some guy," I said.

Mari cleared her throat. *Thank you, Captain Obvious.* "The point is, Papi can't ride it."

"He's not some guy," I said again. Emilio may have been finished with Valentina, on the road, out of our lives, but my heart knew the truth. I'd violated the oath by getting involved with a Vargas, and I'd fallen in love with him. And even if I never got the chance to kiss him again, breaking the oath to be with him was something I *didn't* regret.

"He's Emilio Vargas," I said.

Celi sucked in a breath, her eyes wide with shock, and I pressed on.

"Emilio Vargas is the one who restored the bike. I'm sorry I didn't tell you, and I'm sorry that his brother hurt you, but that's got nothing to do with Emilio. He's been helping us all summer and we finally got the bike running and there's no way I'm letting you sell it."

"What's going on?" Lourdes appeared in the archway between the kitchen and the living room, a towel wrapped around her head. "Hey, is that my Van Halen shirt? Where did you—"

"Not now, Lourdes," Mari said.

"Are you all fighting without me?" Lourdes's teasing smirk faded as soon as she realized that we *were* fighting without her.

"Tell me I heard that wrong." Celi's voice trembled, as if just mentioning the Vargas name unleashed all the memories she'd spent so long repressing.

"You didn't," I said. "I—"

"Juju!" Mari stared at me hard. "This isn't the time—"

"When would be better?" I asked. "Next week? Next year?"

"Stop," Lourdes said. "Whatever it is, let's talk it out. Come on, Juju. Sit down."

"I'm not sitting down," I said.

"You knew about this?" Celi asked Mari.

"Knew what?" Lourdes said.

"Long story," Mari said.

"It's my story," I said. "And I'm saying—"

"Stop." Celi held up her hands, her jaw clenching and unclenching. "Will someone please tell me what Emilio *fucking* Vargas has to do with our family?"

Lourdes scrunched up her face. "Emilio Vargas? What?"

"Juju . . ." Mari slumped backward in her chair. "Maybe you should sit down."

"I'm not sitting. I'm in love with him." The words were out of my mouth, running around like ants on the kitchen floor.

"Aw, Juju's in love?" Lourdes said. "But you were just . . . Wait, who are we talking about?"

Mari, Celi, and I all spit it out. "Emilio fucking Vargas!"

The Holy Trinity stared me down, Lourdes with utter confusion, Celi with a scary mix of pain and anger, and Mari with that subtle I-told-you-so flare. The clock ticked away as my sisters burned holes through my face with their eyes.

Celi finally rose from her chair. She crossed the kitchen and boxed me in at the counter, but before she could speak or scream or pull my hair, Pancake yelped and shot out through his doggy door.

Mari's eyes widened. "Guys, where's Papi?"

Lourdes shrugged. "I thought he was down here with you."

"You were supposed to be sorting his clothes," Mari said.

"We finished," Lourdes said. "He didn't feel like doing any more, and I wanted a shower, so—"

"You can't leave him alone!" Mari said.

"But I thought . . . and then the fighting . . . I'm sorry."

I pushed through Celi's arms. "You guys! Shut up!"

Pancake yelped again, louder than before, and Valentina's helicopter sputter cut through the air.

All four Hernandez sisters tumbled out through the newly repaired kitchen door, tearing it off the hinges for the second time this summer, and bolted for the barn.

Papi sat on the Harley like the king of the road in his old helmet and Las Arañas Blancas jacket, rockin' the best smile ever.

My heart did a backflip. He'd snuck out while we were bickering, went straight for Valentina. He belonged on that bike, and thirty years had vanished from his face with the turn of that little brass key and a jump on the kickstart, and now he looked at us like Clint Eastwood in *The Outlaw Josey Wales* when he was all, *Are you gonna pull those pistols or whistle "Dixie"?*

Papi didn't actually say that, but still. It was a very kick-ass cowboy moment all around. Yeah, it was scary. I didn't know if he could handle it, if he'd fall, if he'd forget some crucial step and zoom off into the wall. But it was his choice.

All along, Papi'd wanted his last ride. And now he'd get it.

My sisters were speechless; they stood at my side with big

gaping mouths and eyes, and I knew they'd seen it too. That glow. That timelessness.

Fuck yeah. Our father was so, so badass.

Valentina growled beneath him, roaring louder as Papi cranked the throttle. He seemed to melt into the bike, as if the machine were merely an extension of his limbs, the thrumming engine his heart and soul. My stomach flooded with butterflies.

Papi winked at me.

If any of my sisters meant to challenge him, she'd lost her voice. We all stood aside, utterly mute as he lifted his feet from the ground. The bike rolled through the barn doorway and zoomed off, joy floating on the air behind him.

Pancake led the charge out of the barn, and we watched as Papi circled the property, Valentina rocketing around the house, back down the driveway, across the front lawn, behind the barn, back around again. He was moving too fast for us to see his face, but in my heart, I knew he was smiling. Valentina and Papi were one, a blur of chrome and black leather, the sun shining down on all of us, and for just a moment I wondered if maybe he'd found a way to outrun El Demonio after all.

I wish Emilio were here.

The thought climbed up and attached itself to my heart. I missed him. I needed him. He should've been there to see Papi take his ride.

On the third loop, Papi and Valentina dipped behind the barn again, our heads turning all at once to watch. Seconds later the bike shot out in another blur. Blue and white and chrome, no leather.

The angle was all wrong.

The speed was off.

Almost instantly Valentina sputtered and conked out in the grass, dropped down on her side.

Papi wasn't with her.

CHAPTER 32

The doctor didn't want to give us any information until Mom arrived, but in our short time at Blackfeather General, Mari had already developed a reputation among the staff. All she had to do was raise her eyebrows, and that fresh-off-the-med-school-boat doctor was singing the whole tale.

Papi had a dislocated shoulder, bruised ribs, and a bunch of scrapes and cuts. On that last trip around the barn, he must've blanked out, forgot where he was, let go of the bike. It rode on without him and sputtered out quickly, but not before throwing him off. He'd thudded onto the earth, landed on his side. He was lucky, the young doc said.

Lucky it was grass and dirt and not concrete or gravel.

Lucky he was wearing a helmet and leather.

Lucky he wasn't going very fast at the time.

It was my fault Papi was here, laid up in a hospital bed not unlike the one he'd probably die in. It was my fault he'd dug up the yard. My fault he'd started that fire. All I wanted to do was help him, make him happy, make him well. It seemed I'd only managed to advance his disease, to shove him a few steps closer to Death's door.

It didn't matter what my sisters threw at me next; no words or threats could make me feel any worse. I tugged the Van Halen shirt over my knees and folded in on myself, wishing I could disappear, wishing I could turn into a tumbleweed and blow on down the road.

I am dust.

"It's okay, Juju," Mari whispered into my hair. I was enveloped by her scent, lavender and cigarettes, as she rubbed my back. "Papi's okay. It's not your fault."

I looked into her face. She offered a tiny smile and wiped my tears with her thumbs.

"I think maybe you were right," she said. "Papi deserved that ride."

Celi and Lourdes nodded too, though Celi had her legs crossed away from me, arms folded over her chest.

"It was stupid and dangerous and crazy," Mari said. "He could've killed himself. But it's not your fault. It was his choice."

Lourdes ditched her chair and knelt before me. She squeezed my hands. "Our father is really sick, baby. Some days he seems fine, other days he doesn't, but either way, he's still sick. We're at the point now where every day could be like today. He's deteriorating."

A whisper was all I could manage. "I know."

"But you did good," she said. "You gave him back something he lost. He's really proud of you, Juju. We all are."

Lourdes took the chair next to mine. Mari was still on the other side—a Hernandez sandwich. I felt warm and safe in a way I hadn't with my sisters in a long time, and nothing would be easier than to stay here. To let them figure it all out, tell me what to do. To follow their rules.

But I couldn't. Not anymore.

"I'm not getting the genetic test," I said.

Mari squeezed me closer. "We'll be there together. No matter what happens."

"It's okay to be scared," Lourdes said.

I pulled away from Mari. "I've thought about it for weeks. It's not because I'm scared. It's because I don't want to know."

"Juju, we need to be prepared," Mari said. "Once we know, we can plan for the future. Or something . . ." She trailed off, ran a hand through her bed-head hair. "Shit. I don't want to know either, tell you the truth."

"I want to know," Celi finally said. She still wasn't looking at me, but talking was better than silence. "I'm not good without a plan."

Lourdes nodded. "I'm doing the test too. Juju, why don't we talk about this later. We'll—"

"There's more." I took a deep breath. I had their attention. No sense holding back anything else. "I'm deferring enrollment for a semester at DU. Just one, so I can help figure things out with Papi this fall."

Mari shook her head, my shoulder suddenly crushed in a vise grip. "You can't—"

"Which one of you is Juju?" A pink-scrubbed nurse approached the plastic chairs, and I looked up into her round face. "Your father is asking for you, honey. He's stable—seems to be aware of the situation and how he got here, so that's a good sign."

My sisters simultaneously rose, flowers sprouting from concrete. Big, annoying flowers.

"Me first," Mari said.

"I'll go," Lourdes said. "You guys stay here and wait for Mom."

"You and Mari should stay with Juju," Celi said.

Mari shook her head. "I'll handle it. Juju, stay with Lourdes and Celi, and—"

"I'm not staying here," Celi said. "I want to see Papi."

"I'm Juju," I told the nurse. I stood from my chair and held up my hand for them to stop talking, and for the first time in our collective history, the Holy Trinity obeyed.

The nurse left me alone in Papi's room, and the sight stole my breath. He was sprawled in the bed looking limp and small, one arm in a sling, hand taped up. With the other, he tugged at the hospital gown that hung from his wiry frame.

"Jujube," Papi said with a great huff, "I don't think green is my color, *queridita*."

"Shh, shh, none of that." Papi kissed my forehead, then leaned back in his bed, motioning for me to take the chair next to him. "'Hey, Jude, don't make it bad . . .'"

Papi's accent made me smile, and I let him sing the first few verses. Unlike Emilio's friends, he actually knew the lyrics.

"What's so funny? I'm an excellent singer," he said.

"I know. People always sing that song to me, but you're the only one who gets it right."

"Of course, *querida*. How do you think you got your name?"

I shrugged. "The medallion. Saint Jude."

"*Ay, Dios mío*. It's from the Beatles, when we first learned English here."

I pulled my chair closer and rested my hand on Papi's good arm. "I thought you learned in a class?"

"Yes," he said, "and the instructor told us to find music to help us practice. Mom and I could never agree on the same thing, and we'd end up in a big fight, always in Spanish, so that didn't help." Papi took a sip of water from a plastic cup on his bed table.

"One night Mom was flipping channels, and she found this Beatles concert, so we watched. It was a few hours long, and at the end she said, 'Looks like we finally found something to agree on.' Next day I bought all the Beatles cassettes I could find. We listened every night at dinner, wrote down all the words, practiced for our class. By the time your sisters were born, we knew English as well as anyone. Which was good, because with all the babies, we hardly had time for dinner together anymore, forget about talking and music."

I knew they'd emigrated here before my sisters were born, knew they'd had to learn English and set down roots. I also knew that things hadn't always been perfect between them, but they loved each other more than anything. It was there in the way Mom put her hand on his shoulder when she leaned over to scoop *ensalada rusa* onto his plate. It was there when Papi looked at her; even through the demon haze, his eyes still lit up the moment she came home from work. They'd built their forever together, raised four kids, woven an entire life of memories and laughter and tears.

And now there was this thing, this awful illness that would finally come between them, taking Papi away from her one memory at a time.

"Don't cry, *mi querida.* I didn't get to the good part," he said. "Fast-forward many years, Mom learned she was pregnant with you. She came to my work to tell me. I thought she was playing a joke. She said, 'I told the doctor the same thing. God must be playing a practical joke.'"

"Is this supposed to make me feel better?"

Papi patted my hand. "We were surprised, that's all. We thought we were done having babies. But we were happy, Juju. We went out dancing that night to celebrate, only Mom was too tired to dance, so we ate a lot of food instead.

"You turned out to be a restless baby," he said. "Mom couldn't sleep because you were always rolling around like you couldn't wait to get out. One night I sang to you to see if it would calm you down. The problem was, whenever I stopped, you'd kick and squirm. So I thought of the longest song I ever knew, 'Hey Jude,' and I sang it, night after night. After a while, it became our song—yours and mine. By then it was my favorite. I told Mom it was like you'd already picked your name and I couldn't imagine calling you anything else, and if she didn't like it, we'd be fighting in Spanish again."

Papi closed his eyes, and I thought he might be drifting off, but instead he started humming the song again. *Our* song. It wasn't a hand-me-down or a last-minute grasp at something because they'd run out of ideas. It was mine and his, just like Valentina.

"It's my fault," I finally said, because I already missed him, already missed the Western Channel and his flannels and the motorcycle, all his Argentina stories. "The fire and this . . . and now they're sending you away. . . ."

"No, no, *queridita*. Is that what you think? No." He shook his head. "They're not sending me away. Mom and I . . . we talked about this a long time ago. When we first got the diagnosis. Together, we made the decision. We found the best place. Everything else was just formalities."

"Formalities? But I saw the brochure, and Mom said—"

"She didn't want me to sign the papers at first; she was scared. Maybe thinking the doctors were wrong. But I knew that when things got bad, you and your sisters and your mother . . . you wouldn't be able to take care of me. I didn't want anyone feeling bad about that. It's just the facts."

"That's crazy," I said. "We're fine."

"Mom didn't want to tell you. She wanted us to spend time together this summer. Just you and me." He looked down at his bandages and laughed. "I'm not sure this is what she had in mind."

Tears blurred my eyes and Papi smiled, his own eyes watery but clear. "You're really something, you know that? Of all my girls, you were always the one with the most spirit. I know sometimes you felt a little lost being the youngest, and with your sisters so much older. . . . I wish I could've spent more time with you, Jujube."

I wished it too, but I didn't say anything. I couldn't; my throat was too tight and scratchy.

He put his hand on his heart. "We sure gave El Demonio a run for the money this summer, eh? You and me. Emilio too."

I snapped my head up at the mention of his name.

"You're lucky to have him in your life, *querida*."

"He's not in my life anymore. He's probably halfway to the Grand Canyon."

"Nonsense." Papi waved away my doubts. "Call him. You have to try. Trust me. I know things."

I brushed away more tears. "What things, *viejito*?"

"I know you feel guilty about your sister and Johnny," Papi said. "I know you want to find your own adventures, not always do what your sisters say. They all made their choices. Now it's your turn. You like Emilio, he likes you, he invited you on the trip. Call him."

Figures Emilio told Papi about inviting me. He probably asked for his blessing. "It's not that simple. Emilio doesn't—"

"Look, Juju." Papi jabbed his finger into the table. "There

are two kinds of people in this world. Those who let other people tell them what to do, and those who don't let other people tell them what to do. Call him."

"*You're* telling me what to do."

"That's different. I'm telling you what's already in your heart. *Soy tu padre todavía.*"

I slumped in the chair.

"I really hoped it wouldn't come to this, but you leave me no choice." Papi coughed and made an exaggerated frown. He looked like a big sad clown. One with a cold, because he kept on with that fake cough. "Don't deny the last wish of a dying man."

"Nice try. Riding the Harley was your last wish. *Poof!*" I made a starburst with my fingers.

"What? That was a warm-up wish."

"So you want to waste your *real* last wish on me calling Emilio?"

"No. My real wish is that you get some clothes that fit." He scanned my outfit and shook his head. "Why do you wear that shirt with all the holes, *querida*? You look like a—"

"I'm not the one in a mint-green dress, *viejito*. What would your motorcycle buddies say about that?" I tugged on his sleeve. "Tell me your wish. For real. And you can't say empanadas, either. You know Mari's putting you on a cardboard diet now."

"We'll see about that." Papi grabbed my hands with his unbandaged one and pressed them to his chest. Beneath the scratchy hospital gown, his heart thudded against my fingers, steady, calm, strong. "Okay. No more jokes, *mi querida*. I need you to do something for me. My wish."

I looked at him and smiled. He'd won, cheated his way to the top. As usual.

"*Sí*, Papi. Anything."

Eventually Papi dozed off. When he opened his eyes again, they were bleary and unsettled, and he looked around the room as if he were trying to get his bearings.

"I should . . . go now," he said. "My family is looking for me."

"They know you're here," I said gently. The nurse had warned me this might happen. The stress of the day, the sedatives. His memories.

"Good, good. I don't want them to worry." Behind him, the heart monitor beeped a steady rhythm, bright green peaks and valleys blurring into a hazy zigzag. "Do you have any kids?"

"No kids yet," I whispered.

A smile settled into the folds of his face. "We have three girls and another on the way. My wife is in labor right now."

"Congratulations," I said. "Get some rest, okay?"

He nodded, eyes vacant and polite. The monitor continued its slow beeping, and I sat in the chair beside his bed until his heart slowed, until he drifted back to sleep.

He looked young and untroubled and whole again, but it was temporary. There was no cure; the force of his illness had come upon him like the Animas in spring, swelling and washing away all that the previous seasons had so carefully deposited.

They say you can never step into the same river twice. And maybe that's how it was for Papi now, memories shifting and re-forming soundlessly beneath him while the rest of us sat on the shore and watched. He was getting worse each day, taking longer to bounce back. No one could tell us exactly when, but I knew it now—the old inevitable I'd been outrunning since his diagnosis had finally arrived. And soon—maybe tomorrow, maybe next month—he'd open his eyes and look at me and no amount of stories or videos or songs would remind him that I was his daughter.

That we'd shared this summer together, rebuilding his old Harley.

That he loved me.

My father would be gone.

But Emilio and I had given him that last ride. And for one moment he was alive, more than I'd ever seen him. Not in the past, but right now. For that, despite the fact that I was losing him by degrees, I smiled.

"*Te quiero*, Papi," I whispered.

"You too, Jude." His voice was groggy and thick with medication, but he'd said my name, I was sure of it, and I grabbed on to those words and tucked them inside my heart.

Screw you, Alzheimer's.

I stopped at the entryway to the waiting room and leaned against the wall, my heart strangely light, full of peace. Mom had arrived, and she sat with her back against the hard plastic chair, Celi's hand kneading her left shoulder. In the chair at Mom's right, Lourdes sat up straight, absently stroking Mom's hair. Mari was across from them, and when she caught my eye, I thought she might wave me over, ask for the update.

But she only tilted her head, some silent understanding passing between us. Her gaze slid sideways, and I followed it to the boy sitting next to her, chewing on his thumbnail.

Emilio Vargas looked out across the waiting room and met my eyes.

I dropped my gaze to the floor and smiled. Tentative. Shaking. And then I looked up again, preparing for the worst, hoping for a chance.

Those dimples were a dead giveaway.

CHAPTER 33

True confessions. I've been wrong about at least six things in my life (not naming names, just saying it happens sometimes). But there's one thing I know with absolute certainty.

Right now, it's *way* too early to be awake.

I won't open my eyes—don't need to. The chill crawls across my skin, bringing with it the dewy cold that speaks of before-dawn, and when a warm kiss lands on my lips, I don't care if it's a dream.

"Almost morning," a gentle voice says. He slowly unzips my sleeping bag, rubs my stomach. "Coffee's hot. Birds talkin' like mad."

"Mmm-hmm. About what?" I ask through my sleep-heavy haze.

"You. They couldn't sleep with all your snoring."

I open my eyes and sit up fast, our noses almost touching. "Let's get one thing straight, Vargas. I do *not* snore."

"Bueno, mi osita."

"Call me a bear again and I'll soak your boxers in raw meat. Then you'll see a real bear."

He flashes his dimples. I'm toast.

Eventually the need for coffee and food wins out over the need for kissing, but only by the narrowest margin, and I crawl out of the tent, shivering in the twilight blue haze. Emilio drapes his fleece over my shoulders and hands me a steaming mug of coffee. Behind him, the fire pops, and here's what I'm thinking:

Wow. For all its ridiculous imperfections, life is pretty damn perfect sometimes.

The first pink sliver of light cracks the deep blue sky, and Emilio smiles. "Take that coffee to go."

I pick up my mug and follow him ten short yards to the rocky rim. We find a good spot to sit, let our legs dangle over the edge.

Fifteen miles across this great gash in the earth, tourists are setting up their cameras, anxious to capture every moment through the lens. But on this side, tucked away from the popular spots, Emilio and I are alone, and neither of us brought a camera.

I drain the last of my Dark Moon blend and slip my fingers into Emilio's hand. The last of the morning chill evaporates. No words pass between us after that, just the feeling of his hand in mine, his lips soft on my cheek. The horizon splinters into pink and yellow rifts, then all at once the light stretches its golden fingers through clouds, streaking the sky and illuminating the red rock floor below.

The sun rises over the Grand Canyon, igniting rocks that have been there for two billion years before we were born and will likely remain two billion years after we're gone. My heart aches with the cruel and unimaginable beauty of it. We're nothing. We're everything.

I am dust.

Emilio coaxes the embers in our fire pit back to life. "Ready when you are, *princesa*."

I nod once. He gives me the space I need.

The fire is perfect in the chilly morning air, and I sit on a boulder before it. I slip the heavy black book from my pack and slide it onto my lap, remembering everything my sisters told me. . . .

"I can't believe you found this again." Celi thumbed through the black book. We'd gathered in her room after midnight, like last time. Emilio would be there in the morning to pick me up, to ferry us onto the open road.

I promised Papi I would go. It was the first in his ongoing series of last wishes—*viejito loco.*

Once I officially accepted the invitation, my sisters and Mom agreed—probably part of Papi's unending "last wishes" preconditions—to hold off on further discussion about Papi's future until I returned. He was released from the hospital the day after the accident, and Mari and Celi were staying in Blackfeather for the rest of the summer. Lourdes would return in the fall. We didn't have forever, but we didn't have to figure it all out in a day, either.

"It's a book of ill repute." I leaned over Celi's shoulder and scanned a page Lourdes had written about sneaking down to the river with some guy.

"It's not a book of ill repute," Celi said. "It's a . . ." Her voice faded as she turned the page, flipped to some other broken-hearted recollection.

"I had no idea you guys got around so much," I said.

"Crushing on boys is not the same as getting around," Mari said. "Some of those boys were just . . . It was, like, one dance in junior high."

"Still," I said. "No wonder you never wanted me to see it. It would've ruined my virgin eyes."

Lourdes gasped. "You're still a—"

"It's a book of old ghosts." Celi had stopped on a page of Johnny's stuff. "Look at this crap! Wedding invitations? Baby names? We weren't even . . . God, I thought he was my entire future." She was in her own world, fighting with the memories all over again.

Shame and sadness burned my cheeks, and I looked out the window and waited for it to pass.

"It's all heartbreak," Celi whispered. "Why did we keep this?"

"It seemed like a good idea at the time." Mari ashed her cigarette into a half-empty Coke can. "And it did help me get over Ham Camari."

"You dated a guy named *Ham*?" I asked, grateful for the redirect. "You didn't list him in the book."

"I used a fake name," Mari said. "Harry Smith. It only lasted a month."

"Thank the Lord." Celi finally closed the book on Johnny and smiled. She was probably grateful for the redirect too. "If you married him, your name would be Mari Camari."

"Oh. My. God!" Mari doubled over. "I never thought of that!"

"Are you kidding me?" I asked. "It's so obvious!"

"His name was Ham!" she said. "I kind of stopped right there, you know?"

"Hello, Simon and Schuster?" I made my best Mari impersonation, which was pretty impressive, truth be told. "I'm calling about that five-billion-dollar book I sold you? This is Mari Camari. Yes, I'm serious. Mari Camari. Camari. C-A—no, it's not a joke."

"At least he didn't have Wesley Laytonitis," she said.

"Mari!" Celi squealed at the same time Lourdes gave Celi the evil eye.

"You weren't supposed to tell anyone," Lourdes said to Celi. "I didn't even put him in the book."

"What's Wesley Laytonitis?" I asked.

"You tell her," Lourdes said to Mari. "Since you know all about it now, thanks to Mouth over there."

"Like I could keep that to myself." Celi laughed.

"The *whole* story?" Mari asked Lourdes.

"You *have* to tell it now, don't you?" Lourdes said.

Mari dropped the end of her cigarette into the soda and scooted down onto the floor. She was, like, giddy. Very un-Mari. Goose bumps rolled down my skin when she looked at me. "Wesley said he was in love with Lourdes, right? Like from day one. And they went out for six months."

"Seven," Lourdes said.

"Hey, you wanna tell it?"

Lourdes shook her head. "You go ahead."

"Six or seven months. Anyway, one night, she decides he's *the one*, and they're gonna do it."

"Lower your voice!" Lourdes was bright red. I'd never seen her so embarrassed.

"Sorry," Mari said. Not that she lowered her voice or anything. "They were supposed to . . . you know. Only right when things were getting hot and heavy, he . . ." She grabbed her stomach to stifle another laugh. "Dude started barking."

"Like . . . yelling at her?" I asked.

"Barking," Mari said. "Straight-up barking like Pancake. *A-rooo! Woof woof woof!*"

Lourdes giggled and winged a pillow at us. "You guys are terrible."

"Anyway," Mari said, "she made up some excuse not to go through with it, thinking maybe he was nervous and next time it wouldn't be an issue. Only it was an issue."

"Four more times," Celi said.

"Five," Lourdes said. "Including once at his parents' house, when they were downstairs watching TV. And even *that* didn't help."

"Guess he liked it doggy style," Celi said.

Mari bent over with another giggle fit, and when she straightened up again, her face was streaked with tears.

"I'm sorry, what was that, Mari Camari?" Lourdes asked. "Did you say something, Mari Camari?"

Mari swatted her with a pillow.

"See what your future holds, Juju?" Lourdes asked. "Don't say we didn't warn you about . . . boys." She flashed a look at Celi, then back to me, and I knew she'd almost said *Vargas* boys. Mari had come around to Emilio, grown to actually like him, hard as it was for her to admit. And after the initial shock, even Lourdes seemed okay; she'd been chatting him up ever since, asking about the bike, how he learned to fix it, how he knew exactly what to do.

But Celi was still struggling with it. She'd graduated from outright cold-shouldering to meaningless small talk whenever he was around, but she still made excuses to leave the room when he came over, to go to bed early or walk to the river to avoid his presence. I knew she wasn't over Johnny, and maybe the idea of Emilio and me would never sit well with her. But she was trying. And I loved her for it.

For once, it seemed that the Holy Trinity and I had finally come to agree on something: I needed to live my own life, take my own chances, make my own mistakes, just like they had.

And maybe, after all that, they wouldn't be mistakes.

My sisters and I eventually drifted into a comfortable silence, each of us thinking about the history in that book, maybe, or everything we'd been through as a family, all the heartbreaks that were still to come. I thought about Zoe and Christina on their way to the Dunes, their last road trip, the places they'd see together. I'd sent them both letters wishing them safe travels. Maybe they'd send me a postcard. Maybe they'd call when they got back, or when they got settled in at college. Maybe they wouldn't, and they'd end up in the book. It was uncertain, like life.

I was starting to be okay with that.

"Girls." Mari clapped her hands once, startling us out of our haze with her usual melodramatic flare. "One more oath." She stood and rummaged through Celi's closet. "To make it official."

"Not this again," Lourdes said.

"Mari, you need to chill. I'm serious," Celi said. "You'll give yourself a heart attack with all that drama."

I raised my hand. "If you bring out a knife, I'm out."

"No knives." Mari rejoined us on the floor. She'd found a tiny little tea light in a ceramic Easter-egg shell and she set her lighter to it. "Jude Catherine Hernandez, it's time we initiate you properly."

Now, at the edge of this great wide gash in the earth, I hug the book to my chest and whisper the new vow my sisters gave me.

I, Jude Hernandez, vow to always and forever, under all circumstances, within or outside of my control . . .

"You need to figure out the rest yourself," Mari said. And that's when she handed me the book.

So this is me, sitting on a rock surrounded by billions of years of everything and nothing all at once, figuring it out myself.

The fire crackles with anticipation.

It seems fitting that the book that held the long and winding record of Hernandez heartbreak would meet its end here, and I take one last look at the cover, trace my fingers over the title. *The Book of Broken Hearts.*

I tip it into the fire.

It bubbles and curls and smokes, and I watch it burn, say my final good-byes to the past.

Eventually the small fire burns down to embers, and I douse the last of it with water and dirt. The oath, the pictures, the flowers, the words, the stories of broken hearts, the old ghosts . . . nothing but smoke and ash, and I take a satisfying breath, exhale it out over the canyon.

I look to the rim where we had our coffee at sunrise, where Emilio has been patiently waiting on the bike. He smiles when he sees me. Stubble, dimples, scar. My heart lights up from the inside out.

He cocks his head to the side, dangles my silver Puerto Rican flag key chain like a dare, and I answer with a raised eyebrow, a grin.

Yes, I'm ready.

He's already packed up camp. We've been on the road two weeks; he's gotten it down to a science. We still have a ways to go, and when we finally return home, I know Papi will be different. He's at the stage where each day costs him a little more.

Yeah, I promised him I'd take this trip, but not because it really was his final wish. I did it because he was right—it *was* in my heart. And even if it ends right now, if Emilio turns us back toward Colorado and the road home, I'll still know it was the most amazing experience of my life. I looked upon ancient rocks and cave paintings, rode a mule to the bottom of the canyon and back up again, watched California condors with a six-foot wingspan float on the currents over the gorge. I rafted on the Colorado River and slept in a cave with baby bats and counted more stars that I had numbers for, including Orion, our self-appointed travel guardian, who follows us on every road, into every forest and ancient riverbed.

And I've done it side by side with Emilio Vargas, the boy I'd been warned against my entire life.

I smile now as I remember that first day at Duchess, how much has changed, how much I'm leaving in the fading smoke as I walk back toward the motorcycle.

Without a word, Emilio holds out his hand, and I take it, no doubts this time. I swing my leg up and over the seat, strap on my helmet, and slip my arms around his waist.

He turns the key.

He jumps on the kickstart.

Valentina roars to life.

We zoom back onto the road in a sapphire blur of blue and white and chrome, the wind at our backs, the morning sun warm on our faces, and then the moment is gone.

I have no idea what the next moment will bring.

But it's a new day. I'm rockin' a brand-new pair of super-cute jeans. And I love the wind in my hair.

I'm ready for the unknown.

No regrets, princesa.

ACKNOWLEDGMENTS

True confessions: the earliest seeds of this story were planted in my subconscious way back in the eighties by the movie *Grease 2*. I spent most of middle school crushing on Michael Carrington, and I learned all the words to "Cool Rider" and "(Love Will) Turn Back the Hands of Time," and I totally ran around singing and pretending I was Stephanie Zinone (only with slightly less awesome hair).

Since then lots of non-imaginary people have worked hard—*without* musical accompaniment—to help me bring this book to life.

Love and endless gratitude to my husband, Alex, who introduced me to all the best things: Spaghetti Westerns, empanadas, Malbec, coffee under the predawn stars, road trips. "You see, in this world there's two kinds of people, my friend . . ." Thanks for being my B.G.O. and for taking such good care of me.

Jen Klonsky, even though you've never experienced the cinematic wonder that is *Grease 2*, you're still an honorary Pink Lady and an Editor of Awesome, and working with you on Jude and Emilio's story has been one of the greatest joys of my career (not to mention, like, totally fun). Those *FNL* references will always be for you!

Ted Malawer, frankly, I'd be lost in this crazy business without you. Six years, several books, and billions of neurotic e-mails (um, mine, not yours!) after our first call, you continue to inspire me, and I'm grateful for your encouragement, patience, and sense of humor every step of the way.

To Patrick Price, who graciously welcomed our new partnership and this book with enthusiasm and dedication, and to the entire crew at Simon Pulse, including Craig Adams, Mara Anastas, Bethany Buck, Jim Conlin, Paul Crichton, Katherine Devendorf, Nicole Ellul, Jessica Handelman, Victor Iannone, Russell Gordon, Dan Potash, Mary Marotta, Christina Pecorale, Lucille Rettino, Dawn Ryan, Emma Sector, Michael Strother, Sara Saidlower, Carolyn Swerdloff, and countless others: You guys are Team Fabulous. Seriously. You need matching leather jackets, and if it were up to me, you'd get Sugar Sweet Sunshine cupcakes every day.

High fives to my fellow writers and readers who offered editorial feedback, moral support, wine, cookies, or some or all of the above, including Zoe Strickland, Amy Mair, Courtney Koschel, Jessi Kirby, Heidi R. Kling, Rhonda Stapleton, Aprilynne Pike, Bronwen Durocher, and the 2009

Debutantes. Your contributions enhanced both this story and my well-being, which is no small feat.

Hugs to my friends and family, especially Dad, who took me out on the Harley way before I thought it was cool, and who patiently read through all the Jude and Emilio kissing scenes just to fact-check my highly questionable biker babe authenticity; Mom, who ensures that the world knows the instant my books hit the shelves; Moma, who taught me how to make the best *ensalada rusa* ever (second to hers, of course); and Popa, my favorite *viejito*, who always laughs when I say completely inappropriate stuff *en español.*

A super shout-out to readers, book bloggers, librarians, teachers, booksellers, and all the other bookworms of the world, without whom I'd be talking to myself. Well, more than usual. You guys rock!

Finally, a very special thanks to Emmalie Conner and Cheryl Parrish of the Colorado Alzheimer's Association, who generously donated their time and expertise to review my manuscript. Though this story is a work of fiction, I endeavored to portray a family's experience of early onset Alzheimer's authentically, and any errors are my own.

Currently, more than five million Americans are living with Alzheimer's disease. To the families here and abroad who've been touched by Alzheimer's, you are forever in my heart.

Things are about to get scandalous. . . .

Read on for a sneak peek of Sarah Ockler's newest novel.

#NOTEVENCLOSE

If a picture is worth a thousand words, a picture tagged on Miss Demeanor's Scandal of the Month page is worth about a million. Especially when the story all those words tell is an absolute lie.

Well, mostly a lie.

The part about falling asleep in his arms is sort of true. I don't remember the details about the horse, or how it got into the living room exactly, but judging from the smell that morning, that part's true too. And yes, the Harvard-bound debate team captain definitely cannonballed into the pond wearing only tuxedo socks and silver fairy wings. *Everyone* got shots of that.

But there's no way the other stuff happened.

Not like the pictures are saying it did.

A SPECIAL MESSAGE TO LAVENDER OAKS SWORDFISH ON THE OCCASION OF PROM

MISS DEMEANOR

2,002 likes 👍

92 talking about this

Friday, April 25

It's prom weekend, fishes, and you know what that means: Sex! Scandal! And . . . glitter?

Yes, glitter, as you'd expect from Lavender Oaks's first-ever Mythical Creatures Promenade. I'm not sure what that even means, but everything's better with sparkle, so let's raise a glass to the planning committee for spreading a dash of pixie dust on an otherwise pedestrian tradition. Cheers!

For those of you who haven't planned the ruination of your innocence at one of the many after-parties, may I suggest popping by the east field for the school-sponsored medieval joust and mutton roast? Principal Zeff assures me that while the lances are made of foam, the horses and meat (mutually exclusive, despite recent legislation) are the real deal.

Chain mail not your thing? Rumor has it the (e)lectronic Vanities Intervention League is hosting a postprom reenactment of the fake moon landing on the grassy knoll, but they don't believe in Facebook; we can neither confirm nor deny reports. Still, if anyone spots any (e)VIL club members at the dance, snap a few pics. I'd love to see those girls rock an updo with their tinfoil hats.

Team Tinfoil Hat pics aside, don't forget to upload and share your juiciest weekend shots here on the Miss Demeanor page, tagged #scandal to enter my Scandal of the Month contest. This is it, kids—the very last #scandal before graduation. Make it count! Winners will be immortalized with a blinking gold star and, of course, eternal humiliation. Can't put a price on that!

Speaking of fame and glory, today we crossed the magic number: 2,000 fans! But it's no time to rest on our überpopular laurels. Millions of Americans have yet to profess their loyalty. I'm saying! So do your part and tell a friend, tell an ex, tell a nana to hit that thumbs-up button!

On a serious note, a message from Students Against Substance Abuse: Driving dry is hella fly. The SASA president will personally monitor the punch bowl for suspicious activity, and the VP has the smoking lounge on lockdown in case you have any nontobacco smoking plans. With all that glitter and gossamer, something tells me you won't need hallucinogenics to have a funky trip, anyway.

While you're out bustin' a move in your satin and sequins tomorrow, I'll be home reclining in my zebra-print Snuggie, knuckles-deep in a box of Fiddle Faddle. Not very mythical, perhaps, but I've got a date with *Danger's Little Darling*, and after last week's killer episode, I can't wait to see what Angelica Darling has in store. God, I love me some Jayla Heart. That saucy starlet's the hottest thing to ever come out of Lav-Oaks. Don't believe me? Check out her fan page, the Jayla Heartthrobs. 200K fans? There's a girl who knows how to bust a move.

In closing, a Facebook message even Team Tinfoil Hat can't protest: Have fun this weekend, fishies. Be safe. And don't forget to smile for the spy satellites!

xo ~ *Ciao!* ~ xo

Miss Demeanor

THE ROAD TO HELL IS PAVED WITH GLITTER

Say . . . *magic pixie dust*!"

Inside the bedazzled Lavender Oaks gym, a photographer blasts me and Cole with the flash of a thousand suns, and the words "terrible" and "mistake" appear in neon bubbles before my eyes.

Dear formerly respectable self: How many lines *will* you cross tonight? Wearing a dress. Riding in a party Hummer. Striking a pose next to a horse festooned with a plastic unicorn horn.

Prince Freckles is normally reserved for the horseback riding elective, but the Mythical Creatures prom committee lassoed him into mascot duty. He doesn't seem to mind his makeshift pen—roped-off section near the bleachers, hay on the floor—but the costume is another story. Sequins? Clearly not Prince Freckles's personal style best.

"Short straw?" I whisper.

He flicks a pink ear in my direction and lets out a pathetic snort. *Don't let the other horses see me like this.*

The camera flashes again, and I wish on some of that magic pixie dust to spirit us both away, far from cowpoke Colorado and the ankle-deep hay and the too-tight hair ornaments.

Sadly, if my fairy godmother's on the scene, her gossamer-winged butt is parked at the punch bowl, and my wish floats up to the disco balls unfulfilled.

"Aww, cutest couple *ever*," the photographer says with a final blinding flash.

Cole winks at me across the speckled horse. His copper-green eyes shine with so much fire my chest hurts, and right before I basically *die*, he gets dragged off by the guys in his band and my half-stalled heart sputters back to life.

Close call, it warns. *Pat-pat-pat.*

"I can't believe they got an actual unicorn. Miss Demeanor will fa-*reak* when she sees this." My friend Griffin and her soul-mate-of-the-hour, an elf-costumed kid named Paul from Saint Paul's Prep, enter the pen. Griff shakes out her dyed platinum curls and tries to snap a selfie, but the phone her parents got her in Helsinki is so complicated, she can never work the camera.

The real photographer takes over, and I find a seat on the bleachers to watch the show of Paul ogling Griffin's succubus dress, a midnight-blue sheath with a sewn-on devil's tail and a deep V down the front. Cute and pointy Legolas ears aside, Paul's getting the Tarts of Apology tomorrow—Griff's method of breaking hearts at the corner table at Black & Brew Café. Bad news goes down better with pastries, she always says.

She has a lot of theories. It's exhausting.

Griffin lets out a high-pitched squeal as Paul palms her ass, and the tea rose corsage near my shoulder tumbles to my lap, scattering petals on the way down. I scoop them into a pile, their edges already curling.

Prom impostor.

It's Saturday night. I should be home slaying online zombies and sneaking people food to Night of the Living Dog, not playing dress up in the land of make-believe. Because fact-check time, for anyone keeping it real:

1. Prince Freckles isn't really a unicorn.
2. Cole isn't really my date.
3. This poof of a dress isn't really my style.
   Vintage rockabilly halter, butter-white chiffon
   with black cherry print and a bloodred sash.
   It's so pretty I'm practically allergic.

From the horse pen, Griff squeals again, and my gaze darts to the doors behind her. Maybe the Hummer's still in the parking lot, still shooting iridescent orbs from its rooftop bubble machine. I can sneak out, catch a ride home. In less than an hour I'll be out of this pinup gear, sucking down a Dr Pepper and roasting undead hordes with a flamethrower.

My fingers squeeze invisible triggers. . . .

"Don't tell me my last-minute date's already bailing." Cole's back, crouching in front of me with a smirk. Normally he keeps a little scruff on his face, but he cleaned up for the occasion, and the late-spring sunshine has left his skin tan and smooth. Kissable. "What's wrong, Luce?"

I heft four thousand layers of chiffon over my black thigh-high boots, the only part of the ensemble that's mine, and crush the fabric in my fists. "I'm a wedding cake topper."

"Not even." Cole takes the wilting corsage from my lap. "You look, um, *really* nice." He leans in close, messy hair tickling my nose. He smells like outside, like campfire and ripe apples, and—

Hey! Prince Freckles's sequined-covered stomp says it all: *Don't even think about it!*

With a heavy sigh, I flick a lone rose petal from my lap. I'd love to follow the horse's advice, but it's too late. Don't even think about it? I *have* thought about it. Every day. For the last four years.

We've never kissed, never cuddled, never been anything more than capital-F Friends. Cole Foster broke my heart anyway. Like the perfect dress and the flowers that refuse to stay put, the only boy I've ever loved belongs to Eliana Pike.

Ellie.

My best friend.

"Thanks for filling in tonight." Cole's breath glances my shoulder as he works to reattach the corsage. Beneath his touch, my heart flops like a beached fish, and I turn my face away from his gaze.

Perfect. How am I supposed to survive an entire night of dancing if I can't even manage eye contact? Honestly, the whole arrangement is getting to be a serious problem.

"Not a problem," I say.

Get it together, Luce. Ellie's in bed with the superflu, missing senior prom—the event she looked forward to more than anything the whole three years she's been with Cole. All I'm missing is a little online carnage.

Please go with him, Lucy. You're my surrogate! You have to send me pictures all night long!

Never one to say no to Ellie, I've been following those orders all night. *omg u & griff r stunners*, her last text said, after she reviewed the series my parents snapped in our driveway. *u r totes keeping that dress!* She's been texting for the play-by-play ever since.

SARAH OCKLER

is the bestselling author of *Bittersweet*, *Twenty Boy Summer* (a YALSA Teens' Top Ten nominee and an Indie Next List pick), and *Fixing Delilah*. She is a champion cupcake eater, coffee drinker, night person, and bookworm. When she's not writing or reading at home in Colorado, Sarah enjoys taking pictures, hugging trees, and road-tripping through the country with her husband, Alex. Visit her website at **sarahockler.com**, and find her on Twitter and Facebook.